Pra

APPALACHIAN JUSTICE

by

Melinda Clayton

Billy May's colloquial narration will draw readers in and make them feel like they are sitting vigil at her bedside as she discusses the injustices of her past. The tale [Clayton] weaves brings Cedar Hollow and its mountain to life in brilliant and horrifying color. *Library Journal*

Serendipity is when you stumble across a book, buy it on the off-chance that it might be an interesting book and it turns out to be brilliant, a superb read. Appalachian Justice is such a rare find....The story and the characters are complex, rich and ooze a quiet strength....[A]lthough this book is about abuse, at times graphic abuse, at the core there is this quiet, positive, persistent message that wherever you are and whatever you experience, you can survive....
The Bookgeek, CurveMagazine

Appalachian Justice is visceral, reaching out to grab your emotions and senses from the first pages....It is a wonderful debut album for Melinda Clayton and deserves to be read by every family trying to teach tolerance and the cost of prejudice....Open the pages, but be prepared, while Appalachian Justice works to break down barriers and to bring about understanding of a few key issues it is raw and at times violent though both factors are critical to the story and are not done simply for shock value. It is a critical story for our time and for the ages to come....
Midwest Book Review

APPALACHIAN JUSTICE

Cedar Hollow Series, Book 1

by

Melinda Clayton

Thomas-Jacob Publishing, LLC
USA

APPALACHIAN JUSTICE

by Melinda Clayton

Copyright 2013 Melinda Clayton

Published by: Thomas-Jacob Publishing, LLC
TJPub@thomas-jacobpublishing.com

Cover Art: Clarissa Yeo,
Book Cover Art: http://www.bookcoversale.com/#

ISBN-13: 978-0-9895729-0-3

ISBN-10: 0-9895729-0-0

WorldCat OCLC Control Number: 910735210

Third Edition

First Printing: July 2013

Printed in the United States of America

Dedication

First and foremost, to the three loves of my life: Donny, Caleb, and Isaac.

And to my grandpa, with a new appreciation for and understanding of the sacrifice he made in the mines.

And to my mother, who explained what it was like to wait by the side of the road, praying her daddy would make it home safely.

"Ain't nobody got the power to destroy you but you. Don't you never forget that." ~ Billy May Platte

Prologue
Cedar Hollow, West Virginia, 2010

The stairway was much steeper than she remembered, dark and narrow, and the railings were not secure. Some of the anchoring bolts were missing, and the banisters wobbled under the slight pressure of her hands. In the stifling humidity, paint was peeling off the walls, the same dark green paint she remembered from seventy years ago, the first and last time she had climbed the bell tower.

She was a slight woman, stooped gently by age, fine wrinkles mapping out a face that was still pretty in spite of the passage of time. One trembling hand gripped the unsteady rail, and she paused to catch her breath, faintly dizzy from the exertion. She felt claustrophobic in the tower, as if the surrounding mountains were closing in, pressing down on the little hamlet, squeezing the very air out of the narrow access. From a distance, she could hear disembodied voices floating outside in the late spring evening. The funeral was over, but people still mingled, reluctant to leave.

Leaning against the rail, she smoothed flyaway strands of silver hair away from her face, tucked the wayward tresses back into the low bun she had worn nearly the whole of her adult life. In her memory, the locks were blonde, and it was pigtails into which she tucked them.

She had just placed her foot on the next step, preparing to resume her climb in spite of her misgivings, when she heard movement below.

"Good God almighty, woman. Have you gone plumb crazy?" The voice echoed in the narrow stairwell. "What in the hell are you doin' up there?"

Recognizing the voice, she glanced down to see the

worried faces of two old men peering up at her through the shadows, their expressions nearly comical in exaggerated concern, what was left of their remaining hair mirrored in identical shades of gray. Seventy years ago one had had hair as black as the coal that was mined throughout the mountains, while the other had been shaved bald, a consequence of a recent lice infestation in the village. She smiled to herself as she remembered that even then, both had been afraid of the bell tower.

Facing forward again, she surveyed the steep climb ahead before responding. "I have to ring the bell," she answered finally, irritated that they hadn't known. "It's the right way to end it." Resolute, she tightened her grip on the rail and coaxed her stiff knee joints to advance another step.

At the bottom of the rickety staircase the two old men looked at each other. One shrugged, and the other sighed, adjusting the straps of his oxygen tank. Without a word they, too, began to climb, muscles quivering with the unexpected exercise. They paused often to rest; after a lifetime of mining, the coal dust made breathing difficult. Slowly but steadily they followed her up the precarious passageway, praying the steps would hold all the way to the cupola. In spite of the difficulty of the climb, they were determined to make it to the top.

She was right, of course. It was the only way to end the story.

Chapter One: The beginning
Crutcher Mountain, West Virginia, 1975

In the chill of the encroaching evening, the girl ran, heart pounding with the effort, lungs gasping for air. Her bare feet, cut and bruised, left bloody smears across the rocky outcrop but she didn't notice, intent only on escape. Panting and gasping, chest heaving, scrawny limbs pumping, she ran down the treacherous wall of the briar-choked gully, tripping over the uneven ground. Clumps of her dark, knotted hair caught and remained on branches that seemed, in her terrified state, to reach towards her, conspiring against her, using their gnarled wooden fingers to hold her hostage.

She was young, certainly no older than twelve, balanced somewhere on the precipice between childhood and adolescence, and painfully thin for her age. The threadbare t-shirt she wore did little to camouflage the xylophone of her ribcage, the knobs of her spine a fragile zipper down her back. She was filthy, too, her battered feet nearly black from the coal dust soil of the mountains. Under normal circumstances, she would have been pretty, her almond shaped eyes a stormy shade of green, her limbs long and supple. But the girl didn't live in normal circumstances, and as such, any prettiness she might have possessed was eclipsed by the ravages of fear and despair.

It was dusk in the mountains, the last warm rays of the sun shining upon the girl's chestnut colored hair and creating momentary sparkles of light among the tangles as she crashed downward through the gully. Ahead of her, squirrels raced for trees, scrambling for higher ground, abandoning the nuts and berries for which they had so determinedly foraged. Snakes raced away from her path, slithering through the impenetrable brush before taking refuge in the cool recesses of the damp rock walls. Even the songbirds fell silent, blue jays and mockingbirds halting their never ending arguments in the wake of the girl's flight.

The girl, however, noticed none of this. Her sensory perceptions having condensed into little more than animal instinct, she knew only that she had to run.

From the top of my mountain, I seen that girl runnin'. It was them hawks that told me to look. I was just finishin' my chores for the evenin' when I heard 'em squawkin' the way they do when somethin' worries 'em. Broad-winged, they was, and there was a passel of 'em, all spiralin' up in the currents over them mountains. They wasn't happy; somethin' had their attention and I remember hopin' it wasn't nothin' serious. A fox maybe, or even a bear would be fine. I didn't pay no mind to the animals; it was the people I feared. Give me a bear any day over a man. Bears is predictable; men ain't.

More than anythin' else, I was just curious about whatever was botherin' 'em. There must have been ten or twelve of 'em, all gathered together for their winter's flight south. Smart birds, I remember thinkin'. The cold on these mountains can kill a person quick, if they ain't careful. The cold, and any number of other things.

I gave the axe a final swing and planted it securely in the choppin' block. Last thing I needed was to trip over my own axe on my way to feedin' the animals. If it didn't kill me right away, I'd be dead of exposure soon enough. It wasn't like nobody was goin' to come lookin' for me, and even if they did, they wouldn't know where to look. I bent down to gather the last piece of firewood and headed towards the cabin, wipin' the sweat off my brow with my shirtsleeve. Fall was comin' but the evenin' was a warm one, and I was a forty-four year old woman swingin' an axe.

I was filthy, soaked through with sweat, but who was to know? I lived alone, had for years, and that was the way I planned on keepin' it. I had no illusions about myself and

4

never had. My thick, black hair was cut short for ease, and thirty years on a West Virginia mountain summit had taken its toll on whatever good looks I may have once enjoyed. I was as brown as my Cherokee momma, my skin as creased as old leather.

With the sweat out of my eyes, I looked up to see the reddish brown underbellies of all them little hawks, flyin' up high above the range and hollerin' to beat the band. I dropped the split wood into the wood box by the front door with a clatter and shaded my eyes against the lowerin' sun, gazin' out over the gully and tryin' to see what had caused the commotion. And that's when I seen her. There she was, Roy Campbell's girl, it had to be, headed for the creek and runnin' as if her life depended on it. I hadn't never met the girl, but there wasn't no one else livin' this high on the range. Keepin' my eye on her, I took off my work gloves, shoved 'em into the back pocket of my dungarees, and felt in my shirt pocket for a cigarette.

Findin' what I was lookin' for, I struck a match along the front of my little cabin and, usin' my hands, sheltered the timid flame while I lit up, sighin' with pleasure as the nicotine went to work. I don't like to admit to vices, but nicotine has been mine, nevertheless. I reckon we all got some sort of weakness, and nicotine was it for me, at least after I took up residence on the mountain. My lungs full of smoke and the cravin' thus satisfied, I leaned forward over the splintered railin' of the cabin's west facin' porch, proppin' my elbows on the weathered wood, danglin' my hands over the edge. This was how I spent nearly all of my evenin's after a hard day's work, but this was the first time I'd ever seen another person so close to my mountain. I drug hard on the cigarette and squinted through the smoke, watchin' the girl's frantic flight down the neighborin' hill.

The sheer desperation of the girl's flight troubled me. I hadn't seen Roy Campbell in nearly thirty years, but I doubted he had changed much. Judgin' by the frightened, filthy state of the girl, he hadn't changed at all. I watched the girl until she cut left around a boulder and disappeared from my view.

Takin' a final drag, I flicked the last of the butt over the rail and into the dust, scatterin' the chickens and causin' a flurry of agitated cluckin'. The sun was just beginnin' to dip below the summit of the mountain, spreadin' rosy streaks across the western sky the way it does on clear mountain evenin's. A cool breeze kicked up sudden like from the north, causin' the dust to dance in miniature tornados and sendin' an involuntary shiver down my spine. The universe has a lot to tell us, if we're listenin'. For thirty years, my survival had depended on listenin', so listen I did.

I still had work to do. First and foremost, I needed to gather them chickens into their coop before the spiralin' hawks decided they'd make for an easy dinner. But I found myself drawn to the girl, unwillin' to leave my perch. Distracted from my chores, I raked my hand through my hair, the calluses catchin' and pullin' as they always did, and gazed down the holler. Truth be told, I was afraid; I ain't ashamed to say it now, and I wasn't ashamed then, neither. The universe was talkin', and I didn't much like was it was sayin'.

Chapter Two: The old woman
Huntington, West Virginia, 2010

I wake up to the beep and hiss of the profusion of medical equipment that holds me hostage. I'm confused at first, the bright lights blindin' me. In my mind, I'm still on the mountain, and they is comin' after me again, pinnin' me down. I fight against the tubes snakin' into my arms, pull at the adhesives holdin' them to my chest. I cain't breathe, and they won't let me go; I panic.

A warm, brown hand stills my own, preventin' me from unpluggin' myself from the machines that monitor my body, and then I know. I ain't on the mountain, and it ain't 1975. It's 2010. I'm an old woman, and I'm dyin'. Funny how in my last days my mind keeps takin' me back up to that mountain.

"It won't be long now until she comes, Ms. Platte," says the young nurse, and her voice is too loud, as if the very act of becomin' old has automatically rendered me either dimwitted or deaf. "You just relax."

I'm annoyed by the patronizin' tone of her voice, but I stop fightin' and tamp down my irritation. The nurse don't mean no harm; she's a sweet girl, really, and I'm just a crotchety old woman she's paid to put up with. She cain't possibly know how I hate bein' restrained, could never understand the fear I have upon wakin' and rediscoverin' that I am, in essence, tied to this bed, held in place by the various tubes and monitors that is supposed to provide me comfort and relief. The irony of it all is astoundin'.

It ain't the nurse's fault she cain't comprehend; after all, she don't know nothin' of my past. My chart don't have nothin' in it but what's needed: my address and phone number, the nature of my illness, copies of my medical insurance card. That's all they need from me, and that's all they is goin' to get.

I look over at the nurse. She's young and pretty, a black girl with smooth skin and a sweet smile. That poor girl don't need me givin' her a hard time; I'll be more patient. After all, she's surely better than that other one, the mornin' nurse, with her beady eyes and sharp nose, forever snappin' on the lights and announcin' at the top of her lungs, "Up and at 'em!" Lord knows, I ain't gettin' up and gettin' *at* nothin' these days, and she oughta be glad for it, because that may just be what's savin' her life. At least this one here is always cheerful, always makin' sure I'm comfortable with fresh water and a fluffed pillow. What's her name? I forget.

One thing that perplexes me is how when you get old you cain't remember what happened three minutes ago but you cain't stop rememberin' what happened three decades ago. Plumb crazy is what that is. Now, what is her name? Somethin' cute and perky. Oh, yes, I remember now. Starlette. Lord, that woman can talk. I'm too tired to respond to all the jabberin' but I smile to let her know I appreciate her kindness.

Starlette has evidently taken my smile as a sign to continue, because she keeps prattlin' on, "How long has it been since you've seen her, Ms. Platte? My goodness, you must miss her. And how did you say you know her? Is she an old family friend? Isn't that nice. You must be so excited." In her chatty exuberance, the blamed woman has rearranged my body into a position that is sure enough guaranteed to result in leg cramps as soon as she leaves the room, but I won't complain; it ain't in my nature. I'll work my legs around later; move 'em into a more comfortable position. It might take a while, but I can do it. After all, I ain't dead yet.

"And do you have any children, Ms. Platte? Will they be coming, too? That will be so much fun."

I close my eyes, plumb exhausted. Starlette don't really expect no reply, and I'm too tired to give her one. If only she would hush; I don't want to talk. Hell, I *cain't* talk. I'm so tired I cain't hardly even breathe. Besides, some things is just impossible to explain and it don't pay to even try. Seem like

8

when you try to explain somethin' important to somebody else, somethin' you hold close to your heart, they don't always right away understand the importance, and that is a frustratin' thing. The answers to them questions she keeps askin' me is important; they is my whole life, and I ain't goin' to take the chance of tellin' someone who cain't understand that.

I keep my mouth shut and breathe deep, prayin' that the nurse will hurry up and finish fluffin' and soothin' and talkin' and move on to the next dyin' patient, leavin' me in peace. My mind is already back up on that summit, whether I want it to go there or not. I will tell you my story if you want to know it, but some parts of it ain't pretty. Then again, some parts of it is just plain beautiful. Ain't that always the way of it? Just know that it is important, my story. It truly is.

Chapter Three: The hiding place
Crutcher Mountain, West Virginia, 1975

That next mornin', the one after I first seen the girl, I was up before sunrise hit the mountain, buildin' a small fire in the stove to ward off the early mornin' chill. It would warm up later, but in the mornin's there was already a nip in the air, particularly in the hours just before dawn, a sign of things to come in the winter ahead. Takin' note of the activity around me, I was anticipatin' a hard one. The migratory birds was already takin' flight and the four-legged critters of the woods was in a flurry of activity, hoardin', storin', or eatin' as their species required. I watched these things. I had learned long ago that the animals knew more than I did, and it behooved me to pay attention.

While the water boiled for coffee I dressed in the same flannel shirt and dungarees I'd worn the day before, pullin' my work boots on over wool socks and lacin' them with stiff fingers. Rummagin' through the steamer trunk at the foot of the cabin's only bed, I pulled out an old flour sack into which I threw some bread and cheese, a quilt and a box of matches. My preparations completed, I stood at the cabin's lone window in the cabin's single room, warmin' my hands on my coffee mug, takin' turns blowin' on and drinkin' the strong, black drink, tryin' to get a handle on my thoughts.

Mall sios, beag amhain, I heard my daddy's laughin' voice in my head. Slow down, little one, he would say to me, his Irish accent so different from the mountain twang around us. *Smaoinigh sula gniomhu tu.* Think before you act, Billy May. *I'm tryin' Daddy,* I thought right back at him. *But you know I ain't never been good at waitin'.* I sipped my coffee and pushed my daddy out of my head. If he wanted me to think, I needed room to do it.

I knew where the girl had gone. I had seen the signs a week before while I was down at the creek fishin' for trout. By then, I had been livin' on that mountain for thirty years and I knew every crook and cranny to be found. I also knew how to track, but I was certain I wouldn't need the skill that mornin'. The girl hadn't been interested in coverin' her trail; she had been runnin' for her life, crashin' through them wild blackberry thorns and honeysuckle vines like they wasn't nothin' but dandelion fluff.

I finished my coffee and set the cup in the washbasin, rubbin' my hands together for warmth. I remember bein' anxious to get started, not because I thought I'd see the girl— I didn't want to see the girl—but because when I was on the move my thoughts was quieter. Gatherin' up the flour sack, I got my rifle down from the rack over my bed. The city folk thought West Virginia mountain lions was all gone by the 1970s, but I still occasionally stumbled across tracks, and more than once I'd heard their spine-tinglin' screams in the wee hours of the mornin'. If you ain't never heard one, believe me, you don't want to; it'll make your hair stand on end. I didn't think I'd run across one that close to sunrise, but I didn't want to be caught unprepared.

I don't like to kill things, never have, and I wouldn't have never killed a mountain lion anyway, not even to save myself. Momma always said they was sacred, one of the only two animals that didn't fall asleep durin' the creation. I don't know as I believed that, but I respected that Momma did. No, I wouldn't kill one, but I would shoot in the air to scare one off if I needed to. Besides, mountain lions wasn't the only danger up on that range. Black bears was all over them mountains back then, and though more than likely they'd head the other way as soon as they captured my scent, I had learned to be cautious, especially when them bears was preparin' for hibernation. If it came down to it, I wouldn't have no problem shootin' a bear to save myself.

What I knew but refused to admit to myself that long ago mornin' was that out of all the livin' creatures on the range, Roy Campbell was by far the biggest threat. I reckon I couldn't admit it because I was scared to. At any rate, I doubted he'd followed the girl; whatever he had wanted from her, he'd already took. Roy was like that. Nevertheless, I shoved some extra ammunition into my shirt pocket. More than anybody, I knew exactly what Roy was capable of. The gun was for him. If it came down to it, I remember thinkin' to myself that mornin', I might actually enjoy shootin' Roy.

Shoulderin' my rifle and the sack, I pulled the heavy planked door shut behind me and stepped off the porch and into the dirt yard, enjoyin' my cigarette and listenin' for a minute to the sounds of the mountain. It was cold; my breath steamed in the night air. The eerie call of a screech owl took over the woods for a bit, echoin' off the mountains and frightenin' the crickets into a momentary silence. Momma always said the call of an owl was a good omen, and I believed it. Owls is known for bein' wise and helpful, and this one was tellin' me to get goin'.

Takin' her advice, I crushed the remains of my cigarette under my boot and set off, headin' south around the side of the cabin and into the hush of the thick woods. The sun still hadn't reached that part of the mountain and the woods was shrouded in mist, heavy with the wet smell of decay. I have always loved the smell of the mountains, and I breathed in deep, inhalin' the sweet fragrance, enjoyin' the expectation that was always a part of the world just before dawn. Nocturnal critters rustled in the brush, preparin' their beds, while others began stirrin' to greet the sun.

I set a steady pace, headin' down in the gray light of the comin' dawn, as familiar with the trail as I was with the floor plan of my one room cabin. After all, I was the one who had blazed that trail. No one ever went up that high on the range, which was exactly why I lived there. The way was steep, but decades of clamberin' around the mountain had made my legs strong, as rock solid as any man's, and my breathin' was unlabored and peaceful as I maneuvered my way past tree roots and rocks, thistles and briars.

My mountain wasn't particularly high as mountains go, only 4,700 feet or so, less than a mile, as are most of the mountains makin' up the Appalachian range. But the goin' was rough, windin' around boulders and gullies, through untamed thickets and brambles, and a mile by the crow was closer to three for me. As the sun worked its way up into the sky, I continued my way slowly downward, makin' good time in the dense woods.

Midway down the mountain I caught a flash of movement out of the corner of my eye, but it was a familiar movement, and I smiled. The old mongrel was back, and just in time. He'd show up at my door the first hard freeze, tail waggin', as he had done for the last dozen years, beggin' to be let in, unaware of how rude he was bein'. For now, though, he tracked me from behind, not yet ready to be noticed. I let him be, confident that he'd come to me in his own good time, happy with the knowledge. The old mongrel and me went way back, and I had come to rely on his company durin' the long winters on the summit. I remember thinkin' it was interestin' that he found me that particular mornin'. The universe was talkin' to me again, gettin' me ready for what was to come. The signs was all around me.

The sun was fully on the mountain by the time I came out of the canopy of trees into a large clearin'. Purple snapdragons and blue lobelia was just greetin' the mornin', their pretty little petals reachin' towards the sky. Before long they'd be covered by snow, gone until the next summer, but that mornin' they was pretty enough to make me stop for a minute in appreciation before continuin' forward toward the rushin' sound of the creek. Kneelin' on the marshy ground, I cupped my hands and scooped up some water, splashin' my face before drinkin' deep. Nothin' is as good as a drink of cold, clear, creek water.

Standin', shadin' my eyes against the now risen sun, I paused and took in my surroundin's. On the far side of the creek a loon, already changin' into his gray winter coat, torpedoed under the water in search of breakfast. He wouldn't stay long; this creek wasn't deep enough for him. He was just passin' through on his way to a larger body of water. In the distance, a mournin' dove called out soulfully and another answered from a nearby tree. *Guledisgonihi, Billy May. A good sign. Doves bring peace.* This time it was

14

my momma's voice in my head, and I listened for more, but she'd said all she had to say. The only sound was the rushin' of the creek on its forever journey down the mountain. The girl was gone now. I felt it in the stillness of the air.

Turnin', I hiked farther up the creek, headin' west, until I came to a rocky outpost. Sometime in the history of the mountain, decades or maybe even centuries before, an avalanche of boulders had created a rough pyramid of sorts, roarin' down the mountainside before crashin' onto the creek bank and becomin' a permanent part of the landscape. It was here that I stopped, bendin' to prop my sack and rifle against an elm whose leaves was just beginnin' to turn. Straightenin' again I stretched, loosenin' my muscles in the warmth of the sun; then I stood still. I knew, of course, exactly where the girl had been headed, had seen the prints and broken vegetation the week before, but I found myself hesitant to continue.

I understood even then that my decisions that day might literally be the end of me. Thirty years I had survived on that mountain top, most of them years alone. I'd been little more than a girl when I had first sought respite in the little cabin. In the years since then I'd stayed far away from other people and demanded the same from them in return. It had been the only way I'd known to survive and put the shattered pieces of my life back together. Now I found myself on the verge of riskin' it all, for a little girl I didn't even know.

I drew a deep breath and tilted my head back, hands propped on my hips, face turned up at the sky. I suppose to anyone lookin' it might have appeared that I was prayin', but I wasn't. Back then, I was at a time in my life where I didn't believe in prayer and hadn't for years. The counsel I sought that day didn't come from God; I was reachin' for Polly. Pauline Henley Crutcher, my *adawehi*, my angel, the one who brought me back to life when I'd rather she had let me die. I knew what Polly would say, what her answers would be, but I needed to ask the questions anyway, so I did. Lord knew, all my other loved ones was in my head that mornin'; I felt sure Polly would be there, too, and she wasn't never one to hold back her opinions.

Finally, havin' come to a truce with Polly, I gave my head a quick shake to clear out my thoughts and forced myself to move. My actions scared me, but truly I didn't have no choice. Whatever happened was meant to be. Good was done to me through Polly; it was a debt I needed to repay. Besides, I reckoned that more than anybody, I alone knew what that girl must be sufferin'.

Behind the boulders I found, like I had known I would, a small openin' in the stone face of the mountain wall, nearly level with the ground and slopin' downward. I dropped to my knees and pressed the side of my face close to the cool ground, allowin' me to peer into the rocky openin'. Seein' no sign of current occupants, I sat on the ground, dangled my legs through the hole, and pushed myself up over the lower rock lip of the entrance. I landed feet first, the thump of my boots echoin' in the little chamber.

Nothin' much had changed over the years. The cave, such as it was, was made of a dirt floor and four uneven rock walls; a very high and narrow openin' in the fourth wall had served as my point of entry. At the highest point, where I had entered, the cave was maybe five feet high, slopin' to a height of only three feet at the back wall, about six feet in. Just enough room for a young girl to hide. I had hidden there myself sometimes after comin' to the mountain, not because I was scared—I wasn't, with Polly—but because I needed a place to be alone with my thoughts, especially on them days when they was chasin' each other around in my head.

Surveyin' the cave, crouchin' under the rock ceilin', I seen where the girl had tried to make a bed out of branches. On the pallet was a blanket, worn nearly to threads, and a book, damp and tattered. Steppin' closer, I read the title, *Jonathan Livingston Seagull*. I wasn't familiar with either the book or the author, a man named Richard Bach. As a young girl, I had loved to read, but that was such a long time ago. It had been decades since I'd touched a book.

I wondered briefly just how long the girl had been hidin' there. Long enough, at least, to have tried to make it more comfortable. It was then that my eyes was suddenly drawn to a shadow on the makeshift bed, so I moved closer and squatted for a better look. Dried blood, not too much, smeared across the boughs and soaked into the blanket. Well, of course. Although I had fully expected it, the reality of that blood squeezed my chest, makin' it hard for me to breathe.

I stood up quick-like, bendin' at the waist and takin' care not to collide with the low ceilin'. All I wanted to do right then was to get the hell out of that cave and head back up the mountain, to the safety of my cabin. But I couldn't yet. Instead, I rolled the flour sack up real tight and placed it on the little pallet. I shimmied back up out of the narrow openin' and began searchin' for stones, then for twigs and dried grasses, for bigger branches, and finally for small, dried logs. Throwin' my finds into the hole, I followed them down and pulled my huntin' knife free of my belt, squattin' again to scrape out a shallow indention in the packed dirt of the cavern's floor. I ringed the indentation with the stones I'd gathered, and then laid out the makin's of a small but efficient campfire, makin' sure it was close enough to the entrance that the smoke would flow out. Finally, there was nothin' else I could do, at least not yet, though I knew in my heart that the day was comin'.

After a minute I wriggled my way back out and stood, breathin' hard in the cool, late mornin' mountain air, pretendin' my hands wasn't shakin' when I lit a cigarette and took a deep drag.

Chapter Four: The old woman
Huntington, West Virginia, 2010

I notice I don't wake up no more so much as I float up. It ain't a fast process; it feels like I'm movin' my way up through somethin' thick and dark, like the molasses Momma used to put on my toast for a special treat. Mr. Smith used to give us that molasses. I just remembered that. He was a good man, way down into his soul. He owned the general store in Cedar Hollow before he passed, and Lord knows he gave more of it away than he sold. The store, I mean, not the molasses, though probably that, too. I feel a sting of sadness rememberin' Mr. Smith, until I realize I'll see him soon, God willin'.

When I'm floatin' up, first I hear the sounds, the steady hum of equipment, and under that, the hurried footsteps of angels in white as they rush down tiled hallways, answerin' to that ever-present call of "stat." When I finally float all the way to the top of the darkness, I open my eyes to the mid-afternoon gloom of an overcast West Virginia evenin'. The glare from the clouds reflects through the uncovered window and causes me to squint in the dim room. I ain't used to such inactivity and it makes me restless, anxious from the quiet atmosphere and the suffocatin' feelin' of doom. They is all just waitin' on us to die here, and that's the truth. They pretend they ain't, of course, but I know.

My throat is parched; I reach a tremblin' hand towards the water glass on my bedside table, prayin' I don't knock it over before I at least get a drink. Dyin', I have discovered, is hard work; even harder is the waitin'. Graspin' the straw between my cracked lips, I drink. It ain't creek water, but it'll do. My thirst finally quenched, I replace the glass and lean my head back against the pillow, closin' my eyes, my energy spent. It's hard even now for me to accept my weakened state. I was always so strong; even as a young girl I could whup half the boys my age. Could, and did, quite frequently. You could ask 'em. Some of 'em has outlasted me. Now, though, now I'm done in by a glass of water and instead of tryin' to beat me at arm wrastlin', Darryl Lane was in here just yesterday bawlin' like a baby over my bedside, bless his heart. He always was a sensitive one.

Encounterin' somethin' hard in the scratchy softness of my pillow, I remember: the book. It arrived yesterday and I tucked it under my pillow for safekeepin'. It ain't that I don't trust the nurses; it's more that things have a way of gettin' misplaced, especially with the crowd of people travelin' in and out of my room all day and night checkin' on the mess of cords and tubes that is supposed to be keepin' me alive. More than that, though, I want the book near me, so I can get to it when I need it.

I twist around the best I can, reachin' behind my head for it, not to read it—Lord, no, I cain't possibly see it in this glarin' light—but as a source of comfort. There ain't no point in readin' it; I done memorized them passages decades ago, could probably recite the entire book by heart. Gropin' awkwardly under the pillow, takin' care not to loosen any of the tubes (I done learned the hard way that pullin' them tubes out means more of them hurtful needle pricks), I find the tattered volume and grasp it in a gnarled, arthritic hand, my fingers still calloused and stained yellow with the damned nicotine I never could shake. I hold on tight.

In my memory, I hear her little girl voice, as crystal clear as it was the day I met her, and it makes my eyes well up. We always enjoyed readin' aloud to each other; we began that ritual early on. Those nights when she couldn't sleep, tortured by them monsters in her dreams, readin' was the only way to keep her fears at bay. On them nights I comforted her the best I could. I'd heat us up some herbal tea and stroke her hair as she read to me, rub her back as I read to her. After particularly bad nights we would greet the sun that way, her exhausted but relieved at havin' made it safely through the night, me exhausted, too, but willin' to do whatever it took to comfort her. Because I knew, you see. I knew, and Polly was there watchin' over both of us. We was like a chain of women, three generations, all holdin' on and helpin' each other through the night, pullin' on each others strength.

The memories flood over me again now, as fickle as always, mixin' the good right along with the bad in a parade that marches behind the lids of my closed eyes. Strange, the way the years flow together with no regard to time and place, no separation of events, as if the whole of my life has been one big, unendin' cycle of emotions. Here laughter and there sadness, terror mixed right in with joy, fury holdin' onto loneliness. Like a creek, I think, all flowin' together, sometimes gentle and peaceful and sometimes bashin' to bits against the rocks.

I hug the ragged book to my chest and keep my eyes closed against the too-bright glare of the overcast afternoon. I want to close the blinds; my eyes is sensitive these days, but I don't have the strength to stand and couldn't unhook from all these dadblamed contraptions, anyway. Instead, I turn my head away from the window and shiver. The room is cold; my body ain't capable of generatin' enough warmth to keep me comfortable, but I am loathe to whine and I am purely disgusted with myself for my helplessness. I have most certainly lived through worse than a little chill in the air. Hell, there's days I would've killed for air conditionin', if I'd known what it was. It strikes me as amusin' that right now I'm hatin' it so. Ain't that the way it goes?

My life has been plumb full of hard times, but good times, too. On the darkest of days, it sometimes seemed to me like God put me here on this earth just to test my strength, maybe to see how strong he made me, see if he'd done a good enough job. I wonder what he thinks now. On the darkest of nights, I rejected him altogether. In the end, though, my life has been full, more than enough.

Soon, I tell myself. She'll be here soon. I can hold on that long. The thought of Jessie calms me, and I relax. As it always does these days, my mind goes back up to that mountain.

Chapter Five: The girl
Crutcher Mountain, West Virginia, 1975

The girl was on the move again, running for her life in the dusky evening. Plunging through the underbrush and past countless unnamed enemies, she continued downward in pursuit of safe harbor. She hurt, but she was *alive,* and this thought drove her onward. Finally, praise God, there it was. The cave. She virtually threw herself into the opening, landing on the cold ground with a resounding thump. Panting, shivering, she closed her eyes and curled into herself, concentrating on breathing, willing herself to calm down, ordering her body to cooperate. At last her body obeyed, her heart rate slowed, and her breathing steadied. She opened her eyes to the damp familiarity of the cave.

She had discovered it by accident, really, only a few short weeks before, when he had first begun his celebrations. Remembering that day, the girl fought an involuntary shudder and swallowed back the bile in her throat. That first time, after he had casually strolled away, she had gotten unsteadily to her feet and begun to run, not knowing where to go but instinctively knowing to head down, towards the creek.

At first she simply sat on the bank, trembling, hugging her knees and gathering her wits. Later, in a state of shock, she had walked aimlessly, finding the pile of boulders and thinking maybe she could hide behind them, too confused in her fright to realize the danger had passed. Searching for shelter, wanting nothing so much as to curl up and hide, she had stumbled across the opening, afraid at first but eventually daring to peek inside. In the weeks since then the small cave had most assuredly saved her, offering her shelter from the monster with whom she lived.

Now she sat up in the semi-darkness, whimpering with the pain. She surveyed her surroundings and was immediately on guard, realizing that someone had been there, and recently, too. She froze, fear clutching at her throat. How could he know? Had he followed her at some point? But no, he would never have followed her; more often than not, those times when she ran for the safety of the cave he was already finished with her. There was no need for him to pursue; even had he wanted to follow, he'd have likely been too drunk to make it down the mountain.

Cautiously she stood, stooping, and approached the boughs and leaves she had arranged as her bed. Hesitating, awkward, she reached for the sack, and then drew her hand back as if expecting to be attacked. Chiding herself, she reached again and pulled the faded sack towards her. Mustering her courage, she looked inside, and immediately her stomach clinched, her salivary glands going into overdrive. She hadn't eaten since early morning, hours ago. Forgetting caution, she pulled out the bread and cheese and stuffed her mouth greedily, barely taking time to chew before swallowing it down her aching throat. Moments later, temporarily satiated, she ventured outside to drink from the creek, glancing around nervously, halfway expecting to see him come crashing through the brush.

Returning quickly to the cave, she emptied the rest of the sack. Matches. A quilt. Desperate as she was, she scarcely paused to wonder at her luck before noticing the carefully dug fire pit, hidden in the shadows by the wall. For a moment, she simply stared. Then she moved into action.

Shivering with the cold, she approached the fire pit and struck a match, holding it to the kindling, blowing gently, patiently, until it took. Sitting back she surveyed the fire, still cautious, wondering who had infiltrated her safe haven and why they had done so. Finally exhaustion overcame her and she wrapped herself in the quilt, safe and comforted in spite of her misgivings. She had no choice; she was too tired, her body too battered, to resist the lure of the warm fire. Eventually the shivering ceased, the pain eased, and she slept.

High above the holler, havin' secured the animals safely for the night, I stood on the porch and smoked. I leaned forward against the rail, elbows propped as was my habit. The moon was full, castin' an eerie glow upon the woods and illuminatin' a fine mist that hovered just above the wet ground. A few wispy clouds was scuttlin' across the sky and a soft breeze was blowin' around the cabin. I remember listenin' to the rustlin' of the tree branches overhead, watchin' the first of the fall's colorful leaves loosen their hold in the fadin' light and drift into my little clearin'. The air was tangy like it gets on early fall nights, and I breathed deep of that smell. As always, I stood alone, watchin' the full moon and listenin' to the sounds of the mountain, both my curse and my savior them past thirty years. The girl was out there; I knew it. I could feel her presence in the wind.

Chapter Six
The trip
Crutcher Mountain, West Virginia, 1975

I had to go into town. I didn't want to, but I had to. By first light that next mornin', I had already seen to the animals and had my breakfast, a cup of strong black coffee, a slab of dry toast, and an egg. I ate slow, puttin' off the time to leave. Finally, I took one last look around the cabin before shoulderin' my rucksack, grabbin' my rifle, and settin' off down the mountain, this time headin' north. I went to town only twicet a year, once to prepare for winter, and again just before summer, and that day was the day. I dreaded the trip, but there wasn't no way around it. It was dang near impossible to get down them mountains once the snows came. Or, more accurately, it was dang near impossible to get back *up* the mountain once I'd made it down, and I wasn't takin' no chance of gettin' stranded in that town.

I provided all I could for myself in my little clearin' on the summit, and did a fine job of it, too, if I do say so myself. But some things had to be bought. I needed flour and sugar, tobacco, chicken feed, beans and coffee. Expectin' an especially long and cold winter, I also suspected I had better stock up on ammunition. In a couple of months I wouldn't no longer be able to fish for meat, and I'd need to rely on whatever small game I could hunt.

I headed down the mountain, distractin' myself from my misgivin's by countin' the different bird calls and namin' the flowers that was still growin' this late in the season. Cardinal, of course, and titmouse, bluejay, and chickadee. Birds that would tough out the winter right alongside me. The golden eagle spiralin' overhead in search of prey was a winter visitor, but the warbler callin' in the distance would soon be leavin' the mountains for warmer ground. The wildflowers would also be gone before long. My own personal favorite, Indian paintbrush, was still blazin' orange on top of the mountain, but pretty soon it would give up and call it quits for the season. Likewise the Queen Anne's lace, the cardinal flowers and even the little bellflowers. That mornin', though, they was still strugglin' on, their colors like little points of light along the trail.

I did love my mountain home, could scarcely remember it any other way. I had learned to live with the seasons, more comfortable with the wildlife than with the people in the town I was now approachin'. It was hard to remember it that mornin', what with my heart constrictin' with dread, but there had been a time when I thrived in the company of friends and lived for the easy celebrations of village life. Not for years, though; not for many, many years. As I hiked closer to the bottom of the mountain, I'd have given plumb near anythin' to be headin' up instead of down.

At first glance, nothin' looked changed in the little minin' town where I'd grown up. The hand painted sign still boasted a population of less than 200, and the town still referred to itself as *Cedar Hollow, the friendliest little town on the map!* What Cedar Hollow really was, was a minin' town, and not much else.

A modern day remainder of the land parceled out in 1772 by Great Britain's King George III to Captain John Savage, the old folks still sometimes referred to the town as part of the original Savage Land Grant. They was proud of that little bit of information, that is for sure. The way I was taught it, in the middle of the Colonial Wars, Great Britain's King George III got worried. He needed more manpower, and to get that manpower he come up with the idea of promisin' free land to colonial soldiers willin' to fight for Great Britain in the French and Indian War. A few years after the war ended, the king made good on his promise and signed almost 28,000 acres over to Captain Savage and fifty-nine other soldiers.

Them soldiers lost out in the end, though, because they was expected to pay taxes on that land. Them men had been fightin' wars; they didn't have no money. The little piece of land that makes up Cedar Hollow was lost to any of the survivin' soldiers shortly after it had been given to 'em. There was court battles and fightin' before, decades later, the land came to be shared by the descendants of two of them original soldiers. Them descendants now hold permanent residence in the Cedar Hollow Baptist Church Cemetery. After they was dead, didn't no one really know who owned Cedar Hollow, and the state swallowed it up, like governments is known to do. The residents didn't really care. They was used to changin' their allegiance to follow whoever they knew to be in charge; it didn't make no difference who it was. Life was still hard and they was still poor; that was all they really cared about.

In the followin' years Cedar Hollow hadn't grown much, drawin' only a handful of new residents with the start of coal minin' in the mid-nineteenth century, poor folks hopin' to scrape out a livin' in the unforgivin' mines. That's how my daddy ended up there. Bein' Irish made it hard to get a job in the city (*Gaeilge nach mbeidh feidhm ag*, he said to me and Momma; there wasn't no point in an Irishman applyin' for them jobs) but the mines didn't care where nobody come from. They was what you'd call nondiscriminatory when it came to killin' men, and Daddy needed a job.

I had to memorize all that history in school as a girl, but it didn't mean nothin' to me. You can recite all the important soundin' history you want, but Cedar Hollow is just one of dozens of little mountain towns, all dependent on them mines, and all so far away from the conveniences of modern day civilization that they seem to be perched right on the edge of the world, ready to topple over into the pits of hell at any given moment. Sometimes, they do. You could ask my daddy about that, exceptin' he's dead. He was one of the unlucky ones that lost his life the last time Cedar Hollow toppled over into hell.

Daddy died in the Wallington Mine explosion back in 1935. I wasn't hardly no more than a baby, but I do remember my daddy. When I think of him he's always laughin' in my mind. He was a big man, and strong, with

29

thick black hair and a loud voice. I remember him throwin'
me up high in the air and then catchin' me up against his
chest, his whiskers rough on my face. And I remember him
teasin' me, callin' me his little tornado and tellin' me to slow
down. *Mall sios, beag amhain.* Slow down, little one, he
always said, but I could tell he liked my high energy. Daddy
had crossed over the ocean to build a better life, he said, and
I suppose if I'm to be fair I'll admit it probably was a better
life than the one he'd had back in Ireland. Daddy grew up in
the slums of Limerick, sometimes freezin', sometimes
starvin', always poor. Havin' a real job and a actual house
must have seemed pretty rich to my daddy. It just don't
seem fair that he only got to enjoy it for such a short time,
but life ain't fair, my momma always said, and she was right
about that; she surely was.

I remember that day, too, when the mine blowed up. I
remember hearin' that big boom and feelin' the house shake,
and I remember standin' out in the road lookin' up at all that
black smoke in the sky. I was tuggin' on Momma's dress
hem, pointin' and askin' her what it was, but she wasn't
answerin' me. Momma was standin' still but she was shakin',
and she had her fist pressed up against her mouth, bitin' it.
That scared me more than anythin', watchin' her bite her fist
that way. The other folks in town was runnin' ever' which-a-
way, all yellin' and cryin' but Momma didn't make a sound,
just stood still in the middle of it all, lookin' up at that black
sky while the blood run down her hand and dripped on the
road. She knew what I didn't yet understand; the mine had
struck again and wasn't nobody goin' to be comin' home that
evenin'. All them sons and brothers and husbands and
daddies was gone.

The mine, shaft number twenty-seven, has been closed
since the explosion, roped off and posted with signs warnin'
curious spectators away. That mornin' on my way to town it
was nearly overgrown, the dirt road leadin' to its entrance all
choked up with weeds. As I passed by that old rusted gate, I
turned my head away. I couldn't look at the place that had
claimed my daddy's life.

Back in them days, the days of the Wallington explosion,

as it came to be called, the United Mine Workers of America hadn't yet established no health and retirement funds and Harry Truman was still a decade away from the White House. After Daddy was killed, me and Momma had to move out of the little house we'd always lived in; we didn't have no money. Even though people had been nice enough to Momma while Daddy was alive, once he was gone she didn't feel a part of the town. To her, it seemed like all of a sudden her Cherokee features was noticed more, and not always kindly.

That was how she felt, and so that was how she acted. She was an outsider, from some place farther south then Cedar Hollow, and that, combined with her heritage, served to make her feel unwelcome without my daddy around to lean on. No one said anythin' bad to her, of course, but no one stepped in to offer their friendship, neither. At least not in such a way that Momma could recognize it, and I reckon that's what counts. If she couldn't recognize it, it didn't do her much good.

Thank heaven for old Dr. Leary, though I don't like to give thanks for somebody else's misfortune. Dr. Leary had a wife livin' at Hopemont, the state sanitarium for tuberculosis. I don't reckon I ever even seen the woman, but Dr. Leary visited her steady until her death. I don't know as he loved her by then, or if he just felt beholden to her in her poor health. Either way, his wife's illness was a sort of blessin' in disguise for me and Momma. When Daddy was killed, Dr. Leary asked Momma if she would consider comin' to work for him. He told her we could live up in his attic in exchange for helpin' to raise his little girl and keep his house in order.

His girl was at that time thirteen years old and in dire need of some womanly instruction. Poor old Dr. Leary didn't know what to do with that child, and she was a willful one; I remember that. Needless to say, we took him up on his offer. We didn't have much of a choice, but that was all right. It was a good shelter for us; we couldn't have asked for no more. And Dr. Leary was a respectful person, though I won't lie and say the same for his daughter.

We lived up in that attic for durn near ten years, and probably would have longer exceptin' that Momma died of the female cancer. It was 1945 when I lost Momma. I was fourteen years old. In the beginnin' I stayed on with Dr. Leary. I didn't have nowhere else to go; Momma's people had disowned her when she married a white man, and I wouldn't have known how to find Daddy's people even if I'd been of a mind to, which I wasn't. Cedar Hollow was my home and I didn't know none of Daddy's people; I hadn't never met a one of 'em, and from the tales Daddy had told me about Ireland, I didn't reckon it was a place I wanted to go.

At any rate, Dr Leary had a kind heart; he wouldn't never have put me out on the street. See, that is the thing about it. Life is hard up in them mountains, but there is always somebody good to help lift you up. Dr. Leary was one of them people. I took on the cookin' and cleanin' for Dr. Leary and tried to earn my keep. His daughter was long gone by then, of course, married down in Memphis and waitin' on her husband to get back from the war.

Dr. Leary and I just kept on the way we always had for a little while. I didn't have no plans for the future; truth be told I didn't even know a future could be planned. If it could, how was it that I was orphaned at the age of fourteen? As far as I could see, you took what life handed you and didn't go off lookin' for more. What life had handed me at that time was an attic in Dr. Leary's house, and I was grateful for it; I truly was. That was all to change, but I hadn't yet known that at the time.

Chapter Seven
The town of Cedar Hollow

That day, leavin' my mountain behind and followin' the dirt road into town, I threw the remains of my cigarette into the dust and blocked them memories from my mind. I needed to contend with the chores on my list, and I couldn't do that surrounded by ghosts. Another mile and I entered what passed for the main drag. A low row of buildin's flanked either side of the road. Although they was nearly all built of red brick most of 'em had at some point been painted white, and after years and layers of coal dust they was now all a dingy gray. A barbershop with a spinnin' red and white striped pole, a butcher shop, and what had, years ago, been Dr. Leary's office, still apparently a doctor's office but not one I'd ever known of. The Cedar Hollow Library was next, and I was pleased to see it was open. Peggy's Diner was still there, with what looked to be the same group of men as had been there thirty years ago, smokin' and cacklin' and coughin' on them worn, wooden benches outside the diner's door.

They hushed their talk and looked up at me as I walked by. They recognized me, and some of 'em gave me a nod as I passed. I imagine a lot of 'em had known my daddy. I nodded back at 'em, and after a minute they returned to their stories, coughin' as before. Always the coughin' with them old retired miners; they have to work hard to catch a breath against the black dust in their lungs. It sometimes seemed like my whole childhood had been filled up with the sound of old men hackin' up little bits of coal and lung while they fell to pieces from the inside out.

The school was farther down, farther than I would go

today, but I figured it was still the same, a smallish red brick buildin' with a playground out front, teachers on the front steps ringin' an old cowbell like they had done when I was a girl. I remembered some fun times in that old schoolyard, playin' chase and baseball and kick-the-can. Behind the school there was an old drainage culvert, and I reckoned it was still there, probably not known by very many, but surely known to me and a handful of others. Yes, indeed.

I made my way to the fourth buildin' on the right, Mr. Smith's General Store, owned by Mr. Gerald Smith for at least the last fifty years, and by his daddy before him. Even the window display looked about the same, showin' overalls and dusty water buckets alongside chicken feed and sorghum molasses. Mr. Smith might have been the one man in town who had altogether escaped the tragedy of the mines, but tragedy had touched him in other ways. He had always been kind to me and Momma, slippin' a little extra cornmeal or a piece of candy into our packages when we shopped for Dr. Leary. Mr. Smith knew times was tough, and he tried to help folks out as best he could, bless his heart. He was one of them people I was talkin' about, one of them who lifts you up. Pullin' open the door, I stomped the dust off my boots and took a minute to let my eyes adjust to the dim light before I walked in. The jinglin' of the bell had signaled my arrival, and heads turned to see who it was, but I didn't look back at none of 'em. I had learned that was the best way.

For a minute there wasn't nothin' but silence, and then there it came, as I had feared it would. "Wal, if it ain't our little Injun queer. How're they hangin' these days, Billy May?" An all too familiar voice yelled out from somewhere in the shadows to my left, over by the old wood stove where the men always gathered between shifts at the mine.

I ignored the voice, along with the nervous laughs that followed, and made my way to the back of the store, past gardenin' tools and bolts of cloth, penny nails and sacks of cornmeal. I was relieved when I seen that Mr. Smith was still there in his usual place behind the counter, more stooped than last time, maybe, but otherwise the same. As I approached the counter I seen the kindness in his eyes, and I

34

had to look away. This wasn't no time for me to show weakness, and the look in Mr. Smith's eyes had brought a burnin' to the back of my own. Lookin' down, I set my rucksack on the counter, untyin' the roll of skins I had affixed to the top and spreadin' them out for him to see. This was our ritual, had been for years. I brought skins, and he traded me my staples. I didn't know if he really wanted the skins, or if he did it out of kindness. It was hard to know with Mr. Smith, but either way I was full of appreciation. I reckon I loved that old man, but I wasn't the type to tell it back then. Later, after everythin' had happened, I was to find out just how much he had loved me, too.

That day at the store, Mr. Smith had adjusted his glasses and leaned forward. "Bear this time," he said, admirin' the skins, and his voice was weaker than I remembered.

"Some rabbit and 'coon, too," I pointed out, my own voice gruff. I wasn't used to conversin' with people no more. The most exercise my vocal chords ever got was me yellin' at the goats or talkin' to the chickens.

Fingerin' the skins and gruntin' his approval, Mr. Smith set about gettin' my supplies, already familiar with what I needed. While he did that, my eye fell on the jars of penny candy along the counter, and before I even knew what I was doin' I made a request of him. "Do you reckon I have enough to get a handful of them Mary Janes?" I asked, no one more surprised than myself at my askin'. Mr. Smith looked back at me quick-like, and then he smiled. "Of course you do, honey. You go ahead and get yourself some." He turned back to the scale, then, weighin' my beans.

When our dealin' was completed, I packed my rucksack, nodded my thanks and turned to go, only to find my path blocked by a burly man a few years older than I was. The owner of the hecklin' voice, he was dressed in brown camouflage huntin' gear, his big old belly strainin' at the buttons, and he had a cap pulled down low over his thick, mottled up face; his veins was broken across his nose. Dark, greasy hair curled out from underneath the crown of that old cap, and I felt my breakfast risin' up into my throat.

"What's the matter, Billy May?" he asked me then. "Ain't

35

you goin' to speak? Seein' as how we're old friends, and all."

He was a bull of a man, leerin' down at me with them rotted teeth, tobacco juice spillin' down his chin. He leaned towards me and his foul breath washed over my face, makin' my breakfast rise up a little higher. I wasn't goin' to let myself be goaded into speakin' to him, but when I moved to go past him he grabbed my arm with his beefy hand. His fingernails was crusted and black against my faded red flannel sleeve, and he was pressin' them through the cloth and into my flesh. I was scared then, that's the honest truth, but I was even more angry than I was scared. The hatred I had towards that man ballooned up in me and I looked at him then, into his bloodshot eyes, and I seen that the whites was yellowed from all the liquor. He was a ugly man in every way there is for a man to be ugly.

"Give me an excuse to shoot, and I'll kill you where you stand," I said to him. I said it soft; I wasn't tryin' to draw no attention to us, but I knew everyone was watchin' us, anyway. I meant it, too. I'd have blown him away in about a heartbeat, and I'd have felt just fine doin' it.

For a minute there wasn't nothin', and then I put my finger on the trigger.

"Let her go, Jimmy." It was the quiet voice of Mr. Smith, and then Jimmy let me go and stepped back, whether from the sight of my finger on the trigger or from Mr. Smith's order I did not know, nor did I care.

I stepped around the sweaty bulk of him and made my way out of the store, fightin' against the urge to retch. I would not give him the satisfaction of knowin' how he upset me. Outside the store, I gripped my rifle hard against me. I hadn't never yet had to use it on them cursed trips to town, but if the occasion arose, I wouldn't think twicet. Maybe that was why the hecklin' never went no further than that. No one moved to stop me, and I retraced my steps, headed back the way I had come, towards the Cedar Hollow Library.

I stepped through the door into the cool, musty air of the library and all of a sudden I felt ten years old again. As a young girl, steppin' into the library had always made me feel

36

clumsy, no matter how quiet I had tried to be. I was a fast child, it's true, always blunderin' my way into things without stoppin' to think. Maybe that's why enterin' the library always made me feel like I'd just interrupted somethin' important, like a religious ceremony or a meetin' of some kind. From the way I'm goin' on, you'd think I didn't like the library but that ain't true. I spent a whole lot of afternoons there, sittin' at one of them wooden tables with my legs curled up under me, lost in the pages of *Little Women* or *Tom Sawyer*, or my favorite, a new addition to the Cedar Hollow Library, *The Long Winter*. It had made me feel special somehow, like a grown up, to sit in all that quiet and read them books. That particular day, the library soothed me. It was a welcome feelin' after my encounter with Jimmy.

As the door swung shut behind me, I found myself hopin' to evade the wrath of Ms. Temple, the old librarian, though if I'd had my head on straight I'd have realized she must surely be dead; that woman had been older than dirt thirty years before. Sometimes I forgot how long it had been. As I moved forward, I seen that the current librarian wasn't nothin' like Ms. Temple; was, in fact, probably a good twenty years younger than me, blonde and petite, dressed in wide-legged dungarees and a sleeveless peasant blouse, a beaded turquoise headband holdin' back her long hair.

"Can I help you?" the young woman asked, glancin' with curiosity at my own getup. I supposed I did look strange to her. I didn't remember the last time I'd looked in a mirror, and I wasn't in no hurry to do it then, either.

I chose to ignore her curiosity and stepped towards the counter, lookin' up at the young woman. When I was a girl, the librarian's desk had seemed huge to me, like a big old throne or somethin', and I had always been a little bit afraid to approach it. I had wondered back then, in my youthful ignorance, if the librarian was more than just a keeper of the books; I had wondered if over the years she had somehow gained all the knowledge out of them books as well.

Given all the things I'd lived through since then, it would have taken a lot more than a librarian to scare me that day, so I said, real steady, "I'm lookin' for a book called *Jonathan*

Livingston Seagull. Do you happen to have it? It was written by a man named Richard Bach."

She plumb lit up at the title. "Well, of course," she said, all excited. "It was a New York Times best seller, you know."

I didn't, in fact, know, but I was willin' to listen.

"It's one of the best selling books in the whole country," the young woman told me. "Let me get it for you."

Gatherin' my thoughts, I held up a hand to slow the young woman down. *Mall sios, beag amhain,* I thought, but I didn't say it. I figured she thought I was crazy enough as it was, and I didn't want to scare her none.

"Hold on a minute," I said. "I live up on Crutcher Mountain. I want to read the book, but I won't be able to get it back down here 'til spring. When the snow comes, I cain't get off the mountain 'til the spring thaw."

She looked at me hard then, like maybe she thought she knew me. "Oh!" she said, and I seen that I had succeeded in slowin' her down, because she stopped dead still. "You must be Billy May Platte. I've heard about you living up on that mountain. That must be so exciting, like a real pioneer woman. What fun!"

Lord have mercy, I remember thinkin', this here is a very young and inexperienced woman if she believes livin' up on a mountaintop is fun. Like I said before, I loved my mountain, and I realized I'd been out of society for a long time, but from what I remembered, swingin' an axe and churnin' butter wasn't ordinarily thought of as fun. But she was a sweet little thing, and I didn't want to hurt her feelin's none, so I just smiled and said, "Well, it can be interestin', I guess."

"Honey, you take the book," she said, "and I know you'll bring it back in the spring. We have several copies," she continued. "And no one in this town reads, anyway, you know? Besides, Mr. Smith will vouch for you, he talks about you all the time."

She was a chatty one, that girl, and my ears wasn't used to so many words. I waited quietly while she fetched the book and made a notation about its whereabouts, then I added it to my rucksack as she returned to her seat high behind that big desk.

"Now you let me know what you think about it, a free spirit such as yourself," she smiled down at me. "Oh, I'm so jealous. I'd love to get off into the wilderness like that, be my own woman, you know? Take care, honey!"

My head spinnin', I made my way towards the door. So far that day I'd nearly been forced to shoot a man and I'd been called "honey" three times. You have to realize, aside from when that old mongrel came around, the closest thing to socialization I had up on that mountain was when them chickens squawked at me or one of them goats head butted me off my feet when I wasn't payin' attention. I wasn't used to all that stimulation, and I didn't think I could take much more of it. I was feelin' crowded. I thanked her kindly and pushed my way outside, suckin' in the fresh mountain air and longin' for the safety and isolation of my cabin on the summit. Not quite yet, though. I still had one more place to go. I reached the road and turned right, headin' east.

The church was white clapboard and needed paintin' somethin' awful. The peelin', hand painted sign out front announced it as *Cedar Hollow Baptist Church*, and reminded people that *There is no SUN without the SON!* It was the only church in town, leavin' those who didn't identify themselves as Baptist without options. My daddy had been Catholic and my momma had been raised with a different kind of religious belief, one that she learned from her people and that didn't really have a church attached to it. We wasn't regular members of the church, but we did go as a family sometimes before Daddy died, and I went by myself sometimes later, not so much to worship but because it was a social meetin' place, and isolated up as we was in them mountains, we took what we could get.

Although the church had seen better days, the settin' was still pretty, stuck back like it was between the stone sides of them mountain walls. Azaleas was planted all along the front walk. They was flowerless now, but from my springtime trips I knew they was deep pink in season. Oaks and elms towered up way higher than the little church, leavin' it in the shadows. Not even the steeple, topped with that big white cross, could compete with them trees for height.

I remembered the day that cross had come, ordered from some exotic far away place. It was made of a new thing called fiberglass, one of the first ever made. The townsfolk had worked so hard to buy that cross, scrimpin' and savin' for the better part of three years. The women had held bake sales and the men had had carwashes, not just in Cedar Hollow but in the city, over in Huntington, nearly an hour away from Cedar Hollow. Back in them days, it was an ordeal to travel that far. Plenty of folks in Cedar Hollow, myself included, had never got any farther out of Cedar Hollow than they could walk to and from in a day's time.

The cross was supposed to be lighter than wood so the steeple could support it, but lookin' at it all them years ago I had had my doubts. It was so big, much too big to fit on that church's little steeple. I can still remember how surprised I was later that evenin' to see how much smaller it had looked once it was in the air, bolted onto that steeple as if it had always belonged.

The whole town had come for the cross hangin', as we called it, which as I reflect was an odd name to give it, but I reckon we didn't know no better. The excitement was just buzzin' through the street; you could feel it in the air. It was the closest thing to a carnival most of the townsfolk had ever experienced; it was also the closest most of us was likely to ever get. I remember the church choir, sweatin' in them robes, singin' "The Old Rugged Cross" without no piano music to help them along. Their voices was floatin' out in the breeze under the elm trees, while Brother Hudson, with his eyes closed like they always was when he was experiencin' the rapture, was praisin' God at the top of his lungs, his voice tremblin' so I was afraid he might cry. I hoped he wouldn't. I hadn't never seen a grown man cry, and it seemed to me back then that it would be a terrible thing to witness. Members and nonmembers alike was there, bein' saved and gettin' dunked in the creek, moved by the spirit of the Lord, or at least by the spirit of the celebration. I myself even considered gettin' dunked. It was mighty hot that day, and some cool creek water seemed to me like a good idea. Only the thought of my momma's ire kept me from it. She didn't hold to dunkin' people in a creek. Brother Hudson did, though, and even old man Pritchett got dunked, reekin' of the moonshine everyone pretended he didn't make down in that still out back of his shed.

I remember, too, how much my mouth was waterin' at the food. Cain't nobody cook like a good Baptist woman, and that is just the truth. There was casseroles and pies, sweet tea and lemonade, even a roasted hog the men cooked up in a hole in the ground. I hadn't never seen nothin' like that. Someone had even put a apple in that pig's mouth, and I could not get over how funny that was. Food was just plumb everywhere, all spread out on red and white checked tablecloths thrown over tables made from planks and sawhorses. The women was fussin' over the food and the babies while the men was fussin' over tools and ladders. Wasn't no one quite sure exactly how they was supposed to attach that cross, but everyone was sure they would figure it out. And they did, too. Thirty-five years later, there I was lookin' up at it.

It had seemed to me all them years ago that the only townsperson absent was my momma. Momma hadn't never been comfortable in crowds, especially not after Daddy was gone. She always found reasons not to participate in social gatherin's, preferrin' to stay by herself in the doctor's house, rewashin' them windows or scrubbin' them spotless floors. Not me, though. Back then, I looked for every chance to escape that lonely old house; it was so dark with them thick draperies and all that heavy furniture. In my imagination, that darkness sucked the air clean out of that house and made me feel like I was suffocatin' if I stayed inside too long. More than anythin', I loved to run around with the other younguns. We was all friends back then; there wasn't a one of us that was on the outs. It didn't pay to put no one on the outs; there wasn't enough of us as it was. I reckon we must have been ten or eleven on the day of the cross hangin'. Old enough to get into trouble and young enough not to care, as Momma used to say.

When the townswomen asked about Momma, I always

answered 'em politely, sayin' only, "She's busy at the house, but I'll tell her you asked about her, ma'am." I wasn't old enough back then to see the things Momma thought she saw, so I cain't speak as to their existence. Don't get me wrong; Momma would not lie, but sometimes the way one person sees somethin' ain't necessarily the way another person does. She didn't feel a part of the town, but I did. I ran and chased and teased and aggravated with the best of 'em.

The townswomen always told me I was a beautiful child, but I don't know if I was, or if they was just pityin' me. I did have Momma's high cheekbones and thick, black hair, and Daddy's strong, slender build. I also had Daddy's quick laughter back then, though that changed later. I am not braggin' when I say I was a favorite with my peers. I didn't have no fear of high ledges and dark places, and I was always willin' and ready to try blamed near everythin', much to Momma's despair. I was as darin' and high spirited as any of them boys, and even faster than freckle-faced, red haired Raymond O'Brien, the fastest boy in school. Lord, that boy's hair was red, and we used to tease him that maybe he was runnin' so fast on account of his head was on fire.

On the day the cross arrived, for the first time in my memory children was allowed up them rickety narrow steps into the tower where the bell was hung. We was even allowed one pull on that thick rope, and if we was strong enough, the bell would ring itself out over the whole valley. Corinne Pruitt and me climbed them steps and pulled together, soundin' that bell clear across West Virginia. We was quite pleased with ourselves, and we teased Darryl Lane and Eugene Cooper terribly when they wasn't strong enough to ring it themselves. To add to Darryl's shame, he'd thrown up on the steps leadin' up to the tower, claimin' the stomach flu, but we all knew that was a lie. Darryl was deathly afraid of heights. He always took sick when he had to climb. We all knew it, but that didn't stop us from teasin' him. By the time the women called us to eat, Darryl had made a miraculous recovery.

Corinne Pruitt, with her blue eyes and white-blonde hair had been, in my opinion, anyway, the most beautiful girl in the world, and she was my best friend to boot. You just couldn't get no closer than we was, back then, before everythin' happened. Corinne's daddy had also worked in the mines, but he had been a foreman, high above my daddy in terms of pay. Still and yet, losin' our daddies at such a young age had brought us close in spite of that difference. Corinne wasn't one of them girls that put on airs; she was just a regular person.

Corinne lived just down the street from Dr. Leary's, in a clean yellow house with white trim. They had a brick walk leadin' up to the door and the yard was surrounded by rose bushes. I thought it was the prettiest house in town. Corinne herself was surrounded by grandparents, aunts and uncles, and even cousins. I visited over there all the time, every chance I could get. Dr. Leary's house was dark and quiet, but Corinne's house was bright and noisy. I suppose I was hungerin' for family, though I didn't think of it that way back then. I loved Corinne's momma, too. She was gentle and nice, and when she laughed, it sounded to me like a little bell tinklin' in the wind. She used to call me her other daughter, and she had this way of smoothin' my hair back off my face. I don't know as I ever told her what that meant to me, but it warmed my heart every time she did it.

Corinne also had an older brother named William, Willy to his family. I didn't know him, other than to see him lurkin' around when I came to visit Corinne and her momma. He was so much older than me when the mine exploded, nearly in his teens. What I remember of him at that time was that he was always frownin', and his tone with his momma was not a nice one. My momma would have washed my mouth out had I spoke that way to her. On the day the cross came he was far away at boot camp, trainin' to be a soldier. The rumor was that the U.S. was goin' to have to join up in the war over in Europe, and Willy wanted to be ready when the call came.

I shook my head, irritated with myself. I hadn't gone to town that day to be rememberin' all them things, and my destination at that time wasn't the tower or even the church. Bypassin' the church, I wound my way along an old stone path, around the side of the church and farther on, until I came to the tall, black wrought iron cemetery gate.

Chapter Eight
Lost loved ones

The gate was unlocked, like it always was, and I slipped through the openin' and stood for a minute, takin' in the rows of tombstones. A lot of 'em was over a hundred years old, gray and crumblin' but still well cared for, I was glad to see. The grass was mowed and clipped, and them tombstones that didn't have no fresh flowers at least didn't have no dead ones, or even worse, plastic ones. I never did care for plastic flowers when there is so many real ones available for the pickin'. I was needin' a smoke, but it would have to wait. I refused to disrespect the dead that way.

On a separate hill behind the main cemetery was an American flag blowin' in the wind, and under it was a special section for war heroes that had passed on. The section was nearly full that day, and that was a sad thing to me. Lookin' at all them graves, it seemed to me like the Forest of Argonne, the black land of Iwo Jima, and the jungles of Korea and Vietnam was like some kind of ancient sacrificial grounds of the gods I had read about in school, and them gods was forever demandin' the blood of young men. Had I been a different kind of woman, a woman who hadn't experienced the things I'd experienced, I might have stopped to ponder on that, but as it was, I wasn't interested in philosophical debates. I was interested in takin' care of my business and gettin' the hell out of town.

Lookin' towards the hill, I stood for a minute out of respect for all them fallen soldiers. Willy Pruitt, Corinne's older brother, was buried there, killed not in battle but by his own hand. The respect I felt for the buried men of war did not extend to Willy Pruitt. Truth be told, I didn't think Willy had no business bein' buried alongside those honorable men, but that hadn't been my decision to make. On the day that Willy had chosen to end his life, I had been strugglin' to reclaim mine.

I continued on, headin' left towards the crooked elm tree across the way, where both of my parents is buried. Approachin' their graves, I knelt down and reached out to trace the letters carved into the stone slabs. *Richard T. Platt, Jr., Beloved Husband and Father, 1905-1935*. And next to him, *Suzanna Clearwater Platt, Beloved Mother, 1910-1945*. So many years had passed by then that my memories was hazy, yet I still felt the loss just as deep as I did the day I was orphaned.

Though Daddy's death had been fast, Momma had suffered at the end; there wasn't no way around that. I didn't know when Momma had first taken sick; she had kept it to herself. That's the way Momma was. When I did find out, it was by accident. Early one mornin', halfway to the schoolhouse, I seen that I had left my lunch pail at home. I was such an active child; I didn't want to have to miss eatin' lunch. I told my friends to let the teacher know I was comin' if I didn't get there in time, then I turned and ran back to Dr. Leary's house as quick as I could. Slammin' through the kitchen door, mussed and out of breath, I found Momma down on her knees on the kitchen floor, her head hangin' low, her hands grippin' that counter top so tight her knuckles was white. She looked up at me, surprised, and struggled up to her feet, stiflin' a gasp as she stood. Momma was a strong woman, and I know that she was embarrassed about me seein' her that way. Even still, I feel bad about that, about catchin' her in a weakened state, and there's a part of me that wishes I could take it back. That day, I was at first just surprised to see her on the floor. I thought maybe she had dropped somethin' or was scrubbin' at a spot of dirt, but when I seen her face, seen how pale she was with them drops of sweat snakin' their way down her cheeks, I was afraid. I truly was.

Momma's health slid downhill quick after that, maybe because she didn't no longer have to hide her pain, or maybe because durin' the months she had surely known about and kept secret her illness it had already destroyed her body. What was certain was that by the time I came across her in the kitchen, Momma was already near the end.

It wasn't but a few days before Momma couldn't no longer stand and was forced to her bed by pain so overwhelmin' I seen it make her cry. I fetched her water and wiped the hair off her sweaty face, tryin' to comfort her when the pain took hold, changin' her sheets and cleanin' her when she couldn't no longer control her bowels. Dr. Leary begged Momma to go to Huntington for treatment at the hospital, but she wouldn't have none of it. I wonder sometimes if she was just ready to die. She wasn't a happy woman; that much is certain. Maybe she didn't feel like there was nothin' to keep her here. Or maybe she wanted to escape what it was makin' her stay. When Dr. Leary seen she wasn't goin' to change her mind, he done his best to prescribe pills to relieve the pain, but towards the end it was all in vain; there wasn't nothin' that could relieve her. It seemed to take Momma a long time to die, an unbearably long and painful time, but in reality it was just a matter of weeks.

I loved my momma. I knew the sacrifices Momma made to keep me sheltered and fed after the mine killed my Daddy. I knew if she hadn't had me, she might have taken her chances with her family, gone back to try and find 'em, askin' 'em for forgiveness. But there wasn't no way for her to do that with me in tow. They would not have wanted a half-breed child comin' into their family.

Momma wasn't the same after Daddy died. She withdrew plumb into herself. She didn't never complain, but she didn't never laugh, neither. I reckon as long as she had Daddy with her, it was worth losin' her family, but once he was gone, she didn't have no one. Don't get me wrong, she loved me the best she could, and she didn't never mistreat me. Momma never raised a hand to me, and I know I must have sorely tested her patience. Her death hit me hard, harder than anyone knew.

After all, I was my momma's daughter, part Cherokee and full Appalachian. Momma wasn't given to talkin' about her feelin's, and so neither was I. Showin' feelin's was a weakness. This is what Momma taught me, and this is what I believed. When Momma died, I was alone in my grief, not because no one cared but because I couldn't let 'em know how deep my sadness ran. I didn't know no different; I just followed my momma's example.

Standin', workin' out the kinks in my knees, I said a silent good-bye to Momma and Daddy and turned right, movin' across the cemetery to the far end. There was less sun on this side, and the gravestones was smaller and had a neglected air about 'em. I squatted in front of the one I was lookin' for, and then I had to sit down on the ground. I was all of a sudden too tired to support my own weight, and I am not a big woman. *Pauline Henley Crutcher, 1880-1956, Wife of David P. Crutcher, missing these many years.*

I ain't never met David P. Crutcher; he has been dead since long before I was born, killed in the Spanish-American War (John Hay's "splendid little war," as it was known, but Polly disagreed with Mr. Hay on that assessment, and it's a good thing he never made it to Cedar Hollow, or he'd have gotten an earful). David's body was lost out to sea, and this late on, I don't reckon it will ever be found.

Although I hadn't known David, I had most certainly known Polly. When you got right down to it, I supposed Polly had gave me the only real feelin' of love I had ever known at that time in my life. I didn't need to see Polly's grave to visit with her; she was always with me, but it wouldn't have seemed right not to stop by since I was there anyhow. I sat with her grave for a little while with my head bowed low as the warm sun passed by overhead. After some time, I pushed myself to my feet, stiff and chilled from sittin' on the cool ground so long. I reached out and patted her stone, sayin' goodbye to her body, I reckon, but not to Polly.

It was gettin' late, the sun already lower in the sky, and I had a long hike home. I was tired, that ain't no lie. Them trips to town wore on me, and I still had chores to do and animals to tend. I shouldered my rucksack and left the cemetery, hikin' my way back to the dirt road that would lead me back to my mountain.

"Billy May." The voice was soft.

I stopped in my tracks, cigarette halfway to my mouth. I knew this voice, too, but it brought on a wholly different range of feelin's. Against my will, I turned towards it. I did not want to, but what else could I do? The owner of this voice was a woman. She was the same age as me but I seen that she looked younger. Her skin was still smooth and there wasn't no gray in her hair. It was long and blonde, caught up in a bun of sorts on the back of her neck. Fine lines was just startin' at the outer corners of her eyes. Them eyes was still the same shade of blue, and they was lookin' at me with somethin' that looked close to fear.

She was thin, and just a wee bit taller than me. She was wearin' a dress in some kind of flowered print and her feet was shod in them practical low heeled shoes all the women in the village wore. She was pretty, not as beautiful as I remembered her, but I hadn't seen her in nigh twenty years, not since I came back to town for Polly's funeral, and beauty is hard to maintain in a poor, coal minin' West Virginia town.

"Billy May," she said again, even softer this time, and I shivered at that sound. I met her look, but I did not answer. I didn't have no idea what to say, so for a minute we just stood like that, facin' each other across the road, the shadows under the oak trees beside the old dirt road growin' out to meet me. It was quiet. I could hear the barkin' of a dog, and then little boys laughin' while they played. She cleared her throat; she was nervous.

"Can you...would you like to stay a minute? I have fresh tea. Maybe we could visit and catch up."

Her voice rose up towards the end, and I remembered that she had always done that when she was feelin' uncertain. While she spoke, she smoothed back her hair, tuckin' a strand back into the bun, but when she let it go, it just fell down again. That almost made me smile. She had forever been tuckin' that strand in, and it had forever been fallin' out again.

I kept my breathin' even, but it was not easy. I waited a

minute before I tried to answer her. I didn't want my voice to give away the thumpin' of my heart.

When I felt like I could speak, I said her name. "Corinne."

She drew in her breath quick-like and held out her hand, steppin' towards me, little puffs of dust kickin' up under her shoes. I jumped back. I did not do it to hurt her, on that I will swear. My reflexes just knew that I did not need her to touch me. "Corinne," I said again, and then shook my head. "No."

She stopped. The sun was lowerin' behind her, and I couldn't no longer make out her face. She waited a minute and then dropped her hand back down. I heard her sigh.

"Thank you for the offer," I said. I tried to make my voice kind. "But I'd best head on back."

When I turned to leave, she ran a little ways after me.

"For God's sake, Billy May," her voice was angry, pleadin' with me in the still air. Her hands was flutterin' towards me, but I knew she wouldn't touch me, not after I stepped back the way I had. "It was so long ago," she said then. "Can't you let it go? Can't you forgive me? Is it worth it to you to hole yourself up on that mountain with nobody? Are you happy that way? Billy May, can't you at least talk to me? Billy May Platte, you answer me!"

But I did not answer her. I forced myself to keep my pace steady and my head up as I made my way back down the road, headed for the mountain and for home. It wasn't that I didn't forgive Corinne; it was more that havin' forgiven Corinne, I didn't have no choice but to move on. The part of my life that had contained Corinne had ended on a stormy night nearly thirty years ago, and in my healin', I just had to let it go. Talkin' about it wouldn't have served no purpose, and pretendin' it never happened was impossible. The events of that night had made me who I was, who I had been for the past thirty years, for better or for worse.

I know she stood there for a while; I could feel her eyes on my back until I rounded the curve and moved out of her sight. It bothered me, and that is the truth.

Chapter Nine
The old woman
Huntington, West Virginia, 2010

They is speakin' in hushed tones, but I can hear the worry in their voices. "I don't know what's wrong with her. Ever since she got that book she's been agitated. She was sleeping peacefully when I checked on her, but then all of a sudden there was a huge crash, and when we got here her lamp was knocked over and she was hanging halfway off her bed." The voice is Starlette's. "It took three of us to get her back on the bed, she was fighting against us so hard. You'd never know she had that kind of strength, looking at her. I can't imagine what upset her so."

I want to tell Starlette I'm okay, but I cain't move. I feel like I am trapped underwater, and their voices is far away, outside of my reach. I'm not afraid, though, and that is purely strange, because of how I hate bein' held down. But this is different. I feel safe, like I'm bein' gently rocked by unseen hands, and I think of Polly. This is a much better feelin' than the one I'd had in my dream.

In the dream, I was bein' held down, too, but not by unseen hands. In the dream, I was bein' held down by the crushin' weight of the devil, my lungs unable to draw a breath, my bones breakin' against the rocks. The devil had his talons buried deep in my scalp, keepin' me still while he sliced me in half with his barbed tail. I think it was a dream, but maybe it wasn't; it's so hard to tell lately. Maybe it was real, and this warmth I'm feelin', this floatin' sensation, is what it feels like to die. If this is what bein' dead is like, I don't mind it one bit. I just wish them troublesome voices would go away and let me rest in peace.

"The sedative should work throughout the night." The voice is deeper now, and I reckon it's the doctor's. "You said she has family coming? When are they due to arrive?"

"Not family," answers Starlette. "At least not that I know of. It's some hotshot producer from California, you know, the one who did that movie about those lost miners in the '30s. Jessica McIntosh."

At the mention of Jessie's name, I remember. No devils, no hooked talons or barbed tails, no respite yet from this pain in my lungs. Just this, the bed and them tubes, the beeps and hums made by all them machines, and the irritation at all them people in and out of my room, never leavin' me alone.

"Really?" The voice is the doctor's again. "What's her connection to Ms. Platte?"

"I don't know," responds Starlette. "If she's family, Ms. Platte has never said. What I do know is that ever since Ms. Platte got that book from her, she's been different. More anxious, but definitely excited about the woman coming to visit her. She's supposed to be here by tomorrow evening. Will the sedative have worn off by then? Ms. Platte won't want to miss her."

"The sedative will be long gone by then," says the doctor. "The bigger worry is whether or not Ms. Platte can hold on that long."

I hear Starlette sigh, the small sound short and sad. "I'll miss Ms. Platte," she says. "I know we're not supposed to get too attached, but there's just something about her. She's so private. So dignified, you know? You never know what she's thinking, and she never complains, although she has to be in pain. She's a strong woman, that's for sure. Got to be strong, to live this long with the cancer." I feel her smoothin' the sheets around my bony frame.

From my warm, fuzzy place below the voices, I allow myself a smile. After all these years, I am still my momma's daughter, I think, before lettin' myself be gently rocked away, my mind floatin' back to the mountain.

Chapter Ten: Billy May and the girl
Crutcher Mountain, West Virginia, 1975

I got into the habit of takin' a little somethin' to eat with me on my fishin' trips to the creek. Not much, just a slice of bread, some cheese, a few wild blackberries before the season ended. I left these things in the flour sack that remained in the cave. After goin' to town, I left them Mary Janes in there, too. I loved them candies when I was a girl, and I wondered if she did, too. Every time I returned to the cave, every three or four days or so, that sack was once again empty, as if it was beggin' me to fill it again.

I hadn't needed to restock the girl's fire makin' supplies, and I was pleased about that. The girl was learnin'. She had gotten better at survival, and I noticed she now kept a stash of kindlin' and wood in the corner of the cave. I left her another book of matches just in case. I seen that she had added a chipped clay pitcher to her stash of supplies, and I assumed that was so she could keep water nearby without leavin' the safety of the cave to get it.

Once, I took a clean quilt, takin' the soiled one home to wash, wincin' at the stains as I did so. I grew anxious about the girl as the nights grew colder, and I hoped she knew how to stay warm.

As for the girl, I didn't know it at the time, but she had stopped worryin' about whoever had discovered her hideout. She was just grateful for the food and supplies and accepted them all without questionin' her luck. After all, she figured, if the person had meant to do her some harm they would surely have done it by now. She was too worn out with survivin' to waste energy on borrowed worry, but I didn't learn all that until later.

One particularly cold mornin', I sensed the girl's presence when I reached the creek bed. The sun wasn't yet fully up, and I had worried about the girl when I awakened to a hard frost, the first of the winter. I had no way of knowin' if the previous night had been one in which the girl sought refuge in the cave, but if it had been, I knew that without a proper fire the girl would be deadly cold.

Besides, I was hopin' to catch a couple more fish before the weather turned. Takin' note of the chill that mornin', I had immediately dressed, puttin' on layers of flannel over my long thermal underwear. Nothin' beats the cold like flannel. Grabbin' my rifle and a fishin' cane, I laced up my boots, threw on my coat, and left the cabin, pickin' my way downward through the underbrush, which was crunchy with the frost.

A quarter mile before I reached the creek I caught the scent of the girl's fire. I continued closer, wantin' to check on the girl, before reachin' the clearin' and spottin' the trail of smoke, lazily workin' its way up through the entrance of the cave in the approachin' mornin' light. I smiled to myself, pleased at the girl's ability to fend for herself. Turnin', havin' no wish to be seen, I left the fish for another day and began my climb back up the mountain.

The girl startled, immediately awake, her heart pounding. Someone was outside the cave. The person was silent, attempting to go unnoticed, but by necessity the girl had learned to live in a state of alert. She had been listening for footsteps in the dark for weeks now. She waited, back pressed tight against the rock wall and eyes on the entrance to the cave. After a few moments she felt rather than heard the person move away. Quietly, she made her way to the rocky opening. She hesitated, then wriggled her way out.

She had been right. There were boot prints in the frost, leading both towards and away from her hiding place. Small prints, she was relieved to see. Raising her eyes, she saw a retreating figure in the grayness of the predawn light, heading up the mountain. The person was slightly built, not much taller than she. A woman, then, or maybe a boy. No, a woman. Something about the movements gave her away. The girl released a pent up breath. While she had never known what it felt like to be taken care of by a woman, she had also never been hurt by one, at least not physically. She was safe.

From her vantage point below, she watched the woman hike powerfully back up the mountain, barely breaking stride as she maneuvered around trees and rocks. Once, the woman paused, as if listening, and the girl was afraid she had been found out. But after a moment, the woman continued on, until the girl finally lost sight of her in the heavy vegetation. The girl rushed back into the hole to put out her fire and prepare for home. She was late enough as it was, and there'd be hell to pay if she didn't get her chores done in time.

———————————

As I headed back up the mountain, I heard the unmistakable sound of a sigh, released in a moment of relief. I stopped for a minute, listenin'. The girl had seen me, I knew, and I cursed myself for it, but I didn't look back; I didn't want to frighten her. There wasn't nothin' to be done now, except to get on with my day. I resumed my pace, trustin' the girl wouldn't follow; she would be too frightened, too tired with her own troubles to worry about followin' a stranger up a mountain.

Chapter Eleven
Jimmy the Great

Down in the valley, Jimmy Williamson rolled over, snorting and muttering, and reached for his wife, not because he wanted her, but because he owned her and expected her to be where he'd last put her. Discovering her empty spot, he cursed.

"Damn you, Sue Ann!" he yelled, spittle hitting the stained and crusted wall beside the bed. "Where the hell are you?"

Receiving no reply, he threw back the sour covers and sat up on the listing mattress, scrubbing his ruddy face with thick hands in an attempt to wake up. Finally he stood, reaching into his yellowed boxers for a satisfying scratch under the testicles, and plodded across the uneven floor into the kitchen, feet sticking to the torn linoleum. No sign of Sue Ann and no goddamned coffee, either. Suddenly furious, Jimmy bellowed at the top of his lungs and kicked the table, which promptly flew across the floor and crashed into the wall, spilling its contents as it went.

"Oh, Jimmy." It was Sue Ann, standing in the open door in her faded Sunday dress, pocketbook in her hands, framed by the morning sun. "Now what did you go and do that for?" Setting down her purse, Sue Ann hurried into the room and began quickly picking up broken pieces of the sugar dish, her hands trembling.

Something about her voice, the exhaustion in it, or the sight of the back of her narrow head, the thin brown hair stringy against her neck, enraged Jimmy even more, and he struck out at her with his right foot, knocking her up against the table. Sue Ann muffled a scream as her ribcage bounced off the table leg. She bit her lip to keep from moaning, knowing that the sound would only anger him more.

Giving her a moment to land and settle, Jimmy watched, his face impassive. Finally, "Where's the fuckin' coffee? And where the hell have you been?"

Sue Ann pointed towards the counter with one hand, holding onto her ribs with the other while struggling to sit up and draw a breath.

"It's on the counter, honey. See? I set it to percolate right before I left. I even set out a cup for you." She gasped at the pain in her ribs. "I was at the school. I had a meetin' with J.J.'s teacher this mornin', remember? About his readin' trouble?"

Jimmy stomped past her without responding, trudging on her outstretched foot in the process, and poured himself a cup of coffee. Cradling the steaming cup delicately in his thick hands, he held it under his nose and inhaled deeply, sighing with contentment. Pinky raised, he lifted the cup to his lips and slurped, eyes closed while he swished it through his mouth.

"Mmmmm." He said. "I do love my coffee in the mornin'." Pulling back the faded red gingham curtain over the kitchen sink, he looked out at the bright sunlight.

"Looks like it's goin' to be a beautiful day," he announced happily.

Smiling peacefully, he turned, stepping gingerly over the mess, taking care not to cut his bare feet, and walked out of the kitchen, leaving Sue Ann alone on the filthy floor.

Chapter Twelve
A gift

Splittin' wood in the side yard in the chilly evenin' air one day not long after my trip to town, I felt dizzy and sat down hard on the cold ground. Quiverin', I leaned back on my elbows, breathin' fast, and took stock of my condition. I wasn't well; it didn't take no doctor to tell me that, no disrespect to Dr. Leary intended. I knew I wasn't well as soon as I set foot out of my bed just after dawn. I felt unusually tired. Ordinarily ready to greet the day, that mornin' I had had to drag myself out of my warm bed, leanin' for support as I pulled on my clothes and built up the fire, boilin' water for my coffee. My muscles was sore and my face was slick with cold sweat. I forced myself to eat a light breakfast even though my stomach rebelled. Refusin' to give in, I pushed myself through my chores, cannin' the last of the beans, churnin' butter and boilin' cheese from fresh milk gathered from the goats. Still, my body rebelled against me all throughout the day.

Frustrated at my weakened condition, I lay back on the ground and sighed, cursin' with impatience. I had things to do, preparations for winter, and no time to be sick. Unfortunately, my body was not on the same calendar as me, and my body demanded rest.

I couldn't complain, really. I wasn't hardly ever sick, was, in fact, generally healthy, at least as far as I was aware. This current sickness was a result of my trip into town earlier in the fall; I often took ill after them visits. There wasn't nothin' to do but give my body, and my mind, the rest they demanded. Them trips down the mountain was taxin' in all sorts of ways.

Resigned, I pushed myself up and gathered the wood I had already split. No sense leavin' it out in the weather when I could use it in the stove. I called the chickens into their coop and herded the goats into their shed, apologizin' for their early imprisonment. I couldn't afford to lose an animal, not with winter comin' on. Finally, I dragged myself into the cabin, more tired with every movement. Latchin' the door, I stoked the fire in the stove and stripped, shiverin', to my thermal underwear. I set the kettle on the stove and, reachin' to the upper shelf, retrieved a tin canister. Openin' my stash of herbs, I added Tsunga needles into the boilin' water. I poured the resultin' brew into a mug and sipped it down, slow-like. The taste was bitter, but the tea would help fight off my fever. Pullin' back my quilts, I climbed in and nestled down, fallin' asleep almost immediately, dusk passin' by unnoticed outside the window of my cabin.

I slept for the better part of two days, barely wakin' to trek to the outhouse for relief or to quench my thirst with an ice cold dipperful from the well. Musterin' all of my strength, I did manage to feed the animals before collapsin', exhausted and tremblin', back into my bed. No matter what, I had to take care of them animals. I worried about the girl, too, but I was grateful that, aside from the cold hours just before sunrise, the weather remained mild. Any immediate danger facin' the girl wouldn't come from rough weather or wild animals. No, the danger would come from home.

On the third dawn, I awoke with energy and knew the worst was over. Shovin' back the quilts, I stood, somewhat shaky, and went to pull open the door, cravin' the sunrise and in need of fresh air and a smoke. As I unlatched the door and heaved it inward, somethin' fell against my feet. Startled, I jumped back, lookin' down.

The flour sack. Always careful, I surveyed the yard quickly, my breath steamin' in the cold mornin' air, before stoopin', curious, to collect the bag. I could tell by the heft it wasn't empty. Latchin' the door, I built up the fire and returned to my bed, pullin' the quilt up over my freezin' feet before turnin' the sack up and emptyin' it into my lap. Out tumbled a handful of little stones. Pickin' them up and lookin' closely, I seen that they was quartz, a mineral Momma had called rock crystal, sparklin' in rosy shades of pink in the reflected fire from my bedside lamp. I examined them little stones, turnin' them over with my fingers. I was touched, that ain't no lie. I gathered them into my hand and held them against my chest, relishin' the feel of their cold smoothness against my palm, swallowin' against the sudden lump in my throat.

Chapter Thirteen
Mr. Smith's General Store

Gerald Smith looked up from his ledger at the tinkling of the bell, pausing in his work to see who had entered. Corinne Pruitt Johnson. He smiled with pleasure.

"Corinne! How are you this fine mornin'?" Squinting, adjusting his glasses to take a closer look, he noticed that Corinne's face was drawn and pale. "Are you feelin' okay, dear?"

Corinne smiled at the grocer, touched, as always, by his kindness.

"Just a little tired is all," she answered. "It's cannin' time."

"What can I get for you?" asked Mr. Smith. "Salt? Lids?"

"I need a dozen more jars with lids and about a pound of salt," said Corinne. "I got to get all the beans in before they freeze."

As Mr. Smith selected the supplies, he glanced covertly at Corinne. He felt sure she knew Billy May had been to town the week before. He didn't know how this affected Corinne, but he suspected it had more than a little to do with her wan appearance this morning. She was still lovely, of course. Corinne had always been lovely. But this morning she looked worn down and a little too thin, as if she had been worrying herself sick over something.

Throughout the years, as he witnessed Corinne marry, have babies, and settle into middle age, Mr. Smith had never been able to see her without also seeing a shadow of Billy May. Those two girls had really been something, he thought as entered the storage room in search of a box of canning jars. One light and the other dark, one rambunctious, the other timid, both as sweet as could be, and both loved dearly by his wife, and by himself, too. He smiled at the memories. How many times, he wondered, had he snuck them a lollipop or a handful of gumdrops? And Mrs. Smith, too. More than a few times he had caught her slipping the girls some sort of treat. They had been impossible to resist, those two girls.

He had watched Billy May grow up, too, from the day she was born until the day she left town amid a storm of averted glances and knowing whispers. Like most folks in town, Mr. Smith didn't know exactly what had happened. He had only heard the whispers, and he didn't put much stock in idle gossip. What he did know, however, was that the town was a sadder place with Billy May gone. Corinne, in particular, seemed to suffer, and the death of her brother Willy shortly afterward certainly hadn't helped matters. Neither girl had had an easy time of it; they'd both experienced more death and tragedy than either should have had to bear. No, life hadn't been fair to them, but life was rarely ever fair, and even less so in these mountains. If it were, he would have children of his own, and his beloved wife would still be with him, working by his side as she always had.

Returning to the counter he rang up the purchases and then, on a whim, reached into one of the candy jars that had lined the counter of the General Store for decades. He reached towards Corinne with a handful of Mary Jane's. He didn't know what possessed him, other than the nearly palpable presence of Billy May.

Once, when Billy May and Corinne were just little things, Corinne had pulled out a baby tooth on one of the sticky candies, later showing it proudly to Mr. Smith. He could still remember Billy May's excited chatter, "Corinne done lost a tooth. She pulled it out on that there candy. She took a bite an' *wham*! It just come right out. I ain't never lost a tooth yet. Can I have some candy so I can try?" Exchanging an amused glance with his wife, he had handed both girls a handful.

Smiling at the memory, Mr. Smith folded Corinne's fingers over the candy and then grasped her hand within his in a quick embrace. When she met his eyes, he saw that hers were full of tears.

"Now, honey," he said, at a loss for words.

"Did you see her?" she asked. "I did, but she won't talk to me."

Understanding she meant Billy May, Mr. Smith nodded. "She came by for some supplies," he answered. "Had a little run in with Jimmy Williamson, but he let her go without too much trouble. I do believe she would have killed him if he hadn't."

Corinne closed her eyes briefly. "Did she seem all right?" she asked.

Again he nodded. "Looked fit as a fiddle, as always. Didn't say much. Never does, anymore." He smiled. "Asked for some Mary Janes, though."

Corinne nodded then, her expression relieved, and looked down at the Mary Janes in her hand. "She don't forgive me, you know, which I understand because I don't forgive myself, either." She chewed at her lip as she put the candies in her purse and snapped it closed. She picked up the box of canning jars.

"Honey, whatever happened, you cain't blame yourself forever. It don't serve no purpose for anyone. You're a good girl. You always have been." Mr. Smith found himself inexplicably on the verge of tears himself as he held the door open for Corinne in the bright morning sunshine.

Corinne didn't reply, only offered him a tired smile before heading home for a final day of canning.

Chapter Fourteen
Old Mongrel returns

As the days grew shorter and colder, I worried more and more about that girl. More than once, I caught myself starin' over at the neighborin' mountain in the evenin's, watchin' for the flash of movement that would tell me she was on the run. It had been a couple of weeks since I'd seen any sign in the cave, and while on the one hand I was hopin' that the lack of activity meant whatever danger the girl had faced was gone, on the other hand I knew such was not the case. I had first hand knowledge of Roy Campbell, after all, and the fact that I hadn't seen the girl scared me. I was fearin' the worst.

Beddin' down the animals for the evenin', I glanced up at the sky and I was greatly disturbed by what I seen. Snow was comin', no doubt about it. A lot of it, judgin' by the look of them clouds. The wind was pickin' up, too, stabbin' through my flannel shirt like witch's fingers against my skin. I hurried to the well, knowin' it would most likely freeze before dawn, and filled several buckets of water to keep inside by the fire. Then, gatherin' enough firewood to make it through the night, I made my way back to the cabin and latched the door against the comin' storm.

No sooner had I gotten the stove goin' than I heard that old mongrel scratchin' at my door. He was whimperin' that it was cold outside, demandin' that I let him in. I couldn't help but grin when I opened up the door to him. He sat there lookin' up at me like he was put out that I hadn't got there sooner.

"You old mongrel," I said to him, and I laughed out loud at the irritated look on his scarred up old face. "I wondered when you'd show up."

I moved aside so he could come in, then I stood back, lookin' at him. He was one of them Heinz 57 varieties; there wasn't no way to tell what all was mixed in. He had long, tannish colored hair that was all tangled up and filthy, all except for his snout, which by then was completely white. He was smaller than a blue tick but bigger than a beagle, shaggier than either one with ears that couldn't decide whether to point or to droop. He was a mystery, for sure, and I had given up tryin' to figure out his lineage. We was both mixed breeds of a sort, and I figured maybe that was why we got on so well.

I had first met that old dog nearly a dozen years before, when he was a just little thing, nothin' but a flash of movement through them woods, chasin' rabbit or squirrel or whatever else he seen fit to pursue. The first mornin' I seen him I had been awakened before sunrise by the angry squawkin' of my chickens. Assumin' fox or maybe even mountain lion, I grabbed my rifle before headin' out to investigate, but I wasn't expectin' what I seen next. This yappin', grinnin' mongrel. After some tense moments we was able to forge an understandin'. If he would leave them chickens alone, I would let him into my cabin. So far, the arrangement had been a success, and I reckoned on that cold night that he was too old and tired to care about chasin' after chickens.

In the beginnin' I did try to think of a proper name for him, but then I gave up, callin' him Old Mongrel when I called him anythin' at all. It suited him. He had stayed throughout most of that first winter, makin' himself at home, comin' and goin' as he pleased. I admired his independent spirit, and I had been grateful for his company. When he disappeared in the early spring, I had grieved him, I ain't embarrassed to admit it. I had grown attached to him by then. When he reappeared late that next fall, I was pleased to see him. More than pleased, if I am to be honest. Since then, we had fallen into a pattern that I think we had both come to appreciate. The older he got, the more I worried he wouldn't show for our winters together, but so far he always had. I didn't know how in the world he had survived to be so old, especially not in them hard mountains, but there he was, movin' slow and favorin' his left hip, his right eye filmed up with cataract, but grinnin' and droolin' on my floor just as he had done the previous dozen years. I didn't know where he went when the weather warmed up, but I did wonder about it from time to time. Maybe he had a whole other home for the warmer months, with a whole other woman lookin' forward to seein' him again. But for that winter, which I knew would probably be his last one on this earth, he was mine again, and I was happy for it.

Once again latchin' the door against the cold, I opened up a tin and handed the mongrel a piece of jerky, which he eagerly accepted, settlin' himself onto the braid rug beside the stove. He had always liked that spot, and I noticed that night that he edged up a little closer to the stove than he had done in previous years. I settled down on the rug alongside him, workin' the brambles out of his hair like I always did, listenin' to the howlin' wind blowin' through them treetops on my mountain. Lookin' back, I reckon I was content in that moment, at least on the top. Underneath it all, I knew somethin' was brewin'. I had this feelin', like I was waitin' for somethin'. Only problem was, I didn't yet know what it was I was waitin' for.

Chapter Fifteen
A roast is more than a roast

Corinne Pruitt Johnson set the roast on the table and went in search of her husband, calling him to dinner. Not finding him in the house, she opened the door to the back porch and made her way into the yard, stepping over engine parts and rusted tools as she went. It seemed that nearly her whole life in this house she had been stepping around and tripping over things, first diaper pails and toys, and then, as the children grew older, bicycles and skates. Now that the children were grown and gone, she was suddenly and inexplicably depressed to find herself still maneuvering her way through misplaced junk.

There he was, hunched over a piece of machinery that was unrecognizable to Corinne, his breath steaming in the cold air.

"John Paul," she called quietly. "It's time to eat." She hugged herself in the sudden blast of cold wind, shivering, gazing towards the sky in the waning light.

John Paul grunted without looking up. "Gotta finish this, then I'll be right there. Need to get it done before the snow comes."

Corinne opened her mouth to ask him what he was working on, but then, suddenly overcome with a wave of exhaustion, closed it again without comment. After twenty-nine years of marriage to a mechanic, she had learned that one piece of machinery worked pretty much like another, when you got right down to it. She shivered again, watching the clouds rush across the sky, obscuring the stars and covering the moon, causing an eerie gray pall to fall over the valley. She sighed, and then turned to pick her way back through the strewn tools and gears, suddenly wishing for nothing more than a deep, dreamless sleep.

She wondered briefly, and not for the first time, about the cause of this sudden melancholy. True, Mother had recently gone to a retirement home in Huntington and Corinne missed seeing her everyday, missed their easy visits back and forth between houses, but they still talked by phone every morning. And Chrissy had moved to Georgia with her husband and the two grandbabies this past year, but even so, Corinne had only seen them a few times a year, anyway. After all, Chattanooga, where Chrissy had lived ever since she had married nearly five years ago, wasn't that much closer than Atlanta. And John, Jr. had been gone even longer, all the way across the country to California. California! She remembered how upset she had been when he first told her he was leaving.

"But you're only eighteen years old!" she had exclaimed, trying hard to keep the shrill note of hysteria out of her voice.

John Jr. had explained to her, his voice agonizingly patient, that he wanted more out of life than a bunch of mountains filled with coal. He had dreams and goals, and none of them had to do with either machinery or mining.

"I know you're content with this life," he had said. "But I'm not. I need more."

Biting her tongue, studying his earnest expression, Corinne had had to fight against a sudden urge to slap his face. *How dare you*, she had thought, *sit in judgment of me? How could you possibly know how content I am? You don't know anything*. Instead of reacting, however, she had simply walked out of the room.

In the intervening years he had come home sporadically, full of tales about his exciting California lifestyle, stories she could scarcely believe, full of women and adventure and an unending supply of new and exciting opportunities. By the grace of God he had never been drafted, and truthfully Corinne had always wondered what he would do had his number been pulled for Vietnam. She had a sneaking suspicion that by whatever means, he would never have gone to war. Her son wasn't a coward; it wasn't that. But he was a gentle soul, adamantly opposed to the war or even to guns in general. He never had taken to hunting, a huge disappointment to his father. In the dark of night, when she was tortured by her thoughts and unable to sleep, she knew that California was probably a better place for him. He would never have been able to survive here as he had been raised.

Still, sometimes, glancing at him in an unguarded moment, she wondered if what she glimpsed was despair, playing itself in shadows over his still face, hiding behind the light in his blue eyes. She wondered, and she longed to connect, but she couldn't. This, she knew, was her undoing, this inability to connect. Oh, sure, she could fake it with the best of them, but children knew. Children always knew the truth, and the truth was that her heart had hardened years ago, before there were even children to consider. She loved her children, she truly did, and by all outside measures she had been a good mother, possibly even a perfect mother, but in her deepest heart, she found herself incapable of those spontaneous expressions of love that mothers are supposed to naturally execute. And her children undoubtedly knew this.

Closing the porch door behind her, she regarded the roast on the table, situated as it was between the mashed potatoes and the peas. Forever mashed potatoes and peas, she thought suddenly, with a flash of unexpected anger. Once, just once, she would like to eat something besides mashed potatoes and peas. There had been a time, so many years ago she could hardly remember it now, when Corinne had enjoyed creating new dishes, had experimented with strange and foreign foods, had even used spices in her cooking, spices that didn't come in a Morton Salt can. But her family hadn't liked it, had complained that she was becoming too fancy, and she had acquiesced to the pressure (didn't she always?) and given in to their demands, reverting back to the staples to which they were accustomed: beef, potatoes and peas or maybe beans, or sometimes—but rarely ever—corn, with on a particularly daring night some applesauce thrown in for excitement.

Corinne breathed deeply, more than a little concerned

about the waves of anger she had been feeling lately. What on earth was wrong with her? Maybe she was going through the change, she thought. She was forty-five this past summer, and Lord knew she was going through *something*. Barely containing her fury and resisting the impulse to splatter the roast all over the floral papered wall, Corinne quietly turned out the light, deliberately walking softly and slowly down the hall to the bedroom. She silently closed the door, locking it behind her.

Later, his task for the night completed successfully before the snows came, John Paul stared, puzzled, at the darkened kitchen. This was unusual. Corinne had always waited for him, reheating as needed, bustling about to make sure he had salt and pepper, a napkin, some sweet tea. John Paul was a good man, and he was worried about his wife, but he was at a loss as to what he could do for her. He called out to her, but she didn't answer. More confused than ever, he started down the dark hallway, pausing outside the door of the master bedroom.

"Corinne?" his voice was tentative, questioning.

No answer other than what sounded like the muffled sound of his wife's crying.

"Corinne? You okay?"

Still no answer. He tried the knob and found, for the first time in twenty-nine years, that he had been locked out of his marital bed and away from his wife. Brow knitted with concern, he turned back towards the kitchen table and sat, staring into space. What in the world had gotten into that woman? Truly worried, he absently filled his plate with roast. And potatoes and peas. Looking about hopefully, he was disappointed to see there was no applesauce.

Alone in her bedroom, Corinne ignored her husband's call. He was a good husband, and she didn't know why she was all of a sudden enraged by his voice, nauseated at the thought of his touch. Shivering again, this time from the force of her own emotions rather than from the cold, she stood at her window and gazed outward, at the upward slope of Crutcher Mountain. The front was moving in, the wind crying over the top of the valley, echoing against the stone walls of the mountains. A blizzard, then. By morning, they'd be snowed in for sure. Snowed in, she thought bitterly. What did it matter, since no one ever left Cedar Hollow?

Corinne found herself suddenly fighting against a desire to flee, to run into that cold wind, forcing her way up the mountain to Billy May, but she wouldn't go. She never had— certainly hadn't when it might have counted—and it was too late now.

Sinking onto the bed, she held her head in her hands and rocked, seeing over and over again Billy May's straight, slender back, rounding the curve and heading forever away from her.

Chapter Sixteen
A stormy night

O n top of my mountain, in the warmth of my cabin, I removed the last burr from Old Mongrel's coat and brushed him smooth in the soft warmth of the fire. Outside, the wind was pummelin' the little cabin like it was angry, tryin' to scare me out of my contentment. With the dog snorin', put to sleep by my brushin', I stood up to reheat some beans on the stove, rustlin' in the tin canister for yesterday's leftover cornbread. I wasn't hungry but I needed to eat. Skippin' through meals up on them mountains meant certain weakness, not a chance I was willin' to take, particularly in the cold of winter, and like the animals had warned me, this winter was already shapin' up to be a hard one.

While the beans was heatin', I went over to the little table beside my bed and picked up that book. *Jonathan Livingston Seagull.* I didn't have no idea what it was about, but I liked the slim, cool feel of it in my hands. I had not held a book in a long, long time. I lit the bedside lamp by an ember from the stove, and settlin' myself into the only upholstered chair I had, opened the cover and began to read.

I, of course, hadn't never seen the sea. I hadn't never seen anythin' beyond a few miles outside of Cedar Hollow. A small sadness landed on my chest for a minute, but then I let it go. I continued with my readin', forgettin' about them beans until the scorched smell brought me back to my senses. I stood and removed the pot from the hot stove, dumped a dipperful of beans into a bowl on top of a slab of stale cornbread, and went back to my readin', enjoyin' the tale of that little seagull. Outside, the blizzard was just a-howlin'.

Down in the valley, Corinne finally fell into an exhausted and bitter sleep. John Paul, still puzzled and concerned, washed up in the bathroom, and climbing into the single guestroom bed, prayed his wife would be back to herself in the morning.

Across town, Gerald Smith sat alone in his apartment above the general store, quiet if not content in the dark, gazing into the fire and smoking his pipe as he had done for the twenty-odd years since his wife had passed on. He missed her still, and thanked God for every day he had been blessed to have her.

Restless, he stood and pulled back the curtain. The storm was moving fast over the mountains; the snow coming down hard. Mr. Smith watched the night and thought of Billy May on her mountain, surrounded by the blizzard. He thought often of Billy May and Corinne, not the women of the present, the silent, stoic woman he had seen a few weeks ago and the sad, weeping one he had seen the other day, but of the girls they once had been.

His wife had loved those girls dearly. She loved all the children of the town, but Billy May and Corinne had held a special place in the hearts of nearly all the residents of Cedar Hollow, not only because they had lost their fathers in such a terrible way, but also because in spite of the loss, they were happy children; it was impossible not to love them. His wife had agonized over her inability to bear children, and spoiling the girls with treats had helped to fill the void. Mr. Smith didn't know exactly what had happened between them, but he did know that whatever it was, overnight they had changed from fresh faced little girls to broken women.

On this frigid West Virginia night, he looked out the window, up towards the mountain, smoking his ancient pipe and reminiscing. In some small way, after the loss of their fathers he had felt a responsibility to look after them, especially since he had no children of his own. Somehow, he had failed them; he had not protected them. That knowledge hurt him to the core. Silly old man, he berated himself. Blubbering like a senile old fool. He wished more than anything at that moment that his wife were there beside him. She had always loved the cozy warmth of a fire on a snowy night.

Farther down Main Street, Miss Valerie Burnett, the town's temporary librarian, tiptoed barefoot across the freezing hall in the boarding home to wash her face before bed. She didn't mind the inconvenience of this arrangement, because in just a few months, her internship complete, she would graduate from Marshall University with her degree in literature and then, as soon as Thomas was honorably discharged from the service, she would be Mrs. Thomas Poindexter the third, living far away from this coal mining town. Thomas had made it safely through Vietnam, thank the Lord; now it was just a matter of time before they could be together. For the time being, though, she was fascinated with the life of the locals. Just a couple of weeks ago, Billy May Platte, local legend, recluse, and mountain woman extraordinaire, had shown up at the library. Where else but here could a girl have an exciting experience like that?

Some folks around town said Billy May was really a man in disguise (and some said much worse than that, but Miss Burnett wouldn't stoop to repeating those things). But Mr. Smith had told her that Billy May had at one time been the prettiest girl in town. Besides, Miss Burnett could tell Billy May was no man. She was too slender, her bone structure too delicate, and up close as she had seen her, Miss Burnett had been surprised to see that in spite of her crop of unruly black hair and her weather-worn face, Billy May still had some of the prettiness that must have been evident in her youth.

The town was small, but it did have its fair share of excitement. Miss Burnett had hardly been able to stand waiting through the dreary afternoon until the library closed. She had rushed home as soon as possible to sit at the tiny wooden desk in her rented room and write Thomas about her meeting with the reclusive mountain woman, relishing the juicy details of the gossip of the townsfolk. Just imagining his response made her smile in anticipation. Climbing into bed, she drifted serenely off to sleep, thoughts of Thomas causing an involuntary little gasp of pleasure as she did so.

Still farther along down Main Street, Jimmy Williamson stirred and finally sat up, wet and frozen and covered with snow, in the gutter into which he had fallen and passed out after one too many drinks of old man Pritchett's nonexistent moonshine, the family business now run by the sons. He wondered, grasping for any memory whatsoever of the game, whether he had won or lost at poker. No matter, he thought now, broke was broke, so what the hell difference did it make? Besides, the poker game had only been preliminary entertainment. The main event, he remembered quite well. Stumbling to his feet, inadvertently passing wind and pissing himself in the process, he lurched his way towards the shack he called home, urine steaming in the frosty air, cursing and mumbling under his fetid breath as he limped his lopsided way down Main Street.

And just off the main road, farther down across the tracks, in the shack for which Jimmy was now headed, Sue Ann sat quietly, staring into the darkness, trying to remember what decisions she had made that had led her to this point. Was it, she wondered, one big decision? One single moment, one option, that had she simply chosen differently would have led to a different life? Or was it a series of small decisions, each unto itself unimportant and forgettable, that, when combined with the rest, resulted in this life? Which ill-fated choices had led her to this? She no longer knew.

What she did know, when she allowed herself to think of such things, was that never in her wildest dreams would she have imagined herself here, in this town, in this shack. True, she had grown up in Cedar Hollow, but she had grown up the privileged daughter of the town's only doctor. Dr. Leary had been respected and loved by nearly everyone in the town. His only daughter had been sought after, with never a shortage of dates and invitations and plenty of suitors from which to choose, not only from Cedar Hollow but from miles around.

And she had married well the first time—*very* well, actually—perhaps most well because she had truly loved the man she had married. She had moved from Cedar Hollow to live near her husband's family in Memphis while her husband served his country during World War II, but he had never made it home. In a wicked twist of fate her first husband had died in the war, at the very end, just before the damned thing was declared over, struck down not by a German bullet but by his own when he tripped over a pile of rubble on a cobbled street in Paris and misfired his own gun. She had received word of his death nine days after Allied forces declared victory over Germany and Japan.

For reasons she could no longer remember (perhaps she had simply had nowhere else to go?), she had eventually returned to Cedar Hollow. Now here she was, in this hellhole of a house, in this hellhole of a town, barely able to take care of one son and unable to bear more, thanks to the monster of a man she had last married. Sue Ann rocked in her chair in front of the empty fireplace, never even noticing the cold.

At first I was confused, thinkin' the poundin' was that of Jonathan, that spunky little seagull, beatin' his wings and tryin' to soar above the earth at seventy miles an hour. Finally, though, the sheer desperation of the knockin' roused me from my sleep. The old mongrel was makin' a noise low in his throat, not a growl so much as a keenin' sound, an anxious whine. His eyes was fastened to that plank door, and his paws was scrabblin' against the wooden floor at its base.

My very first feelin' was panic. No one came to my cabin. No one. That was the way I had planned it, and it was the way I had lived for all them years. Standin', confused at first, rubbin' the sleep out of my eyes, I hesitated for just an instant and then grabbed my rifle from the rack above the bed. Slowly, keepin' quiet, I approached the door. Cockin' the rifle and proppin' it against my shoulder, I hollered out, "Who's there?" Silence. And then...was it my imagination? A thin cry, lost in the howl of the blizzard.

It was then that I knew, and my blood froze with the knowin'. I fumbled in my hurry, finally throwin' open the latch. I yanked the door open, momentarily losin' my breath in that frigid wind. The girl fell forward, crumplin' into a heap on the plank floor, her dark hair covered in snow, her

81

eyelids flutterin', purple with the cold. Actin' fast, I grabbed the girl under her arms and dragged her into the warm cabin, slammin' and latchin' the door behind me.

Chapter Seventeen
The old woman
Huntington, West Virginia, 2010

This time when I float up out of my molasses sleep it ain't Starlette I hear. It's the bird-faced one. Her voice is harsh and nasally, and it grates on my ears somethin' fierce. "They told me to make her look presentable, but I don't know how I'm supposed to do that," she is complainin'. "My God, she's like a hundred years old. What does presentable mean, anyway?"

Another voice, now, an unfamiliar one. "Just comb her hair, honey, and put some rouge on her cheeks. You'd be amazed what a difference that makes. Besides, she ain't that old. It says here on her chart she's seventy-nine. She must have just had some rough livin', and the cancer don't help any."

And again the bird-faced one. "Well, all I know is that she's got some bigwig coming to see her today, some fancy executive producer or something from Hollywood. Ain't that a crock? I tried for ten years to get an acting gig, and here I am in a nursing home in some little podunk town in West Virginia, taking care of people who piss on themselves, and *now* I get to meet a bigwig Hollywood producer. Ain't that the shit to beat all?"

"Why is a Hollywood producer comin' to visit her? It ain't like she's goin' to be actin' in a movie anytime soon." The unfamiliar one says, chucklin', and I am thinkin' that I am glad I can amuse her so.

"I don't know," answers bird-face. "Maybe they're kin?" The nurse stops for a minute and I feel my pulse bein' taken, the woman's cold, bony fingers on my wrist. I do not like her touch. I keep my eyes closed and will her to finish her work and get her hands off of me. "Starlette said it's the woman that produced that movie, what was the name of it? Oh, yeah, *The Devil's Mine*. Remember it? It's the one about that mine explosion back in '35 or '36; I can't remember exactly when it happened."

"Really?" The unfamiliar one sounds interested now. "It was in '35. My granddaddy died in that explosion. I never met him; I wasn't even born yet. My own daddy was just a little boy, decided then and there he wasn't goin' to work in no mines when he grew up. They moved to Huntington after that. That was a terrible explosion, from what they say. Say they could see it all the way to Huntington. My grandmomma used to talk about it. Killed everyone there."

Another pause in the conversation while I feel my IV drip line bein' adjusted. "They closed the mine, after that," the unfamiliar voice says. "Tried to reopen it about ten years ago, but decided it's too dangerous. Methane levels was too high. Besides, it's all run down now, would need too much work. From what I hear, they couldn't even hardly get back to it, it's so grown up around there. That shaft, number twenty-seven I believe it was, was completely caved in." The nurse finishes her adjustments and pulls the covers more snugly around my shoulders. "I wouldn't mind meetin' that producer. I'd like to talk to her about my granddaddy."

I cain't hear the bird-faced one's reply; I am too stunned by the other woman's information. I had not known they tried to reopen that mine. Ten years ago? If they had gotten that mine open they would have been in for a surprise. The closeness of that call scares me.

"Now, why is her heart rate jumping up like that?" the bird-faced one says, and I try to calm myself down.

Chapter Eighteen
Innocence lost
Crutcher Mountain, West Virginia, 1975

Gently, I brushed the hair back out of the girl's pale face. She didn't make no move except to moan. Her eyes was closed and her lips were a frightenin' shade of blue. I threw a couple of bear skins over her and began quickly heatin' up water, fillin' every container I had and usin' every burner on the stove. When they got warm, I emptied all of 'em into the basin I used for my bath, and then I put more on the stove. Reachin' into the cabinet above the stove, I took down my herb tin and put some witch hazel into the basin, pourin' more steamin' water on top. In my tea kettle I put some wild cherry bark, bringin' it to a boil before pourin' it into a mug to cool. Last, I added a leaf of wild lettuce to float on top of the wild cherry brew.

Returnin' to the girl, I began to carefully pull her dirty, torn up coat off her shoulders. I didn't want to scare her, but I had to get her undressed and into that tub. Old Mongrel hovered around, sniffin' at the girl's side while I worked. I finally slipped the coat out from under her and began to gently work her arms out of her threadbare t-shirt, worn so thin I could see her ribs right through it, could see the color of her pale, white skin. When I pulled up the shirt, she stirred, grabbin' at my hands, flailin', fightin' me with what little energy she had left. I shushed her, rubbin' her hands and reassurin' her. I hummed a tune my momma had used, one I didn't even know I still had in my memory. *Osda adenedi*, the good spirits will watch over you, I sung to her while I took off her shoes and socks, tryin' to rub some heat into them cold, cold feet, givin' her some time to calm down. Finally, I had to remove her pants. I just did not want to frighten her, so I talked to her as I did, explainin' that I needed to get her into the tub to get her warm.

The girl's pants was frozen stiff, and when I went to slip 'em down over her bony little hips, she cried out in pain. I stopped right away; more than anythin' in my life, I did not want to hurt that girl. I looked down and what I seen made my stomach drop, and then I felt a rage so big I was afraid I wouldn't be able to contain it. There was blood, a lot of it, stainin' not only the girl's underpants but her pants, too, seepin' through them and onto the floor. Fresh blood, bright red from recent wounds, but darker blood, too. Blood from the womb. Swallowin' back my rage, I worked to get myself under control. When I had that accomplished, I spoke to her, tellin' her it would be okay, though in truth I didn't know if it would.

Liftin' her skinny body in my arms, I lowered her into the warm water, the steam fragrant with the scent of herbs. I took care to settle her directly onto the leaves of the witch hazel; they'd help with the soreness and the pain. The girl groaned, mutterin' somethin' I could not understand, and Old Mongrel whimpered back at her. I spread a quilt over the top of the basin, partly to hold in the steam and partly to afford the girl as much privacy as I could.

Keepin' an eye on her, I set to work cleanin' the floor while the old dog continued his whimperin', sniffin' at the stains. So much blood, not yet dried, clotted on the weathered pine. After scrubbin' the section with snow and rags, I used sandstone to scour away the remainin' color. I would burn them rags in the stove the next day. I couldn't do much for the girl; I surely couldn't remove the memories, but I could at least remove the hurtful evidence of just what she had lost that terrible night.

Checkin' the latch one final time, makin' sure the door was closed tight against whatever ugliness was out there, I stoked up the fire and sat back in my chair, waitin', rifle by my side. Ever' so often I tested the water for warmth and heated up more as needed. The old mongrel laid down by the tub, keepin' vigil as the blizzard raged on.

Chapter Nineteen
Mrs. Lorraine Pruitt
Huntington, West Virginia, 1975

Mrs. Lorraine Pruitt was unable to sleep. Outside, she could hear the wind howling around the window pane, the fluttery taps of snow soft against the glass. She sighed. After living her whole life in the same house in Cedar Hollow, one that her father had built with his own hands before she was born, she was finding it nearly impossible to get comfortable in her new surroundings. Not that the home was a bad one; Corinne would have never let her move away had it been. But compared to her own familiar home, it was cold and sterile. The floors were carpeted in a gold scallop print, the walls an institutional shade of pea green. Pictures of various farm scenes had been hung carefully, and a fresh flower arrangement stood on the bureau. But there was no disguising the fact that her bed was a hospital one, or the fact that one of the two chairs in the bedroom came equipped with wheels.

She could still walk (hadn't she walked herself to the bathroom at least three times already this eternal night?) but after the stroke she found her mobility to be increasingly limited. After her second fall in three days time, Corinne had insisted she move in with her and John Paul, but Lorraine refused to become a burden to her only surviving child. Against Corinne's tearful protestations, Mrs. Pruitt had sold her house and moved into the Mountain View Retirement Home instead, just outside of Huntington. It wasn't quite a nursing home. She did, after all, have her own suite, and the freedom to come and go as she pleased. And there were plenty of other old people with whom to form friendships, along with a wealth of planned social activities. It was considered cutting edge, Mountain View Retirement Home. It wasn't a nursing home. But neither was it *her* home.

She had hated to leave Corinne, but they still talked faithfully every morning and visited every weekend. She worried about her only daughter. She knew they thought she didn't see things, but they were wrong. She knew more than she let on; she always had. She was even fairly certain she knew what had happened to Corinne and Willy all those years ago, and to Billy May Platte, too, though it hurt her beyond belief to acknowledge it.

One thing about getting older, she had learned, was that all the lies you'd told yourself to simply make it through the days were no longer content being silent. The truth, it seemed, refused to be denied upon reaching a certain age. More and more frequently she found herself transported back to that one fateful day. It wasn't a day she wanted to return to; that one day had irrevocably changed her own life and the lives of nearly everyone she knew and loved.

Lorraine had known of the Platte family even before the mine accident. Her husband had been the foreman on duty, had supervised Richard Platte for several years by the time the mine claimed them both. He had always spoken well of Richard and had considered him an honest man and a hard worker. She hadn't known Suzanna well; she had only seen her about town, but she had been struck by Suzanna's dark beauty and quiet reserve. She had never thought of Suzanna as unfriendly or cold, although some of the folks in Cedar Hollow did. Lorraine had recognized that she simply felt shy and out of place among the white residents of Cedar Hollow.

After Suzanna had lost her husband, she had pulled even more into herself, cutting herself off from whatever support might have been offered. Billy May, though, had had none of her mother's reticence, at least not back then, though she certainly did now. Thinking of Billy May the child, Mrs. Pruitt smiled. What a handful she had been, so rambunctious, always laughing, never sitting still. It was impossible, back then, to be around Billy May and not smile at her pure energy. She had loved Billy May like a second daughter. She had known, too, that Billy May needed some softness in her life. Not that Suzanna wasn't a good mother; she undoubtedly was, but Billy May was an affectionate child, and Suzanna wasn't given to displays of affection.

Corinne, especially, had loved Billy May's sense of adventure. Corinne had always been cautious, even timid. She was good child, but she was a follower. The two girls had been perfectly matched, and they had also been inseparable. Corinne had never been the same since the loss of Billy May, and it was a loss, as surely as if she had died. Billy May still came to town once or twice a year, but she was as lost to the Pruitts as if she were an entirely different person, buying her supplies, visiting the cemetery, and disappearing into the mountains with never a word. At first Lorraine had been angry with Billy May. After all, Corinne could have used a friend after her brother's death, and Billy May should have been that friend, but Billy May had disappeared from town without a word. But as the years went by and Lorraine rose above her own pain enough to think objectively about the events of that year, she began to come to a different conclusion, one that both frightened her and hurt her deeply.

She wondered, not for the first time or even for the thousandth, if there had been signs she had missed. Surely there had been, but how could she have possibly known how it would all unfold? She remembered, too, though she didn't want to, the war boys returning home, just the four of them, although more than four had gone. As they climbed off the train she looked past the other boys, hardly noticing them, desperate only for Willy. Was there something then? Some sign she should have noticed? How had Willy been that day?

The death of her husband had been especially hard for Willy; she knew that. He had been at the cusp of his own manhood at the time, full of questions about life and the future and comforted by the presence of a father who was happy to guide him through it all, teaching Willy about the mines, assuming Willy would follow in his footsteps. And he would have, she felt sure; he had adored his daddy. After the accident at the mine, though, Willy was lost. He had always been high strung, but he'd been a good boy up until that time. After the accident he had changed, becoming hard as he grew into adulthood without his father. She had tried to comfort him, but she had been so caught up in her own grief that she had surely not been as available to Willy—or to Corinne, either, for that matter—as they had needed her to be. When the opportunity to join the military had presented itself, Willy jumped at the chance. Lorraine had convinced herself that perhaps it was just what he needed, to leave the mountain and see the world. And hadn't she also breathed a small sigh of relief?

What she remembered seeing now, that day he returned and stepped off the train, was a boy grown into a man, his smile a little forced, his embrace a little stiff. She had swept any misgivings under the rug, however, telling herself that he had been through a lot and needed some time to adjust. She was so happy to see him, so relieved at his return that she had vowed to soothe away whatever painful memories he had brought home with him from the war. How ignorant she had been, unforgivably ignorant.

If only she hadn't gone to that Bible study, but she had felt the need to worship, to thank God for bringing her son safely home. If only she had paid more attention to both Corinne and Willy. Lorraine Pruitt was overwhelmed with if onlys. How had she missed so much?

And how, in the darkest hours, could she grieve for a son who had done the things she suspected him of having done? Oh, Willy, she thought. How could you have? Even in your grief, even in your anger, how could you have? And then her heart broke again, for maybe the millionth time over the last thirty years, not just for Willy, but for all of them. For Willy and Corinne, for Billy May, and also for herself.

Damn this eternal night, she thought, as the snow ticked against the window glass.

Chapter Twenty
Corinne

Corinne woke early the next morning, the sun just making its brilliant appearance over the blinding snow. Struggling into her housecoat, she felt slightly embarrassed. It was hard to believe now, with the sun bringing such fabulous light into the valley, that she had actually locked her husband out of the bedroom the night before. Corinne didn't know what had gotten into her lately. She would make John Paul a good breakfast to try to make it up to him. He would let it go, she knew. John Paul wasn't the sort of man to hold a grudge. She had been blessed with a good husband, a fact for which she was forever grateful.

She had known John Paul Johnson even before the war. In such a small town, everyone always knew everyone, to some extent, but John Paul had been a close friend of her older brother, Willy. Following Willy's example, John Paul had signed up for service right after news of the Japanese attack on Pearl Harbor had reached the mountains, just in time for the beginning of U. S. involvement in the Second World War, but it wasn't until several years later, after he had returned in his crisp khaki green uniform, stepping off the train, that she had really noticed him. He had looked so handsome, and the townspeople were all so happy to have their boys home again, not only Willy and John Paul, but Roy Campbell and Jimmy Williamson, too. Not all the boys of the mountains had made it home, but these four had, and the town had come out in celebration. Standing there with the afternoon sunlight reflecting off his buttons, turning his cap shyly in his hands, she had thought John Paul was the most fascinating man she had ever seen, certainly nothing like the scrawny boy who had departed years before.

She had to admit she had looked pretty fine that day, too, a young woman on the eve of her sixteenth birthday. She had taken special care that afternoon, wanting to look nice not only for her brother Willy, but for all of the returning soldiers. She had brushed her hair one hundred strokes and it lay down her back in a glowing, silken sheet. She had chosen her bluest dress, fitted nicely around her slender waist, knowing it accented her eyes. Smiling, she remembered what a naïve girl she had been back then. Her efforts had worked, however, because she had caught John Paul's eye and he had winked at her in the bright afternoon sun. She had smiled back, too, flirting shamelessly. She had felt so daring that day, even more so because Billy May wasn't with her.

Corinne had gone alone to meet the train, perturbed at Billy May for leaving her on her own on this of all days. The villagers had known the soldiers were returning weeks in advance, and Corinne had been excited about meeting the train. The whole town was there; ribbons were on trees, a makeshift band played *America the Beautiful*, and the men from Cedar Baptist Church set up a carnival of sorts, with horseshoes and croquet, three-legged races and apple bobbing. Eugene Cooper had even arranged for a game of baseball if enough players could be found.

Billy May had never mentioned anything about not going. Corinne had assumed they would go together; they did everything together, and she couldn't imagine Billy May passing up a game of baseball. Stopping by Dr. Leary's house to collect Billy May that morning, she had been surprised at Billy May's appearance when she opened the door. Her hair, usually so full and glossy, had hung limply down her back. Her eyes were red rimmed, her nose runny, and she was barefoot, wearing a plaid shirt and a pair of old miner's pants, rolled up and altered from her father's size. Corinne knew Billy May well enough to know that this was her preferred state of dress when home alone, but certainly not when in public.

She had stamped her foot impatiently, "Come on, Billy

May. You're not even dressed yet. Hurry up or we'll miss everything."

Billy May had shaken her head. "I don't think I can go today, Corinne. I'm just not up to it right now."

Corinne had tossed her long hair, pulling at Billy May's hands, "Billy May, are you thinkin' about your momma again? Even if your momma was here she wouldn't be goin' to meet the train. She never went anywhere, so what difference does it make? Now hurry up and get ready. It'll do you good."

Billy May had simply shaken her head again and softly closed the door, leaving Corinne feeling rejected and abandoned in the street.

Standing now in her sunny kitchen, flipping sausages on the hot skillet, Corinne felt a flush of shame. Billy May had been mourning the loss of her mother, probably more than anyone realized, and Corinne cringed at the memory of the insensitivity of her remarks. The truth of the matter was that Corinne had been a shy girl; she relied on Billy May's outgoing personality for support. When Billy May refused to go to meet the train, Corinne had been not only hurt, but also a little bit afraid. Billy May was like a bridge between Corinne and the other young people in town; without her, Corinne was unsure of herself and her place in the group. This is what she had been thinking about that day; what she had not been thinking about was Billy May's grief. That thought pained her now.

Smiling and flirting with John Paul later at the train station, Corinne had thought it would serve Billy May right if she went around with someone else for a few days. That would teach her, she remembered thinking, and then she had found herself smiling up into John Paul's face, agreeing to meet him at the diner after supper for an ice cream. With one more wink, John Paul was gone, and Corinne was left staring after him, scarcely believing what had just happened. Wait 'til Billy May hears about *this*, she remembered thinking.

———————

Alone in the doctor's house all them years ago, I recognized that I had hurt Corinne, and I hadn't never wanted to do that. I was just feelin' so sad and tired since Momma's death a few weeks before that the idea of dressin' up and goin' out was plumb impossible. I did not have the strength within me to be able to do it. Lookin' out the window, I seen Corinne standin' in the street, her face all sad before she turned on her heel and marched away, her blonde hair flyin' out behind her. I felt bad for her, too; that is true.

Later, when I had finished my chores for the day, I first thought I would just go to bed. More than anythin' else back in them days, I craved sleep, but it was naggin' at me that I had hurt Corinne. I forced myself to bathe and dress. I had missed the arrival of the train, but I would try to catch Corinne at her house later in the evenin', and maybe we could go for ice cream at the diner. The way I figured it, that wouldn't take too much energy, and hopefully it would also soothe Corinne's ruffled feathers.

At her own home later that afternoon after dinner, freshening up for her ice cream with John Paul and the rest of the group, Corinne still felt hurt by Billy May's rejection earlier in the day. She decided not to even tell Billy May about John Paul, relishing the thought of Billy May hearing about it from someone else. Later, in her most honest moments, she had to admit to herself that what she had really wanted at that moment was to hurt Billy May. Let her know what it feels like, she thought, swiping on a final application of Bonne Bell lip gloss.

Startled by a knock on her bedroom door, she had cracked it open and been surprised to see Billy May, her hair damp, her eyes swollen, dressed in a simple yellow cotton dress that fell below her knees, white socks folded down above her oxfords. Touched by Billy May's effort, Corinne realized how thoughtless she had been and was ashamed, her anger draining away at the sight of Billy May's tears. She hadn't seen Billy May cry in years, not since the time Peggy's dog had nipped her on the leg down at the diner, drawing blood. Billy May had been six years old at the time; she still bore the scar, and she loved to brag about the attack to anyone who didn't already know the story. That was typical of Billy May; when something bad happened to her, she moved past it quickly, making lemonade out of lemons, as Corinne's mother would have said.

As a grown woman looking back, Corinne supposed she hadn't realized the extent of Billy May's grief because Billy May never talked about it. She may have been more quiet than usual when the two of them were alone together, but in their group of friends, Billy May was the same as she'd always been. She was the center of attention, the one the others flocked to because she was so good at finding something fun to do. Billy May always had interesting ideas, like the week before when she'd arranged a gambling pool, betting who could climb the oak tree across from the library the fastest. Midway through the bet Ms. Temple had come charging out of the library to yell at them, her veined old legs pumping as she ran across the street, threatening to speak with all of their parents. Although that part had been scary, the kids were still laughing about the whole ordeal a week later, planning to try again, only this time at night. Quite simply, Billy May was fun. To see her sorrow that evening so clear on her face was a shock to Corinne; it was unexpected.

"Your momma told me to come on in," Billy May had said. "She said to tell you she's on her way to the church for the Bible study. I'm sorry I didn't...."

Billy May hadn't finished her sentence before Corinne rushed to embrace her. "I am so sorry, Billy May," she said. "I was bein' selfish. You look so sad I cain't stand it; I'll help you through it, I promise I will. Just please don't look so sad. Come here, honey."

Billy May had reacted naturally, by moving tearfully into Corinne's arms, but as she had done so Corinne was hit by a realization so powerful that even now, thirty years later in her bright kitchen, setting the table for her husband's breakfast, she still didn't completely comprehend it. She was in love with Billy May.

This here is the part I do not like to talk about, but there ain't no sense in tellin' part of the story if I ain't goin' to tell it all.

I do not like to cry in front of folks, I never have, but that day it was like everythin' was weighin' down on me so heavy, like it was squeezin' them tears out of me with the weight, and they just kept on comin'. It had been a few weeks since Momma died and I had tried to move past it, but for whatever reason that day it just wouldn't leave me be. Maybe it was because of all them families goin' together to meet their loved ones, or maybe it was knowin' all the reunions that would take place over dinner. Anyhow, it was hittin' me hard that day that I didn't have no one. I had friends, that is for sure, but if I had been comin' home on that train, there wouldn't have been a single blood relative to meet me. I think that was the first time I really understood that I didn't have no family left in this world, and it was a hard thing to wrastle with.

I seen that Corinne felt bad about our squabble, but I wasn't upset with her. I had too many other thoughts crowdin' my mind to hold onto our little spat. When she came runnin' over to hug me, I felt grateful for the holdin'. I suppose I was needin' a shoulder to cry on, and she was givin' me hers. That's how close we was, you see. I was not used to holdin', but I could let Corinne hold me.

She pulled me close to her and stroked my back, comfortin' me, and I leaned into her with my head on her shoulder, acceptin' it. That was all I had on my mind. I figured she would hug me for a minute, and then we'd go get our ice cream, but then it all changed for us. I felt it, and I knew she felt it, because she stiffened up for a minute and caught her breath. But here is the thing, because I am compelled to be honest in the tellin' of it all. I had always felt it. That feelin' was not new to me. There, now, it's out there, and that is a relief to me.

I do not remember a time when I did not love Corinne. My heart always knew it, even when we was little girls, but as I got older it got more and more confusin' to me. I had kept it to myself, and I reckon I would have always kept it to myself. I was not the type to talk about feelin's, especially not feelin's

I knew was not normal. Now, here she was rubbin' my back and holdin' me close, and my body was feelin' things I hadn't never felt before. I stood plumb still; I was afraid to move. I could feel Corinne's heart poundin' against my own chest.

We stood there like that for a minute, leanin' into each other but not movin', and then Corinne pulled me closer and pressed her face up against my neck. I could feel her breathin' hard against my skin, and my knees went weak.

We was sheltered in them hills. We didn't know much of nothin' about life outside of them mountains. I did not know the word lesbian; to us gay meant havin' fun, and queer meant somethin' strange. This was long, long before people in Hollywood talked about it on the television and walked out in the open holdin' hands. We knew the word homosexual, though, because Brother Hudson preached about it. We had both been taught all our lives that this thing we was feelin' was unnatural, that it was sinnin' against God. Just like killin' and stealin' and lyin', this thing would put us in hell. That is what we believed.

"Corinne," I said to her, afraid, tryin' to pull away from her. "Corinne, we cain't do this." She loosened her hold on me then, and I thought it was over, but it wasn't. She kept one hand gentle against my waist and with her other hand she cupped my chin, forcin' me to look at her. Her face was so close to mine, her forehead nearly against my own, and she was flushed, her eyes wide and bright, and so blue. "Do you feel it, Billy May?" she asked me, and I could not lie to her. "I have always felt it," I said, and she touched my cheek with her fingers. I had to close my eyes then, to keep from losin' myself. "But we cain't do this, Corinne. It ain't right. We'll go to hell for sure."

"No one has to know," she whispered, her breathin' all ragged, and then she pulled me up against her again and laid her face next to mine, and her skin was so soft. "I love you, Billy May."

I do not remember a time when I did not love Corinne.

Corinne set her husband's breakfast on the table and went to find him, arranging a smile on her face, determined to be a good wife to what was, indisputably, her good husband. She was determined, too, to live through this day as she had through all the others in the last thirty years. Even now, her feelings for Billy May confused her but did not shame her; her own cowardice, however, did.

Chapter Twenty-One
A safe haven

I woke quick, sittin' up in my chair, my hand automatically goin' to my rifle. A sound had awakened me and I was irritated with myself; I had not meant to fall asleep. Old Mongrel sat beside me, his eyes watchful and alert. Then the girl moaned again and I realized that was what woke me. I knelt beside the basin and seen that her eyes was opened wide, full of fear and confusion.

"Shhhh," I told her. "It's okay. You're safe here. You knocked at my door. You was hurt, but you're safe now." She let out a breath and leaned her head back again, closin' her eyes.

"Tonight was worse," she said in a whisper. "I didn't know where else to go."

"It's okay," I told her. "You done the right thing. We can talk later, when you're feelin' better. Right now, we're goin' to get you out of that tub."

The girl struggled forward, but I held out my hand, restrainin' her.

"You ain't in no shape to get up. I'm goin' to pick you up and set you on that towel on the bed. Then I'm goin' to help you dress in some of my thermals. But honey...." I stopped. I wasn't sure how much she remembered or even how much she understood of what they had done to her. I was pretty sure she didn't understand the whole of what had happened to her; how could she? She was just a child herself.

"Honey," I started again. "You've been hurt, and you're bleedin' a little bit. I got some supplies you're goin' to have to use, okay? You know what that is, right? You've done that before?"

The girl nodded, duckin' her head, embarrassed. "Twicet now. It should be comin' on again soon. I think it's a little bit late." Her voice faded out on this last piece of information.

"All right then," I said with a quick nod. "There ain't no reason to be embarrassed, honey. Let me just stoke up the fire good so you'll be warm while we get you situated."

I was glad for the excuse to turn away from the girl for a minute. I didn't know what she could see in my face, and I did not want to upset her. Lord knew she was goin' to have a hard enough time of it as it was. That girl's womb was goin' to require some time to heal from the miscarriage, if it healed at all, but I didn't see no reason to burden her with that knowledge yet.

I built up the fire and set out clothes and supplies for the girl. Then bendin' over, I told her to put her arms up around my neck.

"Just hold on, honey, and we'll get you out of there."

She did as I asked. Her arms was weak and frail, her whole body was, and I lifted her easy onto the towel, quickly pattin' her dry and dressin' her, takin' care not to further aggravate all the injuries that covered her body. That girl was plumb covered with cuts and bruises, both old and new. I did not see a single section of her pale skin that wasn't scabbed over, bleedin', or filled up with bruisin'. She was so scrawny her skin seemed like it could barely stretch over her rib cage; her breasts wasn't nothin' more than nubs on her bony little chest. I was guessin' she couldn't be more'n thirteen, maybe even twelve. Still a child, but cursed with a woman's knowledge. My thermals swallowed her up, but they would have to do.

Finally, I pulled back the bedcovers and lowered her down, addin' a extra quilt for warmth and rememberin' for a fleetin' moment doin' the same for Momma all them years ago, and for Polly after that. Helpin' her to prop up against the pillows, I handed her the mug of black cherry tea.

"Drink this, honey. It'll help with the soreness." What I didn't say was that the wild lettuce would also bring her some peace and help her sleep. Sleep, I figured, was probably the best place for the girl to be right now. *It'll heal the body and the soul*, I heard Polly say in my mind.

The girl drank it down fast, and I wondered at the last time she had eaten. Before I could offer her any food, she had already sunk down in the feather mattress, her eyes closed, asleep. I let her be.

Chapter Twenty-Two
Sue Ann's epiphany

In the little shack outside of town, Sue Ann struggled with her own sore body, her ribs aching from the previous collision with the kitchen table, the rest of her hurting from the beating the night before.

Jimmy had come home after midnight, reeking of urine and looking for a fight. Sue Ann had retreated to the bedroom as soon as she had heard him fumbling at the door, but there was no deliverance from Jimmy; after all these years she realized it was futile to even try, yet in spite of that knowledge the instinct for self-preservation made her try, anyway.

Now, standing at the bathroom mirror, she tried to cover the worst of the bruises with makeup. She knew it wouldn't work, knew they'd be noticed anyway, but she was also cognizant of the fact that no one would question it. They'd simply avert their eyes, soothing away their guilt by reassuring themselves that it was a personal family matter in which they shouldn't become involved. Even Dr. Hayden, for whom she did light office work, would remain quiet, though he undoubtedly recognized the truth of her predicament. Sometimes she hated Dr. Hayden for that, but she needed the job.

J.J. was the only one who ever commented on her injuries, and Sue Ann felt terrible about that, but what could she do? A late in life baby, unforeseen, his conception a result of one of Jimmy's nights of abuse, J.J. was an unexpected ray of sunshine in Sue Ann's colorless world. Who would have ever thought, Sue Ann contemplated now, that such a horrific night could have ultimately resulted in so much joy.

He was an exceptionally bright child in spite of his difficulty with reading. Now in the sixth grade, he was still unable to read much of the material he had been expected to master in the fourth. She knew they'd hold him back if he couldn't catch up, but no matter how she tried to help him, he just didn't seem to be able to grasp the letters and their troublesome sounds. Jimmy called him a little retard, but Sue Ann knew differently. Why, J.J. could converse on any subject on earth. He was a whiz at science and math and was artistic, as well, drawing the most beautiful pictures of the mountains Sue Ann had ever seen. But most of all he was sweet, such a good, kind child, touching her bruised face gently this morning, his eyes troubled.

"He hit you again, didn't he Momma? I hate him so much."

"J.J.," she had admonished. "Don't talk about your daddy that way. He just has problems, you know, from the war. It was hard on everybody, honey. War changes people. They ain't the same at the end of it. What we have to remember is that your daddy went over there to fight for us, for our freedoms."

"I don't care what he went over there for," responded J.J. hotly, his small face endearingly earnest. "I just wisht he'd a stayed."

Sue Ann couldn't help but smile at this little love of her life.

"Honey, if he'd a stayed, I wouldn't have you."

With that, she had kissed him on the nose and sent him off to school, watching him through the living room window as he made his way through the snow, nearly thigh high on his slender body. Following his progress as far as she could see, Sue Ann felt a pang of regret. She did the best she could for her boy, but she knew it wasn't good enough.

She wondered how J.J.'s life might have been different had he been born into her first marriage instead of into the hell in which they lived. Her first husband had been a good man; she had always thought he would have made an outstanding father. Sue Ann had met Jack through Ms. Temple, the town librarian. Ms. Temple's nephew had come all the way from Memphis to visit his spinster aunt before joining the service, and as far as Sue Ann was concerned, it had been love at first sight. As soon as they'd seen each other across the aisle at Cedar Hollow Baptist Church that Sunday morning, Sue Ann had known she was in love.

Ms. Temple had been thrilled to see her nephew falling for the daughter of the local doctor, and Sue Ann's father had been thrilled, too, at the prospect of his daughter marrying into a wealthy family of Memphis lawyers. Thrilled, too, Sue Ann had always suspected, because he was so often at a loss as to how to raise a daughter, his wife, Sue Ann's mother, perpetually absent, in the sanitarium more than she was in her own home. The brunt of the work over the last years of her childhood had fallen on her father's hired help, Suzanna Platte, but even so, Sue Ann felt her father was secretly relieved to be done with it all, his daughter now the responsibility of some other man.

By the time Jimmy Williamson returned from the war, Sue Ann had lived in Memphis, Tennessee for several years, had no plans to return to the mountains, and certainly had no reason to think she would ever have occasion to marry Jimmy Williamson, or anyone else, for that matter, happily married as she was. She had known that whole group of war boys, all four of them, the returning sons of the mountain. They were, after all, her age, though not of her social status.

Branded somewhat affectionately, and a tiny bit fearfully, as the town roughnecks, they were seen as boys who could stray a bit outside of the lines, but who did no real harm. Spirited, they were, and mischievous, but not truly bad, at least not yet. They raced their cars down the main drag and drank beer on Friday nights around a bonfire up by the creek, but they'd never been in serious trouble, not a one of them.

When Sue Ann finally did come back to Cedar Hollow after the death of her husband, shocked by grief and barely clinging to her sanity, those four returning war sons of the mountains seemed to have somehow changed the entire composition of the town. Willy Pruitt, to everyone's shock and dismay, had committed suicide, apparently unable to recover from his time on the front. His younger sister, Corinne, beside herself with grief at the suicide of her brother, had up and married Willy's friend John Paul Johnson, though no one had even known they were seriously dating and Corinne was barely sixteen years old. Roy Campbell and Jimmy Williamson had by all accounts been devastated by the war and even more so at the loss of Willy. Rumor had it they'd both turned to drink to deal with their troubles, keeping old man Pritchett happily in business. Sue Ann could certainly attest to Jimmy's fondness for drink, though she wasn't convinced that Willy's death was the cause of it.

To top it all off, Billy May Platte, Suzanna's daughter, had disappeared and no one seemed to know where she'd gone. The town was different, sadder than before if possible, with an air of scandal that even Sue Ann, in her deranged, grief stricken state of mind could sense. But no one was talking about it, at least not to her. The few times over the years she had asked Jimmy about Willy's suicide his reaction had made her wish she hadn't.

As for Billy May Platte, in the first few months of Sue Ann's return to Cedar Hollow she had heard snickering around certain parts of town but thought little of it. With Billy May's parents both deceased, Sue Ann thought the most likely explanation was that she had gone south, looking for her Cherokee relatives. There was nothing in Cedar Hollow to keep her there. Sue Ann and Billy May had never been close, although they'd lived in the same house for several years. Sue Ann remembered Billy May as nothing more or less than the daughter of her father's live-in maid. What few vague memories she had of Billy May were of a little girl always on the run, surrounded by Corinne Pruitt and other children from town.

Sue Ann was already a teenager by the time the Plattes had come to live with them. She'd been wholly self-involved, unconcerned with a pesky little girl, out and about and into whatever little bit of a social scene Cedar Hollow had had to offer at that time. Billy May's absence upon Sue Ann's return home had had no impact on her life one way or another other than as a mildly interesting oddity.

Dr. Leary passed away only a few short months after Sue Ann's return home, and then she herself was orphaned, but she didn't leave town again because although she had no ties in Cedar Hollow, she had none anywhere else, either. She sold the old family home to a woman who was interested in renting the spare rooms. The old house was too big and dark for her tastes, and she settled on a little white house on the opposite side of town.

Sue Ann had made a tidy profit from the sale, which, she now thought bitterly, was gone nearly as soon as she had taken up with Jimmy Williamson. This was also, she admitted to herself, most likely the reason for Jimmy's sudden interest in her to begin with. He had pursued her relentlessly, and back then he had still been able to turn on the charm when it suited him. She had been lonely, and she realized now, somewhat numbed by the losses she had experienced in such a short time period. Like a hunter on the scent, Jimmy had zeroed in and devoured her before she had realized what was happening. They had married and he had moved into her cute little white house and promptly destroyed it, spent all of her money on booze, and beaten the hell out of her.

Sue Ann shook herself from her memories and, giving up on hiding any more of the bruises, struggled into her galoshes in what would turn out to be a futile attempt to stay dry on her trek through the snow. Dr. Hayden had asked her to come early today to help with rearranging the filing system. She picked up her pocketbook and paused, taking a final look around the shabby house to make sure everything was as Jimmy demanded it.

Her attention was arrested by J.J.'s latest painting, hastily tacked up on the kitchen wall beside the stove. As always, she was pleasantly surprised by the depth and detail in his artwork. The mountains were brilliant with fall foliage, the dirt road incredibly real as it wound its way off the side of the picture. And there, smack dab in the middle, J.J. had painted himself, complete with freckled nose and unruly auburn hair. He was holding onto Sue Ann's arm, as if supporting her, and there she was, in all her depressing detail. Thin, bony frame, lank hair, washed out complexion, and the final touch: a big, purple bruise surrounding her right eye.

At that moment, Sue Ann knew something was going to have to change.

Chapter Twenty-Three
The girl awakens

The girl woke to full sunlight, the smell of food in the air. She initially felt so comfortable, so *comforted*, that she didn't want to open her eyes. She remembered immediately her circumstances, partly because there was no angry voice yelling at her to get up, and partly because of the sheer comfort of the bed, the quilts, and the warmth. She didn't want to move, didn't want to break the spell, but her body ached and she needed to shift her position to relieve the pain.

Finally, she opened her eyes. The woman, even more petite than the girl had originally thought, was at the stove, bending down to add more wood. She was dressed in dungarees and a flannel shirt, work boots on her feet. Despite the close-cropped hair, the girl could see that her features were feminine—pretty, really—with high cheekbones and a full mouth, the brows arched and well-defined. And although the girl couldn't see the woman's eyes now, she knew from the night before that they were dark and expressive. Last night, she had seen a mixture of kindness, concern, and at times, she thought, anger, though the woman had tried to hide it, and the girl knew instinctively it wasn't directed at her.

Taking advantage of the woman's distraction, the girl glanced around the tiny cabin. There wasn't much to see. On the wall to the left of the door was the bed in which she rested, with its feather mattress and bundle of brightly colored quilts. A gun rack was fixed to the wall above the oak headboard, and in it sat something...the girl craned her neck to see...a shotgun, maybe. One rack was empty, and the girl knew it was because the woman was keeping her rifle close. Butted up against the end of the bed, the girl could see the rounded top of a steamer trunk, a bear skin thrown haphazardly across it. Directly across from the foot of the bed, against the back wall, was a wardrobe of some sort of dark wood, the doors closed.

The rest of the back wall of the cabin served as a kitchen area, with wooden shelves and a countertop running the remaining length across. Pots and pans hung from hooks, and a small washbasin sat on the counter. On the open shelves, the girl could see an assortment of items, mostly closed tins, but also several chipped pottery plates and mugs in various colors.

The stove sat in the middle of the cabin facing towards the kitchen area. It was a Glenwood from the looks of it, much like the one in the girl's own home. A lot of these old hunting cabins still had wood- and coal-burning stoves. There was no power up on the mountains, electric companies thus far having found it impossible to penetrate the vegetation. Besides, no one lived up here, anyway, unless they were escaping something down below. The stove's top had two shelves and six burners; four of the burners were currently in use, an open tin of something, the girl guessed some sort of herb, open on the upper shelf. In a cast iron skillet on the stovetop something delicious smelling was sizzling, causing the girl's mouth to water.

Against the third wall of the cabin, the wall directly across from the bed and to the right of the door, the girl saw a small, round wooden pedestal table with two matching ladder back chairs, obviously old and probably handmade. On the table sat a book, but the girl was unable to make out the cover, only that it was divided about halfway through by a cardinal feather, presumably holding the reader's place. Built high into the remainder of the wall, leading to the front door, was a series of hooks holding various assorted articles. Under the hooks sat a firewood box, filled nearly to the top with split wood.

Next, the girl's eyes traveled to the front wall and the wide, planked door through which the woman had dragged her in out of the cold the night before. The door was off-center, far to the right of the girl as she lay in bed observing. To the left of the door was the cabin's solitary window, looking out onto the small front porch. The girl saw that a wooden shutter was hinged to the left side of the window, the side furthest from the door. This shutter was now fully open, letting in the bright morning sun.

Finally, closer to the girl, an overstuffed chair, large and comfortable looking, upholstered in something dark (horsehair?). Between the chair and the bed was a small wooden table, rough-hewn, which held a single oil lamp, currently unlit. Next to the lamp was a lace handkerchief, and atop it a small collection of pink quartz, and she felt warmed by the sight of it. The woman had gotten her gift and kept it. She flushed with unexpected pleasure before continuing her inspection of the room.

The floor of the cabin was made of wide planks, pine, the girl thought, with an ancient braided rug spread across the middle. And on the rug, huddled close to the stove, was the dog. He lay with his head resting on his paws, his eyes intent upon her face. She was surprised to see him there; he had kept her company in her little cave on several occasions. Showing up out of nowhere one night he had nearly scared her to death, snuffling around somewhere over her head. At first she had thought he was a bear, or maybe a wild boar, then he had come sniffing around the entrance and she had glimpsed the wagging tail in the glow from the fire. He had kept her warm those cold nights, and she had felt safe with him there, as if he had been sent as a guardian angel to watch over her as she slept.

The girl next allowed her gaze to wander back to the woman, who glanced over just in time to catch the girl's look. The woman paused in her work for a moment and then smiled at her, and it was such a pretty smile, so warm, that to her surprise and amazement the girl found herself smiling back, blushing at the intensity of the pleasure she felt.

Chapter Twenty-Four
Roy Campbell

Roy Campbell was pissed as hell, and somebody was going to pay. The little bitch was gone, Lord only knew where, and he hoped she was ready for an ass-whipping when he found her because she was sure as hell going to get one. Stumbling over beer cans and whiskey bottles, Roy lurched out the front door, unzipping his trousers as he went. It took a moment to locate his shriveled penis in the frigid morning air, but once he found it he leaned over the edge of the rotted front porch and released a stream of dark, steaming urine into the snow, shuddering with satisfaction as he did. His bladder emptied, he re-zipped and stood looking out over the side of the mountain, the glare from the snow like ice picks to his whisky saturated brain.

He wondered foggily where the girl could have gone. He wasn't particularly worried about the storm of the night before or the effect it may have had on the girl. Hell, he could barely afford to feed himself; one less mouth to feed could just be a blessing in disguise. He would miss the entertainment, though. That girl was a regular Jezebel these days. Since she had hit womanhood he'd had more fun than he could remember ever having when her slut of a momma had been around. He had taken it as his due from both of them. Served 'em both right, he thought, as he cleared a glob of thick phlegm out of his throat and spat over the side of the porch. Like momma like daughter. Throw it out in front of a man's face for him to take and then try to deny him. Teases, the both of them, and after all he had done for them, too.

The girl had been just a baby when he had met her

momma. Roy had been called over to the next town to help with a mine when he had first met Lindy. She was standing at the train station holding a baby and a suitcase and crying. Taking in her shapely legs, her high, tight ass and her heavy breasts, Roy had approached her, like a true gentleman would, to ask if she needed assistance.

As it turned out, she did. She had gone and gotten herself pregnant, with no husband to show for it. By starving herself and cinching her belts, she had managed to hide it until nearly the very end, when her momma overheard her cry out in pain and forced her way into the bathroom to see what was wrong. The end result was that Lindy and the baby were out on the streets, Lindy's momma refusing to have a fourteen year old whore living in the family home. So there she was, baby and suitcase in hand, ready to catch the first train out of town. She didn't care where it took her as long it was somewhere away from that hillbilly town.

To Lindy, Roy in his coal dust blackened coveralls had looked like a knight in shining armor in spite of his balding head and pronounced beer belly. To Roy, Lindy had looked like one hell of a good fuck. The baby and the suitcase were both just baggage that came along with the deal. Ironically, when Lindy ran off with a railroad conductor ten years later, she left her baggage behind, both the suitcase and the baby. The baby was no longer a baby by that time, but a ten year old girl.

"Baby doll," Lindy had explained to the girl, "I got to take the younguns with me. They ain't old enough to fend for themselves and you know that asshole won't take care of 'em. But you got to stay behind. I ain't got room to take you. You're big enough to care for yourself, and besides, Roy is goin' to need someone to take care of him. You be good now, you hear me?"

And with that, Lindy and the two younger ones were gone, and the girl was left to cook and clean for Roy. To Roy's way of thinking, that was only fair. She had to earn her keep somehow; hell, she wasn't even his kid. She ought to be damn grateful he had allowed her to stay; he could have just as easily kicked her ass out on the street.

Brooding on the front porch, Roy considered the last two years. When Lindy had left, the girl was still a straggly little kid, but in the last few months she had gone and turned woman on him, tits and all. The first time Roy had seen her little nipples poking against her too-small cotton t-shirt he had had an instant hard on. Here he was, supporting her sorry ass under his own roof, all for a little cooking and cleaning. She wasn't any kin to him; it wasn't like incest or anything, so what was the harm? She *owed* him, goddamnit, and it was time for her to start paying.

Remembering that first time, how she had screamed and struggled against him, he became aroused again. She had liked it too, he knew, or else she wouldn't tease him the way she did, parading around in those tight little shirts.

Reluctantly, Roy pulled himself back to the present. He'd better get a move on or he would be late to the mine. It was nearly time for shift change. Entering the cabin, he poured himself one last cup of grainy coffee, adding a generous dollop of whisky for good measure. Hair of the dog, he thought. Got to stop playing poker on work nights. Who the hell won, anyway? He couldn't remember. Didn't remember the girl leaving, either, but remembered very well the fun they had had before she had gone.

If she was alive, she would be back by evening. She didn't have anywhere else to go. She didn't have any friends; school kids in the valley thought she was peculiar, made fun of her for living up on the mountain with no amenities. Only kid he'd ever heard her mention was Jimmy's son J.J., who was a retard and just as much an outcast as she was. Roy knew beyond a shadow of a doubt she wouldn't have gone to J.J.'s house. No, siree. He chuckled at the thought.

The girl may have hated being isolated on the mountain, but Roy loved being so far away from the nosy bitches in town, up high where he could rule his castle the way he saw fit. He had heard rumors that Billy May Platte also lived up on the range, somewhere over on Crutcher Mountain, but he had no need to look for her. He had finished his business with Billy May years ago. Besides, he had fresh, young entertainment right here at home, ripe for the picking; what did he need with some old Injun queer?

Yes, she would be back by the time he got home, and then they could become reacquainted. Right after he beat the ever living shit out of her.

Chapter Twenty-Five
The old woman
Huntington, West Virginia, 2010

This time I rise up to the sounds of frantic activity; squeakin' footsteps, beepin' machinery, the rustle of clothin', and a flurry of voices, all seemin' to bark orders at the same time.

"There she comes," yells somebody female, and then "We've got her back," this time a male. The beepin' sound slows to a steady rhythm.

Openin' my eyes, I am surprised to see several other pairs of eyes lookin' right back at me, wide and questionin'. I blink. I am not comfortable with such close proximity to so many faces.

"There you are," Starlette says now. "We were worried about you. Your heart rate got a little unsteady there for a minute, but you're okay now."

I try to speak but I realize I am bein' suffocated by a rush of air forcin' its way up my nostrils. I am chokin'. I pull at the tube but Starlette is jumpin' at me, tryin' to make me stop.

"No, no, Ms. Platte," she says, takin' my hands and holdin' them away from the tubin'. "Just relax and let it help you breathe. Your company will be here in a couple of hours, and you want to be nice and strong for your visit, don't you? Relax and go with it. As soon as you relax, you'll see that it helps." She smiles. Her brown eyes is kind, her cinnamon-colored hands warm.

Grippin' them comfortin' hands, I struggle to remain calm against the drownin' sensation in my nose. Trapped. I am trapped. I cain't move against the tubes and restrainin' hands, and I purely cannot bear the stares of so many people. Starlette leans close. "What can I do, Ms. Platte? You look so anxious. Calm down, honey. How can I help you? Tell me what you need."

I am tryin' to let the air flow freely, tryin' to make my throat relax so the air can force its way to my lungs. That's better. I take a few breaths before attemptin' to speak. "Cain't move," I am finally able to say. "Don't like to be tied down."

How can I explain my terror to this kind woman? I feel again the crushin' weight, pinnin' down my arms and legs, squeezin' my chest so I cannot draw a breath. I remember the feel of that concrete pressin' into my back, leavin' cuts and bruises that would take weeks to heal up. I had not been able to move, had not been able to breathe. Death would be better, I thought then, and I thought it again now. But no, that ain't right. If I had died in that moment, I would have missed out on all that was to come later. If I die now, I will miss the girl. I will miss Jessie. I need to hold on.

Starlette rubs my hands. "This tube," she says, noddin' to the offendin' line, "is for your oxygen. This one is for your IV. These wires," she points. "These are for us to be able to monitor your heart. If I pull the machines closer...see? Like this. You'll have a little more freedom of movement. Does that help?" Starlette adjusts the lines, givin' me some slack.

I test my ability to move, raise my arms up and turn my head side to side. I nod. "I thank you," I say. "That's much better."

Starlette nods back. "Good. You call for me if you need something," she says. "Anything at all." She stands up and makes her way to the door, then stops and looks back at me. "Ms. Platte." I turn my head towards the nurse. "You can call me if you're afraid, too. We're all afraid sometimes." With a final smile, Starlette turns to go, leavin' me alone in thoughtful silence. There has been so many kind people in my life, and I am grateful. I am.

Chapter Twenty-Six
Jessie
Crutcher Mountain, 1975

I looked up from the stove and seen that the girl was awake. "How are you feelin'?" I asked as I approached the bed, sittin' carefully on the lower corner, takin' care not to jar the girl.

"Okay, I think," replied the girl, strugglin' to sit up. "I hurt some, though."

I nodded. "You was hurt pretty bad. It's goin' to take a while for you to heal up completely. I'll make you some more tea for the crampin', and we'll give you another witch hazel bath a little later on."

The girl nodded back at me, her eyes, dark green I seen, was intent on my face. "Is that your dog?" She asked, pointin' at Old Mongrel. "He stayed with me some nights in the cave. He kept me warm."

I was not too surprised at this information. "He's his own dog, really," I tell her. "He don't let himself belong to nobody, but he's my friend. Has been for years."

The girl seemed to think on this for a bit. "He's my friend, too," she said presently, like she had just made that decision. Then she looked back at me, her face shy. "Who are you? I ain't never seen you till that day I seen you at the cave. Do you live up here alone?"

I could not help but smile at her. She was full of questions; that was for sure. "My given name is Wilhelmina Platte," I said. "But everybody always just called me Billy May. And yes, I live up here alone. Have for a long time. You're Roy Campbell's girl, ain't you? What's your name?"

"Jessie," she said. "Jessie Russell. Roy is my stepdaddy. My momma married him when I was a baby, but she's gone now. It's just me an' him." This last caused the girl to drop her gaze, and her face turned red.

Lookin' up again, she asked, "You're the one who left the food, ain't you? I know you are. I seen you one time."

I nodded again. "I thought you might need a little somethin' to eat, to keep your strength up. Speakin' of eatin', I've got some breakfast ready. Do you think you can eat now?"

Jessie nodded. "I didn't eat none yesterday. I can eat now."

"Good, then." I stood up and moved towards the stove. "You stay there. I'll bring it to you."

Soon, she was settled back against the pillows with a plate propped on her lap and a steamin' cup of black cherry tea on the side table. I left her in peace to eat, takin' a few minutes to walk outside with Old Mongrel and appraise the mornin'.

The sun was bright, reflectin' off the snow; and the air was clean and crisp the way it always is after a blizzard. Branches bent low under the weight of all that the snow, and drifts had blown against the porch of the cabin, coverin' up the steps and risin' up nearly to the sill of the window. I lit a cigarette and inhaled it deep, the cold air refreshin' after a night of little sleep.

I didn't know what my next step should be, and I was hopin' the universe would tell me. The girl surely wasn't in no shape to walk home, and even if she had been, I wasn't sure I could let her, knowin' full well what was waitin' for her back in Roy Campbell's cabin. How could I let her go back to that? Yet I didn't have no claim on the girl, and I couldn't hold her against her will if she wanted to return home. What she needed was a doctor, but in the state she was in she'd never have made it out of the cabin, much less down that mountain, and I was afraid to leave her alone to go fetch one back. With the snow, it would take the better part of a day to get down the mountain, and at least another day to get back up. What if Roy came lookin' for her while I was gone? She wouldn't stand a chance.

The old dog came putterin' back, his business done, and

struggled up the snow-covered steps to sniff around my feet. Squattin', cigarette danglin' from my mouth, I scratched his tattered old ears. "So you already met Jessie, huh? What do you think, old boy? What do we do now?" Old Mongrel just looked back at me, like he was trustin' I would figure out the answer.

I stood up, stamped the snow off my boots, tossed the remains of my cigarette into the snow and entered the cabin. Jessie had cleared her plate and was fingerin' them quartz on the table beside the bed. "You kept it," she said.

"I sure did," I said. "It ain't everyday I get a pretty gift at my door."

Jessie blushed, and I knew she was pleased.

"Did you get enough to eat? There's plenty more if you want it," I told her.

"No thank you, ma'am. I'm fine now," she answered. She looked sideways at me. "Why are you helpin' me?" she asked. "I mean, I sure appreciate it and all, but I cain't help but wonder why."

Stackin' the dirty dishes in the washtub, I took my time before answerin'. "I guess I'm helpin' you because I was once a young girl too, and someone helped me when I needed it." I emptied the boilin' kettle of water into the tub.

Jessie looked at me, and her green eyes was curious. So many questions, that little girl had. "What happened to you?" She asked. "Why did you need help?"

I scrubbed at them dirty dishes, wantin' to help her, but not wantin' to reveal too much. "Probably about the same as happened to you," I finally said. "But a wonderful woman named Polly helped me through it."

She studied me for a minute, and she did have a very steady look for such a little girl, I have to say. "Who done it to you? Who hurt you?" she asked me, her voice soft.

I stopped scrubbin' and looked at her head on, ponderin' the extent of my answer. I couldn't tell Jessie the truth on that one. The last thing that child needed to hear was that her stepdaddy had been at this business for thirty years that I knew of, and maybe even longer; who was to say? He was evil, and I didn't think he'd just turned evil that one night

121

down in Cedar Hollow. Who knew what he'd done over there in France, or even before that? With the way we was all raised back then, it could be that he'd hurt other girls right there in the village and they'd just never told. I put the clean dishes into another basin to rinse, takin' my time. When I had them all rinsed, I repeated her question out loud. "Who done it to me?" And then I answered it. "Some folks who wanted me to be someone I ain't, I suppose."

Jessie pushed back a sheet of chestnut colored hair. "Did it work?" she asked me next, pickin' at the torn skin around her nails. "Did it make you be somebody else?"

I had to laugh at that one. Jessie had surely been put through things shouldn't nobody have to go through, especially not a child, but in spite of all that she was still so young, with all them questions. "Honey," I said, placin' the clean dishes back on the shelf. "If I coulda been somebody else, I'da sure done it before any of them got ahold of me."

Jessie was quiet then, which was good because I needed a break. I did not think I had ever been asked so much about myself before. After a minute she called to me, and her voice was tired and sad. That little voice that had been askin' me all them questions was all of a sudden much too old for her. "Billy May?" She called. "Can I tell you what happened to me? I need to tell someone. That way I won't be all alone with it." She looked down at the quilts when she finished askin.'

I looked at that girl and my heart was squeezed right through my chest. Lord knew, I did not want to hear that story; I did not, but I understood her needin' to tell it. "Sure, honey," I answered her, keepin' my voice light. "Let me finish cleanin' this kitchen, and then you can tell me whatever you need to tell."

Chapter Twenty-Seven
Jimmy and Roy

Jimmy was hungover, and squatting in a dark mine in a freezing pool of water wasn't helping matters any. Removing a glove, he swiped at his clammy forehead and drew in a deep breath of the stale, dusty air. It was worth it though, he had to admit that. At least, the parts he could remember were worth it. Too bad he had had to come home to Sue Ann's carping, the stupid bitch. She never could learn to just keep her damn mouth shut. You'd think after all the ass whippings he'd given her over the years, she would have learned by now. Jimmy shook his head in disgust, remembering the sight of her cowering in the darkened bedroom when he returned home last night. The worthless cow hadn't even built up the fire, and it was nearly as cold inside as it had been in the snow-filled ditch into which he'd stumbled on his way home from Roy's.

Just the memory of it all was enough to enrage him, her whimpering there in the corner like some pathetic little animal. And then her eyes, widening at the spreading stain across the front of his crotch. "Jimmy, are your...are your pants wet?" she had asked. That was when he had slapped the stupid bitch right across the head.

"Hey Williamson," called Roy, from farther down the vein. "How you feelin' this mornin'?"

"Feelin' well fucked," bellowed Jimmy. "Better fucked than I been in years," he guffawed. "How 'bout you?"

"Hell, yeah," came the answer. "It's a hot little piece o' ass, ain't it?"

Another voice, now, from even farther back in the mine. "What y'all boys been up to? Sounds like y'all need to save me a piece o' that."

Roy cackled. "The last piece o' ass I had that good was Injun ass."

This last caused a chorus of laughter, all but one of the men having no idea what Roy was talking about, just enjoying the easy banter and camaraderie necessary to pass the time in the mines. In reality, the other miners considered Roy to be little more than a braggart, and thus paid little attention to anything he claimed. More than one of them would have been happy for an excuse to fight him, but as most bullies do, Roy only picked on the defenseless.

Jimmy, though, he knew exactly what Roy was talking about because he had had the same piece of Injun ass Roy had had. It still galled him that he had gotten it last, after the others had broken it in. But ass was ass, he supposed, and some was better than none.

After all the years and all the alcohol he could barely remember stumbling into the Pruitt house along with Willy and Roy that evening. They'd already begun drinking, although Willy had been reluctant to at first. His momma hadn't known he'd picked up the habit, and he wasn't in a hurry for her to find out.

Willy had come back from the war a man who was not so very different from the boy he had been, just harder and angrier. Hell, they'd all been harder and angrier. War, Jimmy had discovered, had a way of honing the characteristics a boy had until they were set firm in the man. Out on the front lines, surrounded by enemies who wanted nothing so much as to blow your head off, a wayward boy could easily turn into a criminal man, relying on bad habits just to help him get by. For the four mountain boys, that habit had been alcohol, and with its influence they'd gone from mischievous pranksters to trouble making men.

That night thirty years ago, when all the celebratory family meals were done and the company had all gone home, the boys had made plans to meet up with some friends, girls in particular, at the diner as a sort of celebration of their return home. John Paul was already at the diner, waiting on Willy's younger sister to meet up with him. Roy and Jimmy had also noticed how Willy's baby sister had filled out the last few years and were more than a little jealous that John Paul had snagged her up so fast. Willy, on the other hand, wasn't happy about any of them making a play for his sister. He had insisted on going home to pick her up himself.

"I'll be damned if I'm leavin' any one of you chumps alone with her," he had said to John Paul. "I'll be right there at that diner with you. And don't think you're walking her there, either. This ain't no date, and don't you forget it. I'll walk her there myself, and then I'll walk her home. You just meet us there."

So there they were, Jimmy and Roy, engaged in their usual banter, following Willy up the front steps of the Pruitt home and out of a sudden thunderstorm when Willy burst into the house, yelling for Corinne to hurry up, and threw open her bedroom door, her name suddenly dying on his lips.

The way Jimmy remembered it now, the two girls had been twined around each other like a couple of lovers, faces nuzzled into each other, *kissing* into each other from what he could tell. Their eyes had been closed, their arms wrapped around each other's waists. Billy May had one hand buried in Corinne's hair; Corinne was stroking Billy May's back, gently kneading the muscles. At the unexpected intrusion, they had jumped apart, their faces flushed, eyes wide and alarmed, hair mussed. Their frightened and embarrassed reaction, even more than their embrace, broadcasted their guilt to the boys.

"What the hell...?" At first, Willy had simply gaped with disbelief as his friends snickered behind him; then, fueled by their laughter as much as by alcohol and stunned surprise, he had grabbed Billy May by the back of her yellow dress and flung her thin frame against the wall.

"You freak! What the hell are you doin'? What did you do to my sister?" he bellowed.

Lips parted, Billy May had brought her hand to her cheek, speechless, looking helplessly towards Corinne. Jimmy had always remembered that gesture for its

125

simplicity, the very picture of desperation; it had excited him. Following Billy May's gaze, Willy had turned towards Corinne as well.

"What the hell is goin' on? I always knew she was butch, runnin' around like a goddamned boy all the time. Fuckin' freak of nature. What the hell was she doin' to you?"

Corinne had stared at her older brother, too afraid to speak. She backed against the wall, as far away from his angry tirade as she could possibly get.

Behind Willy, Roy and Jimmy blocked the doorway, chortling with glee. "Ooooweee, Willy! Looks like your baby sister and this little Injun girl got somethin' goin' on. I wanna watch. What about it gals? Can y'all start over again an' let me and Jimmy watch?" Roy had grabbed his crotch, smacking his lips as Jimmy howled with laughter.

Embarrassed by his friends' mockery, Willy was enraged. "Answer me, goddamn it, Corinne. Did she attack you? If it wasn't her that started it, it must have been you and I know my sister ain't no fuckin' queer." Willy raised his hand as if to strike her. "I'm only goin' to ask you one more time," he hissed through gritted teeth, leaning close to her face. "Did this fuckin' queer attack you? Did she force you to do this?"

Corinne had flinched then, for the first time in her life afraid of her brother. Unable to back away any farther and not recognizing the smell of alcohol on his breath, she had been terrified of the angry man in front of her. Swallowing hard, she dropped her eyes to the ground and covered her face with her hands. Finally, a nod, nearly imperceptible, almost nonexistent, but a nod nonetheless. Yes, she said with that nod. Yes, she attacked me.

With that, Willy had grabbed Billy May by the back of the neck and literally thrown her through the doorway, past Jimmy and Roy as they stood smirking at the scene. She landed against the wall in the hallway with a crash, her petite body crumpling to the floor, pain shooting through her left shoulder. As she scrambled to regain her footing, Willy shoved her through the living room towards the door, propelling her down the front steps and into the pouring rain. Her yellow dress, tearing on the banister, was

126

immediately soaked, clinging to her body in the deluge of rain. One shoe flew off into the rose bushes when Billy May struck the ground.

Thunder crashed overhead as Jimmy and Roy whooped with excitement, egging Willy on, urging him to teach the little bitch a lesson. When Willy started down the steps after her, Billy May struggled to her feet and began to run.

In the cold, damp air of the mine, Jimmy smiled at the memory. That girl had put up a hell of a good fight, but they'd gotten her in the end.

Chapter Twenty-Eight
Mrs. Lorraine Pruitt

Mrs. Lorraine Pruitt had slept longer than she had intended. Groping for her glasses on the nightstand, she peered at the clock and saw that it was already after 8:00. A sure sign of age, she thought, awake all night and asleep all day. Grunting, she pushed herself up into a sitting position, lowered the rail, and swung her legs over the side of the bed. Easing her feet into slippers, she gathered what she needed for her bath. The nurses always insisted she call for help in getting in and out of the tub, but she wasn't so far gone that she had lost all sense of modesty, and she felt quite capable, thank you very much, of getting herself bathed and dressed all by herself.

Lorraine adjusted the water and climbed over, holding onto the rails and lowering herself carefully into the tub. She began to bathe automatically, her mind preoccupied with thoughts of Corinne. Her daughter wasn't happy; she knew that. She hadn't been happy in years, for most of her life, as far as Mrs. Pruitt could tell. But she covered it well, well enough so that only her momma knew the truth.

When Lorraine had returned from Bible study all those years ago, she had known immediately that something was wrong. Corinne's light was on behind her closed bedroom door, and the muffled sound of sobbing could be clearly heard. Concerned, she stepped into the dark hallway and knocked.

"Corinne? Open the door honey, and tell me what's wrong."

Corinne, always an obedient girl, had opened the door for her mother as directed. Lorraine was surprised by her daughter's appearance. The girl was obviously very upset and had been for some time. Her face was swollen from crying, her hair was in knots, and her pretty blue dress was rumpled and twisted. Lorraine stepped quickly through the doorway, halfway expecting to find someone else there, someone who was upsetting her daughter. With a frown, she surveyed the room. All was in order; there was no sign of trouble. Corinne's hairbrush and ribbons were on the dressing table, along with assorted lip glosses and perfume bottles. A couple of discarded outfits had been tossed across the bed, probably as Corinne had tried to decide what to wear to meet the train earlier in the day. The blue patterned bedclothes were ruffled, but that was surely from Corinne lying across the bed, sobbing.

"Why, Corinne," she said, turning back to her daughter with a look of concern. "Honey, what on earth? What's happened? Tell me what's goin' on."

For the first time in her memory, Corinne disobeyed. Continuing to sob into her hands, she had steadfastly refused to answer her mother's questions. Lorraine had begged and cajoled, even resorting to threats when Corinne still wouldn't talk. Finally, unable to comfort her daughter and her concern mounting, she had called Dr. Leary for advice. Like the kind old country doctor he was, Dr. Leary had agreed to come over right away.

Stepping into the foyer a few moments later, apologizing for the raindrops streaming off his coat onto the wooden entry floor, Dr. Leary tried to make sense of Lorraine's disjointed exclamations.

"...won't say a word. Just cryin' and cryin'. Didn't know what to do. So sorry to have called you out in this storm...."

Dr. Leary had been no more successful than Lorraine in determining the cause of Corinne's hysterics. After several failed attempts to get to the heart of the matter, he had finally given her a pill to calm her, insisting that she take it and watching carefully to ensure it was swallowed. Stepping out into the hallway, he handed Lorraine an extra pill, explaining, "In case she wakes tonight and is upset again. And if she starts to talk about whatever has happened, give me a call."

She followed him to the door, thanking him again for coming. As he donned his coat, he turned to her suddenly. "Say, you haven't seen Billy May, have you? I thought she was here, with Corinne, but that doesn't seem to be the case."

"Why, no," she answered, surprised. "I haven't seen her since I ran into her on the porch, when I was leavin' for Bible study. She was on her way in to see Corinne, but that was hours ago. They were goin' to go to the diner with the other young people. Something must have happened there to upset Corinne. I'll bet Billy May will know what happened."

"Hmmph," muttered Dr. Leary thoughtfully, absently buttoning his coat. "Well, since she isn't home yet, she must still be at the diner. I suppose she'll be home shortly. I hope she thought to bring an umbrella, or she'll catch her death of cold. I'll question her when she returns home and see what she knows about Corinne. I'll let you know what I find out. It's probably nothing too serious, some boy trouble or something like that. Girls at this age are so emotional, you know."

Lorraine thanked him again, and then he was gone.

She had returned to Corinne's room, where she found her daughter drifting into sleep, the pill working its magic. She undressed to her slip and lay down on the bed beside Corinne, holding her close, not understanding what was wrong but wanting more than anything to provide comfort. Finally she, too, drifted into sleep. She had not heard Willy when he returned home several hours later and stumbled his way into his room.

Thirty years later, in the tub of her new home, Lorraine yanked the plug and wrung out her washcloth, hanging it over the side. Slowly, she pulled herself upright. As soon as she had had her breakfast, she would call Corinne for their morning chat. Something was bothering Corinne, she could tell. Maybe this time Corinne would confide in her.

131

Chapter Twenty-Nine
Jessie's story

Jessie didn't look at me when she told her story, huddled under them quilts on my bed, shiverin' in spite of the heat from the stove. Old Mongrel sat beside the bed, and his eyes was glued to Jessie's face like he understood everythin' she was sayin'.

"Every Wednesday Roy has a poker game," she began.

This one had started no differently than all the others. There were four or five men, as Jessie remembered, no more than that because Roy had few friends. Jimmy Williamson had been there, and two of the Pritchett boys, grown men now, of course, bringing along with them a couple of jugs of corn whiskey. A man Jessie hadn't recognized had come along with the Pritchett's, a cousin once or twice removed on their daddy's side, but he left early, citing a long drive back to Huntington.

They were all drunk, all loud, and as far as Jessie could tell, all meaner than snakes. Her job during those nights was to do whatever Roy told her to do. This time, although it was late and Jessie needed to be in school the next morning, her job had been to keep the men supplied with liquor and cigarettes, empty the ashtrays as needed, and rustle up whatever they decided they were hungry for.

Jessie knew early on that she wouldn't be making it to school in the morning; she also knew she wouldn't be missed. Her attendance had always been sporadic; neither Momma nor Roy had ever put much stock in education. Resigned, Jessie had performed her duties quietly, doing her best to be invisible as she cleaned up spilled messes and poured glass after glass of whiskey, until finally the men decided glasses were unnecessary and simply passed the jug around the table. They ignored her for the most part, other than Roy, who barked orders whenever he caught sight of her.

Finally, as the blizzard revved up and the night wore on, the men began to leave, pulling on coats and gloves and boots, readying themselves for the cold trip back to town. The blizzard was going strong by that point, but the men were confident that with four wheel drive they'd have no problems in the snow. They only had to walk about halfway down the mountain to the road, and Roy's cabin had a well-worn path leading down. In drunken bravado they'd surveyed the storm and taken bets on who could make it down the mountain first.

Jessie had been relieved. She would have to clean up the mess, of course, but then she was hoping to go to bed. She eyed her cot longingly, set back as it was in the furthest corner of the cabin. It had been a long day, and she was exhausted. Plus, if she could get just a few hours of sleep, she might be able to make it to school tomorrow, after all. If Roy were true to form, he'd pass out before the last man stepped out the door, and she would be safe for the night.

But that wasn't the way it unfolded, because all the men didn't leave. Jimmy Williamson stayed behind, and from the looks he and Roy exchanged, it was obvious they had a plan. Roy had been looking at her almost proudly.

"She's all grown up now, ain't she Jimmy? She ripened up good a couple months ago, and we been enjoyin' each other ever since. Ain't we, honeypot?" He had reached out then, and pinched her breast. She clamped her mouth down on the pain. Her eyes slid towards the door, calculating the distance across the cabin, wondering if she could get past them before they caught her. They were drunk; hopefully that would work in her favor. She could go to the cave; surely they wouldn't try to follow her in this storm.

"Now don't even think about runnin', girl," warned Roy, catching her glance. "You know you like it. You been throwin' it out since summer, so don't start actin' all prissy now."

It was true that Roy had first raped Jessie back in the summer, while she had been doing the wash out in the yard. She'd been scrubbing his soot covered clothes on the old washboard, soaked up to her neck with both sweat and soapy water when he was suddenly there, poised over her where she had landed when he threw her on the ground. She had screamed, fighting him, not knowing exactly what he was trying to do but knowing it wasn't right.

"Little tease," he had said, laughing as she struggled. "Goin' all around here in your little wet t-shirt. I'll teach you to tease me, you little slut," he had said, and then the pain had ripped her breath away. Afterward he stood up and zipped his pants, leaving her bleeding into the dust of the front yard. "Get up you little whore," he had said, nudging her thigh with the tip of his boot. "Get that laundry finished." Then he walked away.

She had stood slowly and pulled up her shorts, blinking in shock at the blood dribbling down her leg, not really even sure what he had just done to her. Terrified, she struck off for the woods, running as if Roy were still behind her. It was then that she found the cave, just a couple of weeks before Billy May had first seen her.

Since then it had happened frequently, as frequently, anyway, as Roy was sober enough to perform. His "celebrations," he called it, celebrating her womanhood with his vile attacks. Every few days the girl ran from Roy, sometimes before he had a chance to rape her, but more often afterward. She knew that one day he would kill her with the pain, but she had nowhere to go. This was her life; as far as she knew, no one else's was much different.

Safe in my cabin, Jessie said that the last night had been the worst of it. In spite of Roy's warnin' she had made a run for that door, but they had grabbed her before she'd even gotten halfway across the room, surprisin' her with their speed and agility after consumin' so much alcohol.

She shuddered, rememberin' their laughter. "You wanna make it interestin', huh, girl? Fine by me. I love a challenge. Jimmy, grab her legs. We're goin' to have fun with this one."

Jessie couldn't bring herself to give me the details, but I didn't need no details and Lord knows I didn't want to hear 'em. I had seen exactly what they'd done to Jessie by the evidence on my pinewood floor and by the wounds on Jessie's body.

With the story finally told, Jessie looked up at me, like she was askin' me to say it was okay. I put my arm around her bony little shoulders and pulled her close. Neither of us said nothin'; there wasn't nothin' to be said. Then I pulled the quilt up to her chin, tuckin' her in, brushin' back her hair. "Sleep, darlin', I said. "It'll do you good." Jessie sank down into that mattress and fell right into sleep, soothed, I think, by the touch of my cool hand on her forehead. On the worn out old braid rug, Old Mongrel stood guard. He knew things, that dog did.

Chapter Thirty
Mr. Smith's General Store

Mr. Smith finished restocking the shelves, making sure to add plenty of beer. For anything harder, folks would have to either drive to Huntington or visit the Pritchett boys' non-existent still. It was nearly time for afternoon shift change at the mines, always a busy time at the store, and Mr. Smith wanted to be ready. Sure enough, just as he finished refilling the wood box, the bell above the door began to jingle, followed by the sound of stomping feet and boisterous conversation. Mr. Smith moved to his customary place behind the counter as the men filed in out of the cold and gathered around the stove, warming themselves and jawing back and forth before picking up last minute purchases for harried wives or stocking up on beer for the upcoming night.

Roy Campbell and Jimmy Williamson were in high spirits, discussing a poker game Roy had apparently had the night before. Mr. Smith found himself wondering idly about Roy's girl when a sudden howl of laughter from Jimmy arrested his attention.

"Roy, you are one sick son of a bitch," remarked one of the men, Darryl Lane from the sound of it. "If I took you half seriously, I'd kick your ass myself, but everyone knows you're full of shit."

"Darryl, there ain't no use lettin' yourself get worked up at Roy. You know as well as I do he's a liar and a snake." Eugene Cooper this time, as he placed his purchases – a bag of pinto beans and some corn meal – on the counter. "How you feelin', Mr. Smith?"

"Doin' good, Eugene. How 'bout yourself and the mis- sus?"

"Cain't complain. You take care of yourself now. You're lookin' a little tired." The transaction completed, Eugene and Darryl headed for the door, shaking their heads in mutual disgust when they brushed by Jimmy and Roy.

Roy and Jimmy stood aside and watched them leave. While they enjoyed egging the men on, they were neither stupid enough nor drunk enough at that moment to completely come clean about their actions of the night before. After all, under Nixon the government had started leaning more heavily on states to draw up laws to get tougher on child abuse. Jimmy figured it was the damn democrats pushing the matter, and now that they'd run Nixon out of Washington, who knew what else they'd do? With private matters, it was better to be safe than sorry.

Not that Roy and Jimmy considered the previous night's entertainment abuse, Lord no. That little gal had loved every minute of it. She'd been teasing them all night, running around in a cotton shirt so tight it was nearly a second skin, leaning over them to pour more whiskey or clean up spilled ashtrays. She might pretend she didn't like it, but Jimmy and Roy knew better. That was the way of women, always trying to be coy.

"Hell, she done run off, anyway," This was Roy, his voice muffled as he packed a plug of tobacco against his cheek. "Little bitch took off sometime last night. Wasn't home when I left out this mornin'."

Mr. Smith paused in his rearranging of canned goods, listening more closely, disbelief etched across his face. Was Roy talking about his girl? Last night had been cold, the first real cold of the season, and that blizzard had come fast, out of nowhere and with little warning. The last time Mr. Smith had seen Roy Campbell's girl she'd been a tiny little thing, small for her age, with big, haunted eyes and a skittish demeanor. She had followed Roy into the store, it must have been months ago now, hovering in the background as Roy stocked up on beer and tobacco. She had never said a word, not even when Mr. Smith had tried to catch her eye with the promise of candy. She'd jumped like a scared colt at Roy's voice, though, when he barked at her to stop standing around like a damned idiot and come carry the fuckin' groceries.

Hearing that she had disappeared into the previous night's blizzard filled Mr. Smith with dread. There was no way a child could have survived out in that storm alone.

"Maybe she's with the Injun queer. Ain't she up there somewhere?" Jimmy threw the suggestion out half jokingly, but as soon as it had been said, the two men grew quiet.

Roy looked up from the soda can he'd been using as a spittoon and peered into Jimmy's face. "Do you think so?" he asked. "I'll be damned. I hadn't thought of that, but what if she is? That fuckin' queer ain't got no right to corrupt my girl."

Jimmy grabbed a six-pack off the shelf. "Aw, hell, Roy," he said. "I wasn't bein' serious. Don't nobody even know for sure where Billy May lives. Ain't no way that girl coulda found her, 'specially not in a snow storm. She's prob'ly back at your cabin right now just waitin' for daddy to come home." With this last, he winked, causing Roy to snort with laughter.

"You prob'ly right," agreed Roy. "That girl knows she got a good thing goin'. Hell, who's been takin' care of her sorry ass all these years?"

The conversation changed as the men ambled about gathering whatever they'd come to purchase. Mr. Smith rang them out one after the other, relieved when the bell tinkled with their departure.

Alone in the store, Mr. Smith was distressed. He hoped, for the girl's sake, that she had found Billy May, but he knew very well the trouble that could cause. The thought of those Mary Janes Billy May had requested worried at the back of his mind. He was suddenly very afraid, not only for the girl, but for Billy May as well.

Chapter Thirty-One
Sue Ann learns the truth

Sue Ann walked quickly, nearly running, navigating herself carefully around the slushy puddles and frozen ice of the dirt road. She had to hurry. Jimmy would be home soon, and he would expect his supper when he got there. J.J., thank God, was spending the night with a new friend from church, so he wouldn't have to witness whatever punishment Jimmy decided to mete out if she didn't get home in time. J.J. was spending more and more time with the church folks lately, but Sue Ann couldn't blame him, was thankful, actually, that he had an escape from the violence at home, though she missed him terribly when he wasn't with her. She rounded the curve and saw with relief that Jimmy's truck was not yet in the driveway.

Slipping on the frozen porch steps, Sue Ann stumbled into the house, throwing her purse on the counter and haphazardly pulling food out of the refrigerator, praying for something quick and easy to fix. She had some left over collards and some thawed out pork chops that earned the sniff of approval. She would fry up the chops with the greens and some mashed potatoes. With any luck it would at least all be cooking before Jimmy pulled up.

She hadn't intended to be so late, but Dr. Hayden had given her a last minute letter to type, and she couldn't exactly say, "I'd love to, doctor, but if I'm late gettin' home my husband will beat the hell out of me." So she had stayed, typing as quickly as she could before leaving the office at a run.

Quickly, she peeled and quartered potatoes, throwing them into the pot, wondering what was holding Jimmy up but grateful for whatever it was. She had just put the last chop in the skillet when she heard the splash of the truck tires in the muck of the front yard. A door slammed, and then another one. Sue Ann stood still, listening. Jimmy wasn't alone. Laughter, then, followed by a string of curse words as the men maneuvered their way through the melting slush and onto the front porch. Throwing open the door, Jimmy tracked mud into the hallway, moving aside to make room for Roy Campbell to squeeze past him into the house.

"We got company, Sue Ann. Set an extra place. Roy ain't got anyone to cook for him tonight, so I figured your cookin' is better than none." The men laughed at Jimmy's wit, slapping each other on the back and inadvertently splashing beer out of the open cans they both carried.

Although Sue Ann didn't care for Roy, she was relieved at his presence. Jimmy didn't mind mocking her and cursing her in front of company, but so far he had never hit her when anyone else was around. For now, at least, she was safe, though God only knew what would happen when Roy left. Hopefully he would be too drunk by then to do any damage.

The men went into the living room and Sue Ann withdrew into the kitchen, thankful for the distraction Roy provided. As she busied herself with the last preparations for supper she caught snatches of the men's conversation. "...too damn cold...be there when you get home...nice little piece of ass...." This last caused her to look up from the potatoes she was mashing, her ears perked. It had been Jimmy's voice, and while she couldn't care less who he slept with—was in truth glad it hadn't been her—she was curious nonetheless. She slipped unobtrusively into the dining room, setting the table as quietly as she could so as not to attract their attention.

"We've been through hell together, ain't we Jimmy?" Roy slurped at his beer as he spoke.

"Damn right we have," agreed Jimmy, spitting into his empty can. As Sue Ann placed the flatware carefully by the plates, the men commiserated on their time at the front, during the Second World War. Sue Ann had rarely ever heard Jimmy speak of the war, and she eavesdropped with interest as the men counted down all the comrades they'd known who died.

"And it wasn't much better when we got back, remember?" this was Roy. "There wasn't nothin' to do, wasn't no jobs but the mine, same as our daddies an' their daddies before them. Man takes his life in his hands ever'day goin' down into them mines."

Jimmy grunted in agreement. "Sometimes seems like maybe Willy knew better than any of us, don't it? At least he escaped it all."

The men were silent for a moment, and then Roy said, nearly inaudibly, "If it hadn't been for that damn Injun bitch he'd still be here. You ever think of that?"

Jimmy nodded. "We got her good, though, didn't we? Bitch couldn't even get up an' walk when we got done with her." The men laughed as Sue Ann pulled back into the shadow of the kitchen. "Taught that bitch a thing or two about men, fuckin' freak of nature. You know she's just been sittin' out there in them mountains all this time, wishin' she could get some more of this."

Roy snorted. "Hell man, it ain't you she's wantin', it's me. You know you couldn't satisfy her after she had gotten a taste of mine."

"Fuckin' assholes made me take the leftovers," grumbled Jimmy.

"Wasn't our fault you couldn't run no faster," stated Roy. "Willy caught her first, but she was screamin' and fightin' so much he didn't get to enjoy it the way he shoulda. By the time I got there, she was tired out an' just waitin' to be taken by a real man."

"Hmmmph." Jimmy sniffed. "By the time I got there, there wasn't much left for the takin'." He looked up at Roy, a smile curling his lips. "But I took it anyway."

Roy grinned back. "Them young ones is nice, ain't they? I ain't had another one that nice until my girl turned all woman on me this past summer."

Jimmy lowered his voice, as if suddenly remembering that Sue Ann was in the house. "When's the next poker game? I been thinkin' 'bout that all day. Had a damn hard-on half the day at work."

"Hell, it won't do no good to have a poker game now that she's done run off," said Roy, his tone peevish.

"She'll be back," Jimmy assured him for the hundredth time. "It's too cold for her to stay gone, and she ain't got no where else to go, anyways."

Roy was thoughtful for a moment. "Jimmy," he began, leaning forward in his chair. "D'you really think it's possible she's with the Injun queer? You know she's up there somewhere. What if she done took her in?"

Jimmy stared back at him, thinking over this possibility. Then he shook his head. "I just don't think so, Roy. We don't even know for sure where that Injun bitch went to. How could she? She ain't nothin' but a kid," apparently oblivious to the irony of his statement.

Roy shook his head slowly. "I don't know, but ever since you brought it up earlier today, I been thinkin'. We might not know exactly where she's at, but she cain't be hard to find. We know she's up on that crazy old witch's mountain somewhere, prob'ly as far away as she can get, right at the top. Might take a little hike around the mountain, see if I can find her. And I'll tell you one thing. When I do, she better not be corruptin' my girl."

Jimmy took in Roy's words, then, "Give it a day, Roy," he said. "If she ain't back by tomorrow, I'll go with you. We'll go lookin' for the Injun queer, and if she's got the girl, we'll make last time look like a picnic. She won't know what got ahold of her. Neither of them will."

Satisfied with this solution, Roy sat back and took a deep swig of his beer.

In the kitchen, Sue Ann stood motionless, the horror of their discussion dawning on her. Billy May Platte. They had to be talking about Billy May. Was this why she had left town all those years ago? And Roy's girl, what was her name? Jessie. But she couldn't be more than twelve years old. Sue Ann had never really seen the girl, hidden as she was up on that mountain, but she had heard J.J. mention her fondly a time or two. Dear God, they were in there laughing like lunatics and comparing notes on the rape of not just one girl,

144

but two. Sue Ann bent over the sink and retched, suddenly sick with the knowledge.

"Sue Ann!" Jimmy bellowed from the living room. "Where's my supper, woman? What the hell is takin' you so long? And bring me another goddamned beer. Shag your ass, woman."

Quickly, Sue Ann splashed her cheeks with cold water from the tap. She steadied herself, composed her face into a mask of calm, and went to call the men to dinner. She needed time to think; she knew she had to act, but first she had to survive this night. She was no good to anyone dead.

Chapter Thirty-Two
Billy May

I watched Jessie while she slept, them shadows playin' across her little face from the sunlight filterin' in through the window. Soon, the sun would be settin' on the mountain; she had slept all through the day. I knew I oughta wake her up and make her eat; she needed to regain her strength, but she looked so peaceful and was restin' so easy that I didn't want to disturb her. She was a pretty girl, in spite of all them wounds.

Sleep is the best thing for now. Polly was in my head again, and I was glad for the company. I missed Polly; that is the truth. The funny thing was, I hadn't never met Polly before the night she found me, although she had lived in Cedar Hollow all her life. I never seen her before she heard the sounds and come lookin' for me in that drainage culvert behind the school. I woke up to see her lined face leanin' over me and at first I was scared near out of my wits, but even so there wasn't nothin' I could do about it. I could not get up. Then I felt her strong hands pullin' me to my knees, tellin' me to get to my feet. "Hush now, child," She said. "Hush now. It's goin' to be all right." Up until then I hadn't known I was makin' noise.

Later I found out that Polly stayed to herself. Some folks called her a witch on account of she knew all about herbs and brews, but Polly wasn't no witch; she was a healer. Polly was a woman who knew how to use what the good earth put in front of her.

Other folks said Polly was crazy, and I reckon maybe in some ways she was, but not in no bad ways. She didn't like bein' around people, that is true, and she didn't put no stock in tryin' to impress 'em, neither. Polly did what Polly wanted to do, and she didn't care what nobody thought of it. If Polly wanted to go around without shoes, that's what she did, and if she wanted to skip bathin', she did that, too. She raised her own food and made her own clothes and tried to live in peace with the mountains because, to her way of thinkin', she was just a visitor to them mountains and she needed to be respectful.

Polly was what you'd call a free spirit a long time before them hippies come around and made that a popular thing to be. Polly was a good woman who knew more about life and livin' than anyone else to this day. She wasn't what we used to call book smart, but she was life smart, that is for sure. I find it right funny that nowadays we got politicians spendin' millions of dollars tryin' to do what Polly was doin' all along. I reckon some people might have considered Polly's lifestyle to be crazy, but I'll tell you what; crazy to me is grown men hurtin' little girls. That's what crazy is to me.

Polly only went to town durin' the coldest months of winter, livin' in a little house way back off the main road, down in a little holler. Summers she lived up on the mountain, in the little huntin' cabin that had been in her husband's family for generations.

David P. Crutcher's family, as Polly told it to me, had originally come over from England and had been in West Virginia since before the Civil War, when it was still a part of Virginia. His great grandfather, Peter Crutcher, had been a smart man, and not only smart, but rich. He seen the possibilities offered by the Ohio River and figured out a way to make a livin' off of 'em. He started out in his teens as a ferry operator, and after scrimpin' and savin' for twenty years or better, bought his own ferry, one of the few in Virginia durin' them years.

He worked for a while buildin' up his business, and when he was ready to retire, he sold it. The year was 1848, and as I said, Peter was a smart man. He seen the way the country was headed. The Wheeling Suspension Bridge opened in 1851 and pretty much done away with the need for ferries on the Ohio River. If Peter hadn't sold his ferry, he'd have gone broke. As it was, he was rich. Peter had also figured out that land was the most valuable possession a man could own. He took the money from the sell of that ferry and bought, from the descendants of one of them original Savage Land Grant soldiers, what he was to later name Crutcher Mountain.

By the time David and Polly married, the Crutchers wasn't no longer rich, but what they did have was land, in the form of a mountain, with a tiny huntin' cabin that dated back before the Civil War. A mountain, and a cabin, that, as the eldest son, was David Crutcher's birthright. A cabin in which I sat, watchin' a young girl sleep and ponderin' the mysteries of life.

The first time I came to that cabin I was a young girl myself, only a couple years older than Jessie, and like Jessie, I was plumb full of need. Polly nursed me back to health, and it was my turn to help Jessie. That is the way of the universe; it is all connected. My momma first taught me that, and Polly believed it, too. I have had smart women in my life.

Jessie moved in her sleep, moanin' a little bit. I reached out and stroked her cheek, tellin' her comfortin' words. When she settled back down I leaned back in my chair, *Jonathan Livingston Seagull* in my lap. I had finished the book while Jessie slept and I was restless, my mind preoccupied with hidden meanin's and signs.

I stood up and grabbed my coat, then let myself out to stand on the front porch, pullin' the door closed softly behind me, nearly trippin' on Old Mongrel when he limped quick-like through my legs. I reckon he was restless too, searchin' for some fresh air. Lightin' a cigarette I paced the length of the porch, leavin' tracks in the little bit of remainin' snow that drifted across my path. I could see why Jessie liked that book so much. That little gull thought bein' bored and scared and mad was somethin' that cut our time short. He thought movin' past it all was the way to go. Them words was playin' themselves out in my mind, and I believed 'em.

It is sad to say, but my momma had held onto them things, them fears and spites and angers, and she had died an unhappy woman. I didn't think I had held onto the bad things as much; least ways I had tried not to. I did love my mountain, and my life was a content one at that time. I didn't think of myself as lonely, particularly. Mostly I just didn't think at all; I kept busy, survivin' on that summit. I wondered what thoughts Jessie had of a long, fine life, and if she had ever thought about it. I hoped that she could still consider it a possibility, even after everythin' she had been through.

I was agitated, and I paced some more. The evenin' was calm and the snow was nigh gone, melted from the afternoon sun. It was just about dusk, and it had that kind of quiet that always comes with it up on them mountains. Across the muddy clearin', at the edge of the woods, a bluejay and a squirrel was fightin' over somethin'. They was chatterin' and twitchin' at each other from their own tree branches. A little wind blew across the yard, and I could hear the chickens settlin' for the night in their coop. A goat bleated, soundin' irritated, and I heard her shufflin' around for a minute before gettin' situated.

From where I stood everythin' looked calm, but I knew that one way or another everythin' was about to change, and I was afraid; I am not ashamed to say it. I looked up at the sky, and I began to pray. I had not believed in a god for a long time, but I figured now was as good a time as any to start.

Chapter Thirty-Three
A restless night for the folks of Cedar Hollow

Down in the valley, Gerald Smith finished tidying up the small kitchen above the store, drying the single plate and fork and putting them in their proper places. When Marla had been alive, supper had been one of their favorite times of day. Marla had been a terrible cook, overcooking things to a fault, he remembered now with a chuckle, but the meal hadn't been about the food; it had been about the company.

Supper had been their time to compare notes, sharing their individual observations of the day. From their vantage point as the owners of the only general store in town, they were often in the best position to keep an eye on the welfare of the townsfolk. Marla had always been a sort of unofficial goodwill ambassador for the town, taking a loaf of warm bread to the family that had fallen on hard financial times or a bottle of cough syrup to the household that had been felled by a lingering case of the croup. He had often teased her that she was giving the store away, but in truth he loved her generous heart.

All these years later, he was still sometimes stunned to find she was no longer by his side. She had been taken so quickly, an invisible enemy ravaging her heart without anyone even knowing, until one day she simply collapsed on the stairs. They had been on their way upstairs after a typical day at the store, Gerald looking forward to nothing so much as kicking off his shoes and putting his tired feet up for a rest. She had been in the middle of a sentence—he could still remember it—"Did you see Lou...." when she had grasped her chest and fallen backwards. He caught her before she tumbled down the stairs. Hoisting her into his arms, he had rushed into the apartment and frantically dialed for Dr. Leary. Though the good doctor had arrived in a matter of minutes, Marla was already gone. He wondered now if she had felt the same warning signs he often felt lately, the palpitations, the shortness of breath, the pain. If she had, she had never let on. Marla was like that, though; she was modest about anything to do with the body.

Not a day had gone by since she passed on that he hadn't longed for her company. He missed her chatty observations, her kind spirit, and the cowlick above her right ear that she never could tame. He missed her freckled face, her ginger-colored hair, streaked with gray in her later years, and the tiny droplets of sweat that always gathered above her lip in the unbearably humid summers. Most of all at this moment, however, he missed her wise counsel. Marla had always known just what to do, and Gerald desperately needed to know what to do.

The conversation he had overheard between Roy Campbell and Jimmy Williamson continued to worry at him. He hadn't missed the sly insinuations, but still, as a kind and gentle man, it was all but impossible for him to wrap his mind around the idea that what they had hinted at could be true. Men—decent men—simply didn't do such things. And they hadn't ever come right out and admitted to wrong doing, they'd just laughed those wicked laughs, cutting their eyes at each other as if they had a secret almost too big to contain. Gerald had been witness to enough gossip over the years to know that Roy Campbell and Jimmy Williamson were not nice men, but surely they weren't that evil. Were they?

Those concerns, however, took a backseat to the more pressing realization that the girl had apparently run off, heading right into the first blizzard of the season. Gerald removed his glasses and rubbed his tired eyes absently, pacing around the small living room of the upstairs apartment. Had she come home? Was she, even now, sitting down to supper, warming her hands by the stove? He would ask Roy tomorrow. He would find out if the girl was safe.

And if she wasn't, he would summon help. He didn't know how he would do it, but he would.

Farther across town, in her little shack across the tracks, Sue Ann had retreated quietly into the bathroom, washing her face and brushing her teeth in preparation for bed. The men had wandered back into the living room after supper, picking up their conversation where they'd left off when she had called them in to eat. Drunk enough now to be more careless with their words, they openly discussed just what they would do to Billy May if Jessie had not returned home by morning.

Taking care not to be seen, Sue Ann tiptoed quietly down the hall and let herself into the bedroom, silently pushing the door closed behind her. After a moment's hesitation, she braced her feet against the side wall and shoved hard against the dresser, finally managing to push it across the bedroom door, effectively blocking anyone who tried to enter. There would be hell to pay eventually, but right now she needed the protection. Jimmy was an ugly man, she knew that, but the conversation she had overheard tonight was a whole different level of evil, and the men were working themselves up into a state of high excitement. She would worry about the consequences tomorrow; she first had to make it through the night. Sue Ann rolled up her sleeves and set to work pulling the wardrobe towards the door.

On the opposite side of Main Street, John Paul Johnson took one final look around the machine shop before locking up for the night. Satisfied that all was secure, he trudged across the yard, taking care to miss the muddiest spots, and let himself into the enclosed back porch, latching the door behind him. Corinne, he saw, had finished the dishes and was nowhere in sight. At least she had left the stove light on for him this time. He took this as a sign that things were getting better.

John Paul had always considered their marriage to be a good one, especially given the circumstances surrounding it. Funny, he thought now, he had never really noticed Corinne before the war, other than as Willy's baby sister. But that day, after the war, when the four of them returned to town and stepped down from the train, Corinne had stood out like a bright blue flower, her golden hair falling down her back; she had been impossible to miss.

He had scarcely believed his luck when she had agreed to meet him at the diner, and when she had failed to show up he hadn't known quite what to make of it. At first he had thought maybe Willy had refused to let her go. He knew Willy wasn't happy about John Paul making eyes at his little sister. He had wondered, too, where the three boys had gone. Roy, Jimmy, and Willy all failed to show up that night, which was odd, given that the four of them were the reason for the gathering in the first place. John Paul had finally shrugged it off, assuming they had probably passed out somewhere from drink. Though he wasn't averse to a few beers himself, he had never been able to keep up with the three of them when they were determined to go on a binge.

As the night wore on and the crowd grew, getting feistier by the minute, he finally stopped worrying about his missing friends and allowed himself to mix and mingle with all the folks he had been so afraid he would never see again. He'd see the rest of them tomorrow, and he would bet money the three boys would be nursing hangovers, with Corinne angry that Willy had made her miss all the fun.

He had been right about the hangovers, he reflected now, as he turned off the stove light and padded down the hall to the bathroom. But wrong about everything else. When he dropped by the Pruitt house later the next day, Corinne had been eerily silent, pale and withdrawn, her eyes swollen nearly shut from what appeared to have been a night of crying. Willy, too, was silent and withdrawn, snapping at John Paul to go away and leave him alone. Their mother, Lorraine Pruitt, seemed as mystified as he.

Wandering around town that evening, John Paul had stumbled across Jimmy and Roy, either drunk again or not yet sobered up from the night before. They, too, had been uncommunicative. The whole town had suddenly seemed silent, John Paul thought now, as he showered away the grime of the day. He had been gone for nearly five years, and he hadn't known when the eerie silence had started, but it had bothered him.

The only good thing to come out of the strangeness was that suddenly Corinne seemed desperate for his company. Her best friend had disappeared into the mountains and her brother...well, that had been an ugly business for sure. It was a clear blue Sunday morning two weeks later when Corinne and her mother, sitting down to breakfast before church, heard a shot from upstairs. Rushing up the stairs, they had found Willy, slumped backwards across his bed, eyes open, one leg caught awkwardly underneath him as if he had fallen on it, bits and pieces of blood and brain on the wall behind his head.

Corinne had turned full force to John Paul then, and it had only been natural that they would marry. Jimmy and Roy hadn't seemed happy for him; in fact, they had been downright ugly about it. He didn't know why they didn't care for Corinne, but they clearly didn't, their tones mocking when they spoke her name, uncomfortable silences stretching out when he unexpectedly appeared at the general store, the diner, or anywhere else in the tiny town.

Once, after Roy had made a particularly nasty comment about Corinne, a comment that hinted that she wasn't as pure as she pretended to be, John Paul had punched him right in the mouth. That had been the final wedge in their friendship, which was just as well with John Paul. Jimmy and Roy had seemed to be on a downward spiral ever since their return home. A spiral, John Paul thought now as he leaned over the sink and spat out mouthwash, that they seemed to have continued until this day.

Regardless of whatever Jimmy and Roy had thought, it had been a good marriage, although John Paul often sensed that Corinne held a part of herself back, away from him and even away from their children. And he couldn't help but worry about this recent behavior. She was clearly unhappy, and he couldn't fathom why. Towel around his waist, he headed for the bedroom door and gingerly tried the knob. It opened. Maybe things were getting better after all.

Chapter Thirty-Four
Billy May

Jessie woke up while I was restockin' the woodbox early the next mornin'. I hadn't yet thrown the shutter open, and the cabin was lit only by the fire in the stove. Jessie wasn't much more than a shadow over in the bed. I had kept her there since she showed up, makin' a pallet on the floor by the stove for myself. I knew she had woken up because I felt her watchin' me. She was a curious child, Jessie was. Old Mongrel sensed her, too, and he left my side and padded over to her, nose snufflin', leanin' forward for a scratch behind the ears. Jessie leaned over and obliged.

"Good mornin'" I said, placin' the last of the wood. "We need to get some food in you, and get you a soak in the tub. How'd you sleep?"

Jessie struggled to sit up. "Okay," she answered. "The soaks are helpin'. I don't hurt as much this mornin'." Duckin' her head down like she did sometimes, she looked up at me from under her hair. "I thank you for all you done. I'll get out of your way soon's I can walk," she said.

I pulled off my gloves and tossed 'em on the table, goin' over to sit on the edge of the bed. She was grippin' the bedclothes tight, and I patted her hand. "Jessie, I cain't make you stay if you want to go," I said. "But you're welcome here as long as you care to stay."

Jessie's head jerked up and she looked at me, grabbin' onto my hands. "Do you mean it?" she asked. "Can I stay for good? I don't want to go back there, ever. I hate Roy. I thought about goin' to try to find my momma, but I don't have no idea where she went, and I don't reckon she'd want me, anyway, else she wouldn't have never left me with him."

She was squeezin' my hands hard.

I squeezed her hands back. "I mean it," I said. "Now, I don't know what kind of trouble Roy will cause, but I'm sure as certain there will be some. I don't know how that'll all work out, but I ain't goin' to make you leave here. I cain't send you back to that, knowin' what's waitin' on you there."

She leaned back against the pillows. "Is this how that woman took care of you? Is that why you're doin' all this for me?"

She was partly right, but she wasn't wholly right. I was doin' it for her for a lot of different reasons, but mostly because it felt like what I was supposed to do. The universe put Polly there for me when I needed it, and now it had put me there for Jessie when she needed it. That is the way it works, all connected together.

"Polly did take me in, yes," I said. "I lived with her in this very cabin until she died, when I was full grown. She was like a momma to me. But that's not the only reason I'm helpin' you honey. I'm helpin' you because you're a good girl and you need help."

Jessie was quiet, mullin' this information over. "But where was your own momma? Did she leave you, too?"

I shook my head. "No, honey, she died, just a little while before Polly found me. And my daddy was already dead, killed in the mine when I was just a little girl. Polly became my family then, and she was all the family I needed."

"I don't know my daddy." Her voice was sad. "I ain't never met him. He might have loved me, though, better than my momma did." She looked down at the quilt.

I let go of her hands to reach over and smooth her hair. "Well, honey, it's his loss that he never met you, and her loss that she left you behind. You seem lovable enough to me."

Jessie smiled, and it was a sweet little smile. That girl was doin' strange things to my heart. "Will you tell me about Polly?" she asked. "I wish I'd have known her. She sounds like a nice lady."

Lord, this child with her questions. "You wasn't even born yet when I met her," I said. "And I was just a little bit older than you when she brought me here."

158

"And you were hurt," prompted Jessie, reachin' for more.

"Yes, honey, I was hurt," I said. "Just like you were."

"Can you tell me about it?" asked Jessie. "It might help you to tell it, like it helped me. It ain't good to be alone with that stuff. It gets in your head and won't get back out."

That was true, for sure; it did get in your head and try to stay put, but over all them years I had pushed mine so far back in there that I didn't never think about it no more, until somethin' happened to stir it up again. My trip to town and the run-in with Jimmy, findin' Jessie...things sure was happenin' to keep it stirred up. I didn't know why, but I did believe there must be a purpose for it; otherwise, after all that time, why would so many things be happenin' different?

I felt like things was churnin' towards somethin', and I felt like whatever it was was meant to be. I had not talked about myself in so many years, hadn't never told anyone but Polly about what happened to me. There hadn't been no one to tell, and it wasn't somethin' I wanted to dwell on.

"Honey, I will tell you some of it," I said, "but not the ugliest parts. I know you done been through it yourself, but tellin' you all of it wouldn't be right; it ain't somethin' you need to hear. And then I don't want it discussed no more. It was a long, long time ago and I don't like draggin' it back out. You're young enough that maybe you can work it out of your soul by the tellin', but I done spent a lot of years pushin' it away. That is how I learned to survive with it, and tellin' it now don't serve no purpose for me."

I did not know how long I had lain in that culvert behind the school that stormy night before Polly found me. One of my last clear memories is of runnin', jumpin' across ditches and over fences, with Willy and them boys hot behind me. I knew why they was mad and I knew that they was goin' to punish me. That was what I had been afraid of all along. Brother Hudson had said them feelin's was a sin, and sins have to be punished in one way or another. I didn't have no business holdin' onto Corinne that way, feelin' them desires. I knew I had to pay for that mistake. As I was runnin' from them, guilt and fear was at war in my heart. I was scared, that is for sure, but bein' a young girl, I didn't have no clear idea of what they was goin' to do when they caught me.

When I found myself comin' into the school yard I remembered the culvert. I was glad for rememberin' it, because I was thinkin' I could hide in it and wait for them to give up and leave me be. I knew they'd still get me sometime, but maybe their anger would die down before they seen me again. I was a fast child, one of the fastest in town, and I was feelin' certain that I could get far enough ahead of them to hide without them seein' me, but I hadn't taken into account that I was runnin' from full grown men. When I say that now I think it drives it home, the predicament I was in. I was a fourteen-year-old girl runnin' from grown men. I don't hurt no more for the person I am, but I hurt for that little girl I was.

And they wasn't just men, either, they was soldiers, and they had been conditioned strong in the time they was gone. The other thing I hadn't taken into account was that these was not just angry boys tryin' to yank on my hair or trip me up. These was bad, bad men. They had outgrown callin' names and trippin' games durin' the war. My idea of hurtin' and their idea of hurtin' was two wholly different things.

I nearly flew around the side of the school and headed for the culvert, splashin' through that ditch that was already rushin' with cold water from the storm. No sooner had I ducked inside than I felt myself yanked backwards by my long, soakin' wet hair. I lost my footin' and fell backwards into Willy Pruitt's chest. He had me, but even then I did not fully understand what that meant.

"What's the matter, Billy May? You so eager for love you think you got to get it from my baby sister? Don't you know you need a man for that?" His breath stank of beer, and he twisted my arm up behind my back until it popped, pullin' me tight up against him. I was so surprised I could not make a sound. All the times I had wrastled with boys to see who was the strongest, it hadn't been nothin' like that.

He shoved me down, tearin' what was left of my yellow dress off of my body. I was terrified, then. I hadn't never had nobody handle me that way, and I was ashamed and embarrassed about my nakedness in front of him. I fought against him, kickin' and screamin', tryin' to claw his face, and all the while he pinned me down, layin' on top of me so I could not breathe. I was an active girl, and I was strong, but he was so much stronger than anyone I had ever come up against. He had his hand all twisted up in my hair, holdin' my head under water, and then I felt the pain, like the *deabhal*, the devil, tryin' to rip me in half with his barbed tail; that is what it felt like to me.

When he was finished he laid still on top of me, breathin' hard before lettin' go of my hair and movin' off and away. I sucked in air, my head finally above the water, my lungs free of his weight and able to expand. I was hurtin', and I seen blood in the water around my legs. I had no idea what had just happened to me, and that is the truth. I didn't know nothin' about them things; more than anythin' at that moment I was just glad I was still alive. Then, just when I started thinkin' it was over, I found myself lookin' up into the face of Roy Campbell, his pants already down around his ankles in the rushin' water. He stepped on one of my legs with his boot and held it down while he kicked the other one aside and pinned it there.

I tried to fight again, but I wasn't no match for them men. I reckon I passed out for a while, and the next face I seen was that of Jimmy Williamson. I do not know how many times they had hurt me by the time it was over; I don't even remember it endin'. The next clear memory I have is of Polly's worried face, just in front of my own, tellin' me to get up. She half-carried and half-dragged me to that tiny little house on the edge of town. I remember her wrappin' me up in a blanket and talkin' to me. I don't remember what it was she was sayin', only that her voice was kind. I remember the smell of her herbs and the taste of somethin' bitter and sweet all at the same time. And then I slept.

That first night, Polly wanted to call Dr. Leary, but I begged her not to. I was too ashamed, and in my own heart I still believed I had deserved the punishment they gave me. I couldn't stand the thought of Dr. Leary witnessin' my sins, after all he had done for me and Momma. In the end, Polly gave in and doctored me herself. Things was different in them days; people knew how to take care of themselves.

My shoulder had been dislocated from bein' twisted up behind me, and my backside was cut and bruised from bein' slammed so much against the concrete of the culvert. My feet were tore up from runnin' barefoot through the village, and my scalp was torn, with big patches of hair gone. In my dreams that night, I seen my long, black hair floatin' away through the culvert, washin' into the river and bein' carried away to a ocean I hadn't never seen. I don't know why that is what I seen, but it is. After that, I cut off all my hair. I did not want it long again.

I don't know what the rest of me looked like. Polly did not tell me; she just clamped her mouth shut and shook her head. She made up poultices and soaks and made me drink somethin' bitter and rotten tastin', sayin' it would get rid of anythin' they left in me. I did not know at that time what she meant, but I did as she told me to do. It was a few days before I could stand up and even longer before I could walk, and all the while Polly was there, nursin' me. She asked me who she could fetch for me, and I told her there wasn't no one; all my people was gone.

Polly didn't never mention callin' the law, not that first night and not later. Cedar Hollow hasn't never had its own police station; it is under the jurisdiction of the county, and with a population of only 189 back then, it wasn't never high on the list of priorities. No one in town ever called the law, and truthfully the law wasn't really ever needed. The folks of Cedar Hollow handled their own problems just fine; nobody wanted an outsider mixed up in their business.

Once or twicet a week Officer Wimbley would drive into town and stop in at the diner for a cheeseburger and a piece of key lime pie. After shootin' the breeze for an hour or two, he'd drive back out; so far as he knew, the law wasn't never broken in Cedar Hollow. In the end, Polly didn't tell nobody I was holed up in her house, and I thank her for that even unto this day.

It took a long time for me to tell Polly the whole story of what had happened, but when I did, Polly told me I didn't have nothin' to feel guilty about. "God made you the way you are, honey, and you ain't got nothin' to be ashamed of. If he made you to love that girl, that's the way he meant you to be, and it ain't up to us to question it even if we might not understand it. Them boys, though," she said, "that's a different matter. That wasn't no work of God, what them boys done to you. That was the work of the devil." She spat on the ground at her feet. The *deabhal*. Then I knew it to be true.

After a while, I quit worryin' about God. Polly believed in him, but I didn't think about him one way or another. I think that hurt her some, but it would have hurt her more for me to lie about it; she was a truthful woman.

"She became like my momma," I told Jessie, brushin' out her hair while I talked. That hair was a mess, I tell you. It was all matted up and tangled, but as I brushed it I could see it would be pretty again; she just hadn't had no one to teach her to take care of it. Brushin' out that hair made me remember how proud I used to be of mine, back when I was a young girl.

"Polly took care of me," I told her, "and when I was strong enough, she sold her house in town and we came up here to live. I didn't want to go back to town. All I needed was Polly and this here mountain." I started to plait her hair when I got it all brushed. I figured we had enough to mend up on her without worryin' about her hair gettin' all ratted again.

"We lived quiet. We fished and we hunted. We had a little garden and a few animals, like I still do. We quilted and sewed. There was always somethin' that needed doin'; there always is. But it was peaceful and healin'. It was what I wanted, and Polly hadn't never been a social person. She was a woman of the earth; she didn't understand social things, and didn't care for them neither. We lived that way for the better part of eleven years. I didn't go into town that whole time; I couldn't make myself leave this mountain. Polly went when we needed somethin'. She knew I would go when I felt strong enough to go."

All of a sudden I felt like I was drownin' in them memories. Polly did more than save my life, she made me whole again, so that I didn't blame myself or hate myself no more. She had a way of talkin' that soothed them feelin's right out of me. When she passed on, I finally had to make myself go into town. I found Brother Hudson, and he got some men in the church to come and get her body. I fixed her up fine for the funeral, in one of them Sunday dresses she'd saved back for just that purpose. She looked restful, and I was comforted by that. We buried her in town, by the grave meant for her husband's body.

I was thirsty; I wasn't used to talkin' so much. Seemed like lately I was doin' a lot of things I wasn't used to doin'. I went to the stove and put water on for coffee before returnin' to Jessie's side and continuin'. "Polly didn't have no younguns of her own. Her husband died before they'd ever had a chance. I reckon we did that for each other; I needed a momma, and she needed a child. She left her land to me, and here I am. Someday, I'll be buried next to Polly. She arranged it before she died, and that's the way I want it to be."

Jessie had been listenin' like I was tellin' her the secrets of the world. She didn't even scarcely blink durin' the tellin' of the story. Now, lookin' into my face, she said in that straight manner she had, "And you ain't had nobody since then to be your family."

I was not expectin' that question, and for a minute it left me without words. "No," I said when I got my bearin's. "I guess I ain't, but Old Mongrel and me do just fine."

That little girl just kept lookin' at me, and I swear to you it was an old soul in that child's body. "Well," she said, and she patted my cheek. When was the last time another human bein' had touched me the way that girl kept pattin' on me? Years and years before. Then she told me, like it was a matter of law, "Now you got me, and I reckon I need a momma, and you need a child."

I was caught off guard by them words, but even more so by the clutchin' in my chest. I surprised my own self when I laughed out loud. "Yes," I said, smilin' at her. "I reckon I do."

But I knew it would not be that easy. The devil was still out there.

Chapter Thirty-Five
Corinne
Cedar Hollow, West Virginia, 1975

Corinne Pruitt Johnson was up early, relieved to see the first rosy streaks across the sky signaling the end of a long night. Buttoning her robe and feeling in the darkness for her slippers, she decided to let John Paul sleep in a little. He deserved it; he worked so hard, always had. Another few minutes wouldn't hurt.

Corinne sighed, as confused by her recent behavior as was her husband. He was a good man, she reminded herself for the hundredth time, as if repeating the words would calm the irritation she felt. She didn't know why she felt such anger lately, after so many years. She had always felt sadness, but the anger was new. Her mother was concerned, too, and had been pressing her for answers, but Corinne didn't know what to tell her. Lately, she felt so full of vying emotions she thought she'd explode from the pressure, but too many years had gone by to talk about it now.

Cracking eggs for John Paul's breakfast, she gazed idly out the window, noting that the snow of two nights ago was nearly gone. She wondered fleetingly, as she had so often over the years, how Billy May had fared during the storm, up in her little cabin on the mountain. Unbeknownst to everyone else, Corinne knew where Billy May was living; she had followed Billy May up the mountain once, years ago, after Pauline Crutcher's funeral. She had been unable to help herself, longing for a connection, and Billy May had been too distraught to notice her following far behind.

It had been so many years since she had seen Billy May that she had felt nearly faint upon first glimpsing her in the sanctuary of the church. Billy May had looked older, and she had cropped off all of her beautiful hair. She was still a pretty woman, nothing could hide that, but she had none of the vibrancy Corinne had loved so much in her girlhood. Billy May had been silent, standing and kneeling as called upon to do during the service. She had quietly thanked Brother Hudson afterwards and then slipped nearly unnoticed out the back door of the church. Corinne, however, had noticed.

She followed Billy May at a distance, thankful for her low heeled shoes as she began the climb up the mountain. Billy May followed a trail that would have been undetectable to Corinne or to anyone else unfamiliar with the mountain. The narrow trail made the climb easier, but even so Corinne had to take frequent breaks, fearing she would lose Billy May when she did.

Ahead of her on the trail, unaware that she was being followed, Billy May had cried quietly as she climbed. Corinne knew this only because she saw Billy May wiping away her tears; she made no sound. This woman was so different from the girl Corinne had known, with her silent tears and rigid posture, and Corinne felt responsible for the change. Her heart had clenched with guilt as she witnessed Billy May, and she longed to make it right. She didn't know how to fix what was broken, but she knew she had to talk to Billy May, to explain things. There was no peace to be found until she did that.

Once there, though, once she had climbed the summit and seen the little cabin, she had found herself unable to call out, unwilling to disturb Billy May in her mountain sanctuary. It had somehow seemed wrong to trespass into the safe world Billy May had created for herself. Corinne had been afraid, too, she admitted to herself now, of Billy May's reaction.

She watched from the cover of the deep woods as Billy May stood on the cabin's front porch, leaning against the rail and smoking, looking out over the gulley, lost in grief. Silently, Corinne had turned and retraced her steps, leaving Billy May alone.

This morning, eggs sizzling in the cast iron skillet, Corinne found it hard to believe that just yesterday morning the town had been blanketed in white. Today was shaping up to be beautiful, crisp and clear. As she took in the morning through the kitchen window, she caught sight of Roy Campbell's green Chevrolet truck, headed through town and towards the mine, and she experienced an involuntary shudder.

Corinne had never spoken to either Jimmy or Roy about what had happened; in fact, she couldn't remember ever speaking to them again at all. But she knew, nevertheless, what had happened, and the knowing had made grieving for her dead brother particularly difficult. He hadn't killed himself because he was traumatized by war, as all the townfolk believed. He was not the hero they wanted to believe him to be. He had killed himself because he was traumatized by guilt. She had seen it on his face, recognized it in his eyes in the days leading up to his death, though they, too, had remained silent, unable to reach out to each other in the aftermath of all that had transpired.

As for Jimmy and Roy, what she felt for them was pure revulsion, not only for what they'd done and for who they were, but also because she had been forced to share secrets with them for the past thirty years. They lived in the same town and attended the same events, walking around as if they had every right to be free. But she knew better, and some days she hated them for it almost as much as she hated herself.

Chapter Thirty-Six
Morning in the town

Across town, pealing into the mine area, Roy scanned the mingling workers as they readied for morning shift change, looking for Jimmy. The bitch hadn't come home last night, and he meant to keep his word. This morning he had made certain his rifle was in the truck rack and he had thrown in some rope for good measure. The more he thought about it, the more he had become convinced that Billy May had taken his girl. Come evening, there was going to be a revolution. He'd be damned if he'd let some Injun queer take what was rightfully his.

Finally he spotted Jimmy, hanging back by the mine entrance. Roy could tell immediately from the dark expression on Jimmy's face that he must have had a row with Sue Ann this morning. He couldn't imagine what it had been about; Sue Ann had made herself scarce last night, which was fine with Roy. She had always been a little too hoity-toity for his tastes. Oh, well, he thought, as he watched Jimmy pace angrily at the time clock. It would serve to fire him up. The angrier the better, when they went looking for the Injun bitch.

Farther back down the main drag, across from Peggy's Diner, Valerie Burnett, the town's temporary librarian, stared down the street towards the mine. Jerk, she muttered to herself, and was immediately sorry for voicing such a negative thought; she didn't like to mess with karma. But some idiot in a green truck had nearly run her down. She had had to jump onto the sidewalk to avoid being hit, and the driver never even glanced her way. Although she had managed to escape becoming a part of the road, her skirt was splattered with mud, and it was her favorite broomstick, the one with the paisley print.

Maybe *he* should worry about karma, she thought, and then immediately banished the negativity from her mind, took a cleansing breath, and continued on towards the library. She hoped it was quiet today so she could study for her comprehensive examinations. She felt confident that it would be; no one in this little old town ever read.

In the diner, Peggy Mitchell shook her head in amazement. That Roy Campbell, they just didn't make them any meaner than him. He had nearly run that cute little girl over, but he never even stopped to make sure she was all right. Peggy could remember when Roy was just a little boy, hopping up onto the barstool with his dirty little face, asking for a coke float. More often than not, she had taken pity on him and served him one even though she knew he couldn't possibly pay. You would think he'd have tried to make a better life for himself, but in the end Roy had grown up to be just like his daddy, she was sorry to say. The apple didn't fall far from the tree, and a rotten tree it was. With a grunt of disapproval, Peggy turned the "Closed" sign to "Open" and waited for the morning crowd.

Officer Wimbley parked his cruiser right up in front of Peggy's Diner just in time to see her switch the sign. Good timing, he thought as he heaved his hefty bulk out of the patrol car. He hitched up his pants, tucking in the loose tails of his uniform shirt, and looked up the street, quiet now after the near accident involving Roy Campbell and the cute little librarian. Officer Wimbley, of course, knew nothing about the near miss. As he turned to look back down the street, he puffed his chest up a bit, confident in his ability to keep the residents of Cedar Hollow safe.

The only person in view was the son of Dr. Hayden's receptionist, what was her name? Sue Ellen? No, Sue Ann. The kid was a slow one, a scrawny little boy with glasses and an awkward gait. He was wandering aimlessly along Main Street, swinging a Superman lunchbox. At the rate he was going, Officer Wimbley thought, he'd surely be late for school. That was the trouble with young people these days;

none of them cared. They were irresponsible, the whole lot of them.

Although the morning was brisk, he dug around in his pocket and pulled out his handkerchief, mopping the sweat off his forehead. Satisfied that he had the town under control, he waddled in for some coffee, and maybe even some pancakes. He'd already had breakfast, but Peggy's pancakes just couldn't be beat. His stomach rumbled just thinking about them. Town was quiet today, he reflected. He had been patrolling this town for over thirty years, and nothing had ever happened yet, but Peggy's Diner had the best food around. That alone almost made the beat worthwhile.

At Dr. Hayden's office on Main Street, Sue Ann was just settling in behind the counter when the bell jingled and she looked up to see Mr. Smith, his face pale, his breathing labored. Sue Ann jumped up to help him through the door, swallowing her own groans of pain from this morning's beating. She'd known there'd be hell to pay when she moved the dresser away from the door this morning, but even she hadn't realized it would be as bad as it had been. Moving slowly, gritting her teeth against the pain, she settled Mr. Smith on the nearest lobby chair.

"Why, Mr. Smith! What in the world is wrong? You look terrible," she said as she removed his heavy coat from his perspiring body.

"Oh, just a little short of breath," he replied weakly, struggling to breathe. "I don't have an appointment, but I was hopin'...."

"Of course," answered Sue Ann. "You just wait right here and I'll run get Dr. Hayden."

Sue Ann ran down the short hallway, holding her sore ribs, before bursting through the door to Dr. Hayden's private office without knocking. He looked up from his notes, startled by her abrupt arrival, and quickly scanned her face, as he did every day, taking in the healing bruise around her eye, the fresh, vivid finger marks around her throat, and the red and swollen ear, partially hidden by an awkward flip of her hair.

He noted, too, the awkward way in which she was

carrying herself, favoring her right side. Recent injuries, probably done as recently as this morning. He felt a pang of guilt at her appearance, but he was unsure of what he could possibly do to help her. Although he had practiced in Cedar Hollow for nearly fifteen years, according to the code of the locals, he wasn't one of their own, and he didn't know how to reach out without offending.

There was no time to reflect on local customs that morning, however, because Sue Ann was worriedly urging him down the hall to the lobby where Mr. Smith was lying prone across several chairs, his hands clutching at his chest. Dr. Hayden was immediately concerned; Mr. Smith was sweating profusely in the cool lobby, and his breathing was labored, his ribcage contracting and expanding with each panting breath.

He bent over him and took his pulse, listening to his heart. Mr. Smith had been coming to him for some time now, his heart disease fairly advanced. "Gerald," he said finally, after completing his assessments, "let's get you back in the back where you can lie down. We've got to get that heart rate steady."

Mr. Smith shook his head and pushed the doctor's hands away. "Patch me up, doc," he said, "and then let me be on my way. I've got to be at the store this afternoon."

"What's so important at the store today that you'd risk your health for it?" asked Dr. Hayden, impatience in his voice. "You need to take the day off and let me monitor you. We may need to send you to Huntington if we can't get that heart rate under control."

Mr. Smith grabbed Dr. Hayden's hand, his grip surprisingly strong. "You don't understand, doc. Today of all days, I have to be there. If I'm not, it's not my health that's in danger. There must be some pill you can give me."

Dr. Hayden peered at Mr. Smith, his gaze quizzical. "I'll see what I can do, Gerald. But first and foremost, I have to do what's best for my patient. If I think you need to go to Huntington, I'll have to arrange it. Right now, though, come back here with me and we'll see what we can do to keep you out of the hospital today. Okay?"

Nodding, Mr. Smith got slowly to his feet and followed the doctor down the hall, leaning on Sue Ann for support. He would do what Dr. Hayden said, for now. But come hell or high water, he was going to be at the general store when the miners got off for the afternoon.

Chapter Thirty-Seven
Shift change

Late that afternoon, just before shift change at the mine, Dr. Hayden finally agreed to release Mr. Smith. His heart rate had steadied and his color, although not good, was certainly better. It was against Dr. Hayden's better judgement, but short of tying him down, he was finding it impossible to control his patient. After a stern lecture and a list of orders for the night, Mr. Smith was free to go.

"But at any sign of trouble, get yourself right back here, you understand?" asked Dr. Hayden sternly, looking over his glasses at the grocer. Mr. Smith nodded meekly, although he had no intention of coming back until he knew exactly what Jimmy Williamson and Roy Campbell were planning and had taken steps to stop it.

"Sue Ann, why don't you walk him home?" suggested Dr. Hayden. "It's nice out, and you haven't had a break yet today. Besides, he might need a little assistance."

Sue Ann was happy to oblige, and within a few moments she and Mr. Smith were arm in arm, headed for the general store.

"We have to hurry, little lady," informed Mr. Smith. "I need to be there when the miners come by after their shift."

"Well, ain't you sweet," responded Sue Ann. "I'm sure they can do without you for just a day."

"It ain't sweetness I'm talkin' about," said Mr. Smith. "There's trouble brewin', I just know it. But I won't know exactly what it is until they come in and start talkin'."

Sue Ann slowed her steps even more, and turned to look directly at Mr. Smith. "Mr. Smith, if there's trouble brewin', you know as well as I do that my husband is a part of it. Is this about Billy May Platte?" At Mr. Smith's surprised expression, she patted his arm. "You can tell me. I ain't under no illusions. I just haven't known what to do about it."

After a brief hesitation, Mr. Smith nodded. "I'm afraid you may be right. Roy and Jimmy...."

Sue Ann interrupted him with a wave through the air. "I heard them last night when Jimmy brought Roy home for supper. Does Billy May have Jessie? Do you know?"

Mr. Smith shook his head. "I don't know yet. That's what I got to find out. You scoot on back to Dr. Hayden's now, and let me unlock this door. Your husband don't need to see you here, does he? He might suspect somethin'." He gestured gently at the fresh marks on Sue Ann's throat, causing her to blush with shame. "You're still young, Sue Ann," said the grocer, his voice soft. "It ain't too late for you, you know. It ain't never too late."

On impulse, Sue Ann leaned forward and kissed him on the top of his bald head as he stooped to unlock the door to the general store. He gave her a shy smile and then stepped inside.

"If they're goin' to do what they was talkin' about, Jimmy'll have to come home first," said Sue Ann. "He ain't got his gun." She put a hand on Mr. Smith's arm. "Mr. Smith, where is Billy May?" She looked imploringly at him, her forehead creased in a frown. "I know she don't want people to know where she ran off to, but someone's got to warn her. I didn't never know her very well; she was just a little girl when I left home, and I'm sorry to say I wasn't the most thoughtful girl back then. I never paid her no mind, nor her momma either, really, but I swear I didn't know Jimmy had done that to her until I overheard it last night. It's horrible."

Sue Ann shook her head in disgust and looked off into the distant mountains. "They was braggin' and laughin' to beat the band," she said. "Not just about Billy May, but about the little girl, too. Lookin' back now, I don't know what I was thinkin' to marry a monster like that. I don't reckon I *was* thinkin'; I was too upset at the time to think. But I cain't let him get away with what they was talkin' about yesterday. Someone has got to help them." She looked into the kind old man's face and tightened her grip on his arm.

Mr. Smith sighed. "I don't know exactly where she is, Sue Ann." He patted the hand on his arm. "All I know is that she's up on Crutcher Mountain somewhere near the summit, in David and Pauline's old huntin' cabin. I ain't never been up there. But...." He pointed a shaky finger at Sue Ann. "You stay out of this, now, girl. You got enough troubles for yourself as it is, and you got to take care of that little boy of yours. He's goin' to make somethin' of himself one day."

"You're right on both counts," responded Sue Ann as she handed him his prescriptions. "J.J. is goin' to be somethin' fine someday, and I got plenty of troubles myself. But this might just be the way to fix 'em." Leaving Mr. Smith staring after her, ignoring his questioning look, Sue Ann turned and hurried back to wrap up some odds and ends for Dr. Hayden before rushing home. She had a plan, and she needed to set it in motion before Jimmy got home.

No sooner had Sue Ann reentered Dr. Hayden's office than the miners began pulling up to Mr. Smith's General Store, looking for whatever odds and ends they needed to take home for the night. The usual customers came in, looking for the usual items, fishing line, beer, tobacco, maybe some candy to surprise the little ones at home.

Raymond O'Brien struggled over the purchase of a scarf for his wife, finally settling on one with a pattern of wildflowers nearly the same brilliant red his hair had been years ago. He approached the counter and handed it to Mr. Smith, who spread it out, holding it up for Raymond to see.

"Are you sure, Raymond? I mean, this one is purty, that's for sure. I'm just askin' because it seems to me June has always been fond of purple. Just last week she was in here buyin' some purple material, talkin' 'bout makin' herself a new dress. I reckon she would love a new scarf to go with it. I got a purple flowered one, right over there under the green one." He pointed.

Raymond hurried back to the rack and swapped scarves. "I sure do thank you, Mr. Smith. I didn't know she was makin' herself a new dress, but you're right, she would prob'ly love this here one to wear with it."

As Mr. Smith rang him up he handed Raymond a roll of Necco wafers, explaining with a wink, "It was her favorite when she was a little girl. Tell her happy birthday for me. And here, take this lollipop for Isabelle. She sure is a prettier red head than you ever was." Raymond smiled and thanked him again, promising to pass on the good wishes before hurrying back out to his truck and heading home.

Jimmy and Roy were among the crowd but stayed to themselves, huddled back around the stove even though Mr. Smith had not yet had time to build a fire. One by one the miners made small talk, paid for their items and left, until only Roy and Jimmy were left, whispering in the shadows.

Ignoring the fluttering in his chest, Mr. Smith called over to them, "Anythin' I can get for you boys?"

The men looked up, then stepped out of the shadows and into the main aisle of the store. Exchanging a look, they moved towards the counter. "Yeah, old man," said Roy as he set a six-pack of beer on the counter, a wad of tobacco distorting his jaw. "I need some ammo for my .22."

Mr. Smith struggled to show no visible reaction, instead reaching down behind the counter and searching through the ammunition. "You boys goin' huntin'?" he asked, keeping his tone casual.

The men exchanged another look, this one accompanied by a loud snort from Jimmy. "You might could say that," he replied. "Huntin'. Yeah. We're goin' huntin' all right. Need to find some huntin' dogs first, though. Lost a couple of bitches up on the mountain and got to go find 'em this evenin'."

The men laughed uproariously at the double entendre, and Mr. Smith was filled with dread. He rang up the purchase, then peered over his glasses at the two men. "You ain't goin' lookin' for trouble, are you, Jimmy?" he asked.

Jimmy cocked his head to one side, looking down at Mr. Smith for a moment before answering. "Old man," he said, "don't you worry about what I'm lookin' for. I ain't the one causin' trouble here, and I ain't the one stealin' somethin' that don't belong to me. Any trouble goin' on here, it ain't me that started it. It's just me that's finishin' it."

Mr. Smith handed the men their bags, then placed both palms on the counter and leaned forward towards Jimmy. "Leave 'em alone," he said quietly. "Just leave 'em alone, Jimmy. They ain't done nothin' to you, neither one of 'em, and she's just a little girl. You ought to be ashamed of yourself."

Mimicking Mr. Smith, Jimmy placed his own hands palms down on the counter and leaned forward, his face only inches from Mr. Smith's. "What are you goin' to do about it old man? Nothin'. You just stay here in your little store and make change and leave the rest of us to our business."

Turning, the men strode quickly out of the store, popping open their beer cans, and jumped into Roy's old Chevy, revving the motor and spewing mud and gravel as they peeled out of the parking lot and headed across the tracks to Jimmy's side of town.

As soon as they were out of sight, Mr. Smith moved into action as quickly as his physical condition would allow. Securing the register and turning out the lights, he grabbed his keys and rushed outside, locking the door behind him. Breathing heavily, he headed north, opposite the direction in which Roy and Jimmy had driven. He was so focused on his destination he didn't notice Raymond O'Brien's truck until it had stopped right beside him, Raymond leaning out the window.

"You closin' up early, Mr. Smith? I forgot to get some candles. The kids was goin' to make June a birthday cake today and I was supposed to pick up the candles."

Startled, Mr. Smith turned towards the truck, sweat beads gathering on his pale forehead and trickling down his nose, though the day was crisp and the breeze was cold.

"You okay, Mr. Smith? You don't look too good today."

"I'm okay, Raymond. I just got some business I need to take care of. Here, you let yourself in." He reached out with the keys. "Just leave the money on the counter and lock up when you're done. Drop the keys off at Peggy's Diner and I'll get 'em later."

Raymond reached out the window for the keys. "All right. I thank you kindly. But I sure wish you'd tell me what's goin' on. You're whiter than a ghost and sweatin' to boot. Did them boys upset you somehow? Jimmy and Roy? I seen 'em hangin' back waitin' on everybody else to leave, and they're meaner'n hell, the both of 'em."

Mr. Smith turned his full attention on Raymond then as he worked to catch his breath. "Raymond, they got some evil plans, them two. Got somethin' to do with Billy May up on the mountain. They think she's got Roy's girl, and they're goin' after her."

Raymond nodded thoughtfully. "They been whisperin' a lot about somethin' at work lately, and I been catchin' Billy May's name in it all. And they been crackin' some downright vulgar jokes that I sure as hell hope ain't true. One thing's certain; if Billy May is keepin' Roy's girl, there's a reason for it. She's helpin' that girl somehow." He scratched his chin. "You said they was goin' after her. What're they plannin' on doin'?"

Mr. Smith shook his head in despair, shoved his hands deep into the pockets of his trousers and looked down at the sidewalk. "I found out today that what I was afraid of all them years ago is exactly what happened. They raped Billy May, Raymond. Hurt her bad, and she wasn't but a little girl. That's why she left. Sue Ann heard 'em braggin' about it last night. And Roy's girl. Jessie. Raymond, they was braggin' about her, too."

Mr. Smith's voice cracked, then he continued, removing his hands from his pockets and pushing up his glasses. He swiped at his eyes. "And Raymond, Roy just bought some bullets for his rifle."

Raymond sat up straight in alarm. "My Lord, Mr. Smith, are you sure about all this?"

Mr. Smith nodded. "I am, Raymond. And they're vowin' to make it worse this time."

Raymond ran a hand over his face, still taking in Mr. Smith's information. "You think they're goin' to kill Billy May? What about the girl?"

"I wouldn't put anythin' past 'em. I got to get Billy May some help, her and the little girl both. I ain't goin' to let them hurt her again. Her or nobody else."

Raymond ran a hand through his hair. "Alls I ever heard was rumors, and young as I was, I didn't know what half of 'em meant. My girl ain't much older than Roy's, is the same age Billy May was when she left town." He put the truck in gear and handed the keys back out the window. "Keep your keys, Mr. Smith. June'll understand. I'm goin' to see if I can find Darryl Lane and Eugene Cooper. Maybe we can help. Is Billy May still somewheres up on Pauline Crutcher's mountain?"

"As far as I know," Mr. Smith nodded, feeling some of the weight lift from his shoulders. "Somewhere up on top."

His mouth grim, Raymond pulled away from the curb in search of his friends, and Mr. Smith continued towards his destination, hoping like hell John Paul Johnson was home.

Chapter Thirty-Eight
On the move

Sue Ann burst into the house, slamming the front door closed behind her as she raced down the hall to the bedroom. Stripping quickly out of her dress, she pulled on thermals and wool socks, then jeans and a sweater, reaching for her snow boots under the bed. Throwing open the closet, she stuffed her discarded dress inside and snatched one of Jimmy's hunting coats off of its hanger. The coat nearly swallowed her whole, but it was warm and it would have to do.

Next, she grabbed his shotgun out of the closet, checking to make sure it was loaded. She grabbed extra shells just in case, and shoved them deep into the pockets of the hunting coat. He would look first for his rifle and hopefully wouldn't even notice the shotgun was gone.

Finally, she swallowed a couple of aspirin for her aches and pains, took a flashlight from the junk drawer in the kitchen, then let herself out the back door and locked it behind her. She prayed Jimmy would think she had had to work late. He would be furious, but that didn't matter now. With any luck, she would be way ahead of them on the way to finding Billy May.

She wasn't sure exactly when the plan had begun to take form in her mind. At first, overhearing the men the other night, she had been shocked and repulsed. Later, she had realized she had to do something with her knowledge. She couldn't simply sit by and let two grown men do irreparable harm to a little girl, nor could she do nothing as the men plotted revenge against a woman they had, according to their own accounts, already tortured.

Gradually, a plan had begun to take shape. She would go up the mountain and find Billy May and the girl. She would warn them. Sue Ann knew the violence Jimmy was capable of; she fully expected the encounter to be dangerous, possibly—probably—even deadly. If things went the way she hoped, that could work to her advantage. There was no other way; Jimmy would kill her before he would let her leave him. She realized she might very well be killed up on the mountain, but at least she would go down fighting. And if she survived....Well, if she survived she and J.J. might get a whole new chance at life.

Staying off the road, Sue Ann cut through back yards and across pastures on her way out of town. The sun was just beginning to sink lower in the sky and the breeze had become colder. Overhead, dark clouds were building on the horizon, creating an eery glow as they filtered out the sunlight. Glancing towards the sky, Sue Ann hoped she wasn't on a fool's errand. Lord knew, she had been a fool plenty of other times in her life. She could see the top of the mountain in the distance, shrouded by purple clouds. Shouldering the shotgun she picked up her pace.

Across town, Mr. Smith gripped the handrail and hauled himself up John Paul and Corinne's front steps, struggling to keep his balance as the world swayed in and out of focus. He leaned against the bell, panting against the front door.

"Mr. Smith!" It was Corinne, drying her hands on a dish towel. "Come on in. Lord have mercy, Mr. Smith, what's wrong? You look like death warmed over. Come and sit for a spell. Hold on one minute while I get you somethin' to drink."

"No time for that," gasped Mr. Smith as he sank gratefully into the deep cushions of Corinne's couch. "Where's John Paul? I need to speak to him."

"He's out back in the shop," answered Corinne. "I can go get him, but what's wrong? Is there somethin' I can help you with?"

"Oh, mercy....." Mr. Smith panted, trying to catch his breath, impatient with the questions. "Corinne, it's Billy

186

May. I think Jimmy and Roy are goin' up there tonight, and I think they're goin' to hurt her, maybe even kill her, and Roy's little girl, too. They think Billy May's got her. I need to speak to John Paul. I need him to go up there...warn her...."

Mr. Smith paused, breathing rapidly, his head leaned back against the couch, eyes closed. "I did her wrong, Corinne. I let them hurt her. I ain't talkin' 'bout that night, cause didn't none of us know what they was doin' then. I'm talkin' 'bout after that. I should have gone after her and found her, let her know she had friends in this town, people who cared about her. She left here thinkin' she had nobody. I should have let her know she wasn't alone." He lifted his head, fastened his eyes on Corinne's face. "Now I got to make it right. I need John Paul." His voice trailed off as his head fell back again.

Just then the back door slammed, and John Paul came walking into the living room, pulling off his gloves. "Corinne, I'm callin' it quits for the day. It's nearly dinner...." He stopped at the sight of Mr. Smith, a concerned expression crossing his face. "Mr. Smith, I didn't know you was here. How are you? Is everythin' okay? You don't look too good."

"Mr. Smith says Roy Campbell and Jimmy Williamson are headin' after Billy May. They think she's got Roy's girl with her. John Paul, we've got to do somethin'." As she spoke, she was already pulling snow boots out of the coat closet, searching for her gloves on the top shelf.

"Now hold on a minute, Corinne. We don't even know where she lives. Mr. Smith, are you sure about this?" John Paul sat down in the chair across from Mr. Smith, his brow furrowed.

"I am," replied Mr. Smith. "As sure as I can be. We ain't got much time." He wiped the sweat off his brow with the back of one hand.

Having finally found her gloves, Corinne slammed the closet door. "John Paul, you can sit here all day and try to figure out what to do if you want to, but I'm leavin'. I know where she's at, and I'm the reason she's there. I been livin' enough years with regret. I ain't livin' no more that way. Mr. Smith, you ain't the only one who done her wrong." With

187

that, she walked out the front door and jogged down the steps, headed for the road.

"Now you just hang on a minute, Corinne!" yelled John Paul, hurrying out to the porch. "You ain't even got a gun with you, Corinne." But Corinne was already gone, moving at a jog in the direction of Crutcher Mountain.

"I'll be damned, Mr. Smith, I don't know what's gotten into her head lately but I think she's about plumb lost her mind." John Paul re-entered the house and stood, hands on his hips, thinking of the best course of action.

"John Paul, you cain't let her go alone. Them boys is dangerous. You know 'em. You know what they're capable of. They didn't come back the same boys they was when they left." Mr. Smith attempted to stand.

"No, now, you sit down here," admonished John Paul, placing a firm hand on Mr. Smith's shoulder. "I ain't goin' to let her go on her own, but I got to get my head straight. I'll need my gun, and a flashlight, and damned if we ain't about to get more snow. You sit tight while I get ready. I'll be right back." Mr. Smith sat where he was, too weak to protest, and prayed John Paul would hurry.

Meanwhile, Corinne set a steady pace, sticking to the road, never even noticing as she bypassed Sue Ann, who was just cutting through the backyard of her childhood home, now the town's boarding home. From Sue Ann's old bedroom window on the second floor, Valerie Burnett, the town's temporary librarian, looked down in surprise. What on earth? For such a backwoods town, some mighty strange things went on around here. In her head, she was already composing her next letter to her fiance. *And when I looked out the window, what did I see but Dr. Hayden's receptionist, dressed in hunting gear and sneaking through the backyard with a shotgun in her hands!* Thomas would get a kick out of that. He loved to hear her stories about the town.

Up on the road, Corinne jumped to the side to avoid being splashed by Officer Wimbley's car. Squinting through the dirty windshield, Officer Wimbley vaguely recognized Corinne as the wife of the town's mechanic, and waved as he crawled on by. Another quiet night in Cedar Hollow, he thought. Seems like these people would want some excitement every now and then. Shaking his head, bemused with the sleepy little mining town, he turned on the radio and fiddled with the knob, finally crooning along with George Jones as he left the little town behind, safe for another day.

In the little shack across the tracks, Jimmy Williamson and Roy Campbell had already finished off the six-pack and were partway through a bottle of moonshine, all the while gathering rifles and bullets, flashlights and rope. Satisfied with their cache, the two men looked at each other, eyes gleaming with a mixture of alcohol, fury, and lust.

"Ready?" asked Jimmy.

Roy lifted his empty beer can, spat tobacco juice into the opening, and nodded.

"Let's go raise some hell," he answered.

Moonshine and rifles in hand, the men set off for Crutcher Mountain, the summit of which was nearly invisible in the growing bank of purple clouds.

Chapter Thirty-Nine
Billy May and Jessie

Jessie was up and about for the first time since showin' up at my cabin door. She was movin' slow, but she was determined to get out of bed. When I went outside to secure the animals for the night, Jessie followed along and sat on the porch, lookin' for some fresh air.

Outside, the sunset was showin' off its colors through the buildin' clouds; the sky was streaked with dark purple rays, and Jessie looked up at it in wonder.

"It sure is pretty, ain't it? All streaky and colored like that."

"It sure is," I agreed, answerin' around the cigarette in my mouth while I used both my hands to wrangle the goats safely into their shed. "Looks like another storm might be comin', though." I glanced up at them gatherin' clouds, scuttlin' across the sky the way they was. "Comin' from the north," I decided. "Goin' to be a cold night." The chickens squawked, irritated at me when I shooed them back into their coop.

"What's wrong with Old Mongrel?" asked Jessie, pointing. "Look at what he's doin'."

I turned to see Old Mongrel pacin' in circles on the north side of the cabin, his nose lifted up in the air, nostrils flarin' as he sniffed the air. I could hear a strange keenin' sound comin' from deep in that old dog's throat, the same sound he had made the night Jessie came to the cabin in the middle of the storm. It was comin', that thing I'd been feelin'. *Asgina*, my momma whispered in my ear, the demon, and a chill ran over me.

Shieldin' my eyes against the sharpness of the wind, I

turned north, followin' the old dog's line of vision, and scanned the woods for whatever he was sensin'. I couldn't see nothin' out of the ordinary. The breeze had picked up, blowin' the treetops towards us, them bare branches scrapin' at the sky. The last of the leaves tumbled across my muddy clearin', comin' to rest against the side of the cabin. Everythin' was quiet, the only sound that of the rustlin' trees, but I was uneasy, the hair risin' up against the back of my neck. I shivered, anxious to get the girl back inside where we could latch the door against the thing that was worryin' Old Mongrel so.

"I don't know what he's doin'," I said to Jessie. "Maybe the wind has got him nervous. Let's get you back inside before you get chilled." I stamped out my cigarette and turned towards Old Mongrel.

"Come on ol' boy, let's get back inside. It's goin' to be cold out here tonight. I'm comin', too, Jessie, just let me get a couple buckets of water." I lowered the bucket into the well, distracted-like while I scanned the woods. I couldn't see nothin', but I knew it was there.

For a minute it didn't seem like that old dog was goin' to come, but then he took one last look at them dark woods, growlin' low in his throat, and followed me up the steps. Safe inside, I latched the plank door. Old Mongrel gave up his favorite spot by the stove and settled up against the door, his nose pressed to the floor, still sniffin' that thing out in the night. My heart was poundin' watchin' that dog.

"What is it?" asked the girl. "Is somethin' happenin'?"

I turned to Jessie and forced my face into a smile. I didn't want her worryin'; there wasn't nothin' she could do. "He probably just smells an old bear or somethin', maybe one that ain't hybernatin' yet. They come around sometimes. Good thing we got them animals locked up tight, ain't it? I'll just keep my shotgun by me if it'll make you feel better, but they cain't get in here. They ain't never bothered us, have they Old Mongrel?" In my nervousness I was chatterin' away like a school girl. I needed to get my disconcerted nerves under control so I could think.

"Let's get this fire built up," I said, turnin' away and

busyin' my hands, hopin' Jessie didn't see them tremblin'. "And then why don't you and me read for a while. I see you like the story about the seagull, too."

At the mention of the book, Jessie's eyes lit up. "I ain't finished it yet," she said. "I'm at the part where all them other gulls done kicked him out and they ain't speakin' to him. Can you believe they done that? And he didn't even do nothin' wrong! He's just different, is all."

I smiled to myself, wonderin' if Jessie understood the meanin' behind what she was readin'. I suspected she did. Jessie herself was a different kind of child. "All right, then," I said. "We'll read it out loud together. You read first, and then after a few pages I'll read to you. How does that sound?"

"That sounds fun," squealed Jessie, clappin' her hands, and I was touched at the sight of her bein' a child, just a regular little girl excited by a bedtime story.

"Wash up and get settled in bed, then, and we'll get started," I said.

While Jessie washed up at the basin, I studied that dog. He wasn't no longer keenin', but he was still sniffin' at the bottom of the door, ears perked up and tail all stiff out behind him. That dog knew what was comin'; he was talkin' to me, and I was listenin'. My hand was ready on the shotgun. I did not usually use my shotgun; the pellets from them is too hard to get out of game, and it ruins the meat. But that night I knew the shotgun would be best. No need to aim, and no way to miss at close range. I tightened my grip.

Chapter Forty
Up the mountain

Sue Ann kept falling, slipping down the mountain, finding it hard to make progress in the mud and muck of the melted snow, the challenge made worse by her injuries. She grabbed at tree branches and hauled herself forward through the thick underbrush, jockeying for a solid foothold. Frustrated, she realized she had grossly underestimated how hard it would be to climb this mountain; it didn't look that high from the valley, but the boulders, gulleys, and thick vegetation made it nearly impossible to traverse, and the wind buffeting her in the face wasn't helping matters. Billy May, she thought, if you were tryin' to make sure no one could find you, you done a good job of it. She stopped for a moment to rest, and that's when she heard them.

Not far behind, just a little ways down the mountain and to the right, over the sound of the moaning wind, Sue Ann heard the unmistakable voices of Jimmy and Roy, cursing loudly and crashing through the brambles, discussing their upcoming plans.

"I say we take the girl first, make the old bitch watch." That was Roy. "We can tie her up and take her when we're done with the girl."

"Hell, naw," responded Jimmy as he hacked up a wad of phlegm and spat into the brush. "You get one and I'll get the other'n. I ain't takin' seconds this time around. There's enough for both. It don't matter which is which. You seen Billy May lately? I seen her in the store back a couple months ago. She's still got a tight little ass on her. We can swap up when we're done if we want to."

Farther up the mountain, only several dozen yards away, Sue Ann froze, her heart galloping in her chest. Now what? She couldn't move or they'd spot her, but they were catching up to her fast. Her boot slipped in the mud and she grabbed for a branch.

"Shut up a minute," barked Roy, holding out a hand to still Jimmy. "Did you hear somethin'? I know I just heard somethin'."

"Hell, Roy, there's all kinds of stuff out here. Bears, cats, wild boar. You oughta know that; you live up here, too. They ain't goin' to bother us. Besides, we got guns, and they don't."

"Naw, it didn't sound like that. I know them sounds. This was more like...." Roy was interrupted by a loud crash up ahead and to the left. Both men looked up just in time to see a body come sliding towards them, grabbing wildly for roots and vines along the way, finally halting the fall by clutching onto a sapling. Desperately, whoever it was tried to scramble to his feet, and it was then that Jimmy recognized his very own hunting coat, dwarfing the petite body inside.

"*Damn it all to hell, Sue Ann!*" roared Jimmy. "What the hell do you think you're doin', you stupid bitch?"

Frantically, panicked, Sue Ann struggled to regain her balance and swing the shotgun off her shoulder. "I'm not goin' to let you hurt that girl, Jimmy Williamson. You pervert; you're goin' to burn in hell, you and Roy both...."

The blast, coming so close to Jimmy's ear, temporarily deafened him, and he blinked, mouth gaping, and looked over towards the source of the noise. Roy lowered the rifle and spat a stream of tobacco juice onto the ground.

"Sorry, Jimmy," he said, using his tongue to rearrange the wad of tobacco against his left cheek. "But you should have taught that bitch when to shut up."

Jimmy blinked again, looking back to where Sue Ann lay motionless on the ground. Finally, he shrugged. "Ready to move on?" he asked, and at Roy's nod, the men continued up the mountain.

With one last troubled look at Mr. Smith, who was leaning back on the couch, his face pale and drawn, John Paul gathered his rifle and went to meet up with Raymond O'Brien, as Mr. Smith had directed. Raymond had already called Darryl Lane and Eugene Cooper, and the four men had agreed to go together to offer whatever assistance they could to Billy May and the little girl.

It was an odd assortment of would-be rescuers, given that none of the men had spoken to Billy May for the better part of thirty years. John Paul had never known Billy May other than having seen her running around town with Corinne when they were little girls, but he hadn't really ever paid attention. He hadn't even been paying attention to Corinne back then; he had only known her as the annoying baby sister of one of his best friends. He had learned, of course, that Billy May had been Corinne's best friend and he knew that Corinne had been devastated when Billy May disappeared. That alone was enough to spur him into action; he would do anything for Corinne, and Corinne obviously wanted to help Billy May.

And then there was the business of the young girl. Try as he might, John Paul had a hard time believing that Jimmy and Roy might do something to harm a young girl. Although they hadn't been friends for decades, John Paul simply could not accept that his old schoolmates and war buddies were capable of doing something so heinous. Sure, they had gotten into their share of trouble over the years; an argument could easily be made that they weren't nice men. But John Paul couldn't fathom that they were the monsters Mr. Smith and Corinne seemed to believe them to be. To put their minds at ease, he would go and make sure the girl was okay. He didn't anticipate much trouble on the mountain; surely they could settle whatever the dispute was without resorting to violence.

Unlike John Paul, Raymond, Darryl and Eugene had known Billy May quite well. She had been a playmate of theirs as far back as they could remember, playing shortstop during pick up games of baseball and being the first of their group to jump from the Rugged Creek Bridge into the freezing water down below. When Billy May had disappeared from town all those years ago they had still been children themselves, Raymond fifteen and the other boys fourteen, all three too young to understand the whispered rumors floating about the town.

They had missed her, of course, but none of the three of them had known precisely where she had gone until many years later, when Billy May started making trips to town. By then, it had seemed too late to approach her. She had been different, closed off to all of them. One by one they had married and started families, structuring their lives around the mine and the church, busying themselves with the comings and goings of the people in town. Curiosity about whatever had happened to Billy May Platte had taken a back seat to the simple routine of family life in a small town.

When Mr. Smith confided in Raymond earlier that afternoon, he had had no idea Raymond would participate in trying to save Billy May. At first, Raymond himself hadn't known, but as he absorbed Mr. Smith's words he had a clear vision of Billy May's laughing face, daring him to race across the school yard so many years ago, beating him as always. At the memory, he had felt a pang of sadness for the girl he had known. She had been as close a friend to him as had any of the boys in town. He had a daughter of his own now, and the thought of anyone hurting her was enough to drive him into a frenzy. He couldn't let them hurt Billy May again, and he damned sure couldn't let them hurt the girl. He was no longer a boy. This time, he understood exactly what was happening; he also understood exactly what he needed to do.

He had been surprised at the reactions of Darryl and Eugene when he called upon them for help. Both men had been eager to jump on board; both men had expressed some of the same sadness and guilt he himself was feeling. They had just been gathering their gear when John Paul called. The four men agreed to meet up at the diner, and from there they set a quick pace towards the mountain, hoping to catch up with Corinne and warn Billy May before Jimmy and Roy could get to her. They didn't know, of course, that Jimmy and Roy were already ahead of them.

Chapter Forty-One
The cabin

Jessie stopped readin', markin' the page with her finger so as not to lose her spot. "What do you think about this part, Billy May? Do you think there's a heaven?"

I had to think on that before answerin', because at that moment I was not completely sure what I really believed. I had prayed to God just the other day, so I was hopin' he was there, but I had a lot of years of denyin' him behind me at that point. Finally, I decided to be honest. "I don't know, honey. I wonder that myself. Sometimes seems like maybe heaven an' hell are both right here, and some days we live in one, and some days we live in the other. I just don't know the answer, but I'll tell you one thing; if there is a heaven, there won't be no sufferin' there, not like you been through here, honey."

Jessie nodded, apparently content with my explanation. "Some days have been like hell," she answered, her voice soft. "But some is also like heaven. Like this one, here, Billy May, and like yesterday, too."

I squeezed her shoulders, hopin' beyond hope that that thing Old Mongrel was sensin' wouldn't get a chance to change Jessie's assessment of the day.

Jessie opened the book to read again, but before she could get started Old Mongrel jumped up to his feet, whinin' and diggin' at the floor in front of the door. It was here, after all.

I motioned for Jessie to move back on the bed, into the shadows by the far wall. I put my finger to my lips to tell her to stay quiet, and then I propped the shotgun against my shoulder and moved quiet-like in front of the door, aimin' at the center, right where I figured the heart would be. A sudden knock startled me, but not nearly as much as the voice did that followed it.

"Billy May, let me in! Hurry! Open up!" The poundin' continued.

I froze for a minute out of pure surprise; then I threw open the door. "Corinne? What in God's name are you doin' here?"

Corinne rushed inside and leaned against the door, closin' it and latchin' it behind her. "Oh, God, Billy May, there ain't much time. They're comin' for you. Jimmy Williamson and Roy Campbell think you got Roy's girl...." She interrupted what she was sayin' to follow my eyes, and that's when she saw Jessie, huddled up against the wall with the quilts pulled high, only her eyes showin', scared in the dim light. "I'm sorry, honey," she said to the girl. "I don't mean to frighten you, but there ain't no time to be delicate." She turned back to me.

"They're on their way up here. They don't know exactly where you live, so there's a little bit of time, but Billy May, you know what them boys is capable of."

"Whoa, Corinne, slow down." *Mall sios,* my daddy echoed in my head. *I cain't slow down, Daddy. There ain't no more time.* I gripped my shotgun close. "How do you know all this?"

"Gerald Smith came to the house, lookin' for John Paul. He said they bought ammo today. Said they was talkin' 'bout comin' back to take what was rightly theirs. Billy May, the things they said...." She glanced again over at Jessie.

I shook my head, cuttin' my eyes towards the girl. There wasn't no need for Corinne to go on. Jessie probably knew as well as I did what them men likely had planned for us, but there wasn't no need to spell it out.

"Billy May, we got to hurry. We got to get off this mountain. We'll go the back way, circle 'round." She grabbed at my hands, remindin' me of years ago. Corinne was always grabbin' my hands when she wanted me to get a move on. "You can stay with us," she said, "and Jessie too. They won't come there." She stopped when I shook my head at her.

"What do you mean, 'no'? Billy May, you *got* to, don't you understand? They ain't just goin' to hurt you this time; they're goin' to *kill* you!"

I reached out and put my hands on her shoulders, willin' both of us to be calm. I kept my voice low, tryin' to shield Jessie from what I was about to say. "I know what you're sayin', Corinne, but goin' into town ain't no answer. It ain't goin' to work. You and I both know they'll just come after me there. It won't never end. And Jessie...." I stopped, my eyes flickerin' over at the girl. I lowered my voice even more. "She's been hurt. They hurt her." I looked hard into Corinne's face. "She won't make it down the mountain; she cain't walk that far. You understand what I'm sayin'?"

Corinne grew still, realizin' the horror of what I was tellin' her. "You mean...." She looked over at Jessie and lowered her own voice. "His own stepchild? *Both* of them? Oh, dear God, it's true, what Mr. Smith said. I knew it was, but I was hopin' it wasn't." She swallowed, looked down at the pine floor. "How bad?"

"Bad," I said simply. "Corinne, you go. There ain't nothin' you can do here. I 'ppreciate you comin' to let me know."

Corinne stared at me, and I recognized the look. She wasn't goin' to listen to me; I knew that. Corinne had been a shy girl, but she had a stubborn streak in her a mile wide, that is for sure, and when she made up her mind, there wasn't no changin' it.

"No, Billy May. I cain't leave you again." Her voice was firm. "I took the coward's way out the first time, but I ain't doin' it again. I know you got another gun somewhere. Now, where is it? Hurry up, Billy May." She was grabbin' at my hands again. "We ain't got but minutes, if we even got that."

It wasn't goin' to do me no good to argue with her no more, and at that point we was just wastin' time we didn't have to waste. I let go of her shoulders. "It's over there, above the bed. It's already loaded. Get it, and stay there with Jessie. If they get past me, kill 'em."

She lifted down the rifle and double-checked to make sure it was loaded, I reckon just easin' her own mind.

Satisfied, she scooted back on the bed next to Jessie, puttin' an arm around the girl's shoulders. "You're goin' to be all right now. If anyone can take care of you, it's Billy May. I've known her my whole life. She ain't goin' to let nobody hurt you."

Jessie didn't say nothin'. Her face was pale and pinched, and she curled even tighter into a ball and pressed herself against Corinne.

Chapter Forty-Two
The conclusion

In front of the door, facin' that thing on the other side, Old Mongrel stood stone still. His hackles was raised, a growl rumblin' in his throat. He wasn't keenin' no more. That old dog was ready to attack; his fangs was bared and I seen the saliva drippin' off of 'em. That growl kept buildin' up, risin' into the room and fillin' the cabin, almost like it was alive.

I hadn't never seen that old dog look like that, not in all the years we'd been acquainted. He was tellin' me how bad it was, and I believed him. I looked over at the bed one last time, makin' sure they was okay. Corinne hugged Jessie close and cocked the rifle, noddin' at me, tellin' me by her posture she was ready. Her eyes was steady on mine.

I stood back from the door, back near the stove, shotgun against my shoulder, heart poundin', and we waited. It didn't take long. There was dead calm, and then all of a sudden the whole world exploded. The door come crashin' in, breakin' free from its hinges and slammin' into the wall...

... and Old Mongrel flew forward, airborne...

... and I could see only Roy Campbell's face, leerin', laughin' at me, cursin' me as that old dog knocked him off balance, knockin' his rifle to the side...

...but he come up fast, swingin' the rifle towards me, tryin' to get his aim, and in the middle of the explosion the world stood still for just one second...

... and I seen his face; it was so clear to me at that moment, so in focus that I could see the tobacco particles stuck between his two rotted front teeth, could see, too, the drops of brown spit that sprayed out of his mouth while he cursed me, could see the yellow crust in the corners of his pale blue eyes, the angry blackheads on his temples...

... and suddenly I was fourteen years old again, lyin' in the bottom of that culvert, naked and hurtin', freezin' in the rushin' rainwater while them men destroyed me from the inside out...

... and I had known I was goin' to die that night, maybe had even *wanted* to die, but I didn't, I did not, and I wasn't goin' to now, no way in *hell* was I goin' to die now, and I realized then that they had not destroyed me after all....

I squeezed the trigger and it was a deafenin' noise, bouncin' around them cabin walls. I watched in slow motion as Roy's chest caved in, suckin' his huntin' coat in with it, knockin' the rifle out of his hands where it clattered to the floor and discharged into the woodbox...

...and there was Jimmy Williamson, the front of his coat spattered with the chunks of red that come out the backside of Roy Campbell...

...but Jimmy was still comin' even as Roy fell down; Jimmy was pointin' a rifle at me and I wasn't ready, there wasn't no time to get ready, but maybe Corinne...

...Jimmy was linin' up level with my face and dear God I could not pump that shotgun fast enough...

... and then Jimmy's head exploded from his right, just blew clean off, leavin' one eye, his left one, and I remember it was open wide in surprise, and only half a mouth, open but without no sound comin' out, and he fell sideways onto the porch, and then...

"God*damned* son of a bitch left me to die. God*damned* son-of-a-mother-fuckin' *bitch*." And there was...who was it? Sue Ann Leary? Comin' around the side of the porch, leanin' heavy on the rail, holdin' onto her left shoulder with slick red fingers, blood soakin' through the front of a big ol' huntin' coat that must be Jimmy's...or must have *been* Jimmy's, since I was fairly certain nothin' would ever be Jimmy's again, because there appeared to be a part of his skull layin' on my front step...

... and then Sue Ann was draggin' herself up the steps,

kickin' Jimmy's skull aside as if it weren't nothin' more than a withered up leaf, and I seen the hair on that skull blowin' in the wind, I swear I did, and then Sue Ann was sayin' somethin', but I could not hear her over the roarin' in my ears...

... and then Jessie was there, face buried into my chest, and suddenly I could hear again and the world stopped spinnin' me around. Jessie was cryin'.

Pushin' Jessie behind me, usin' my body as a shield, I held tight to the shotgun, eyes on the open doorway where Corinne was supportin' Sue Ann, leadin' her into the cabin.

"Who else is out there?" I demanded of Sue Ann, and my voice was hoarse, like I had just woke up from a long sleep. "Are there any more?"

Sue Ann shook her head, wincin' as Corinne led her to one of the wooden chairs at the table, lowerin' her down careful-like. "Just them," said Sue Ann. "Mr. Smith and I both heard 'em talkin' and I tried to get up here to warn you but they overtook me...shot me...left me for dead, the no good sons of bitches." She focused then on Corinne, really seein' her for the first time. "What in the world are you doin' up here? Lord, it's busy up here tonight."

"Mr. Smith came lookin' for John Paul, told him what was goin' on, and while they was talkin' I left to come warn Billy May. Speakin' of which, Billy May, John Paul may be out there, too. Oh, my God, I hope they didn't kill John Paul! He was comin', too, but I didn't wait on him to get ready; I just left without him. I knew the way up here and I wanted to hurry and get to you. Sue Ann, did you see him?"

Sue Ann shook her head, groanin' softly as Corinne tried to work the huntin' coat away from her wounded shoulder. "I didn't see nobody else, just them two." She jerked her head towards the open doorway.

Followin' her movement, I seen Old Mongrel standin' in the splintered frame, leanin' over the dead bodies of them men. He wasn't no longer growlin' but sniffin' still, his nose raised up in the wind, that keenin' sound comin' from his throat again.

I led Jessie away from the busted door, shieldin' her

from the terrible sight of them men. She did not need to see that. Settlin' her back onto the bed, I sat beside her and held her hand. My knees felt like they was too weak for me to stand.

"If Old Mongrel is communicatin' as well right now as he has been all night, it sounds like John Paul is on his way," I told the women. They looked over at the dog, with his head lifted up at the dark sky, that cryin' sound risin' up in the wind. "He ain't angry now," I said, "he's just lettin' us know someone is comin'."

I hadn't no sooner said that then we heard a voice. "Corinne? Honey, are you okay? We heard shots...oh, Lord, honey please let me know you're okay."

Corinne and me both stepped up to the doorway in time to see John Paul break through the heavy woods in front of the cabin. Just when he cleared the tree line and Corinne run down the steps to meet him, three other forms come out of the darkness behind him, and I raised my shotgun again, finger on the trigger.

"Goddamn, Billy May. We got here as fast as we could, but it looks like you're still faster'n me." Squintin' in the light spillin' out from the open doorway, I could not believe what I was seein'. A head of red hair, not as bright red as it had used to be, but red nonetheless.

"Raymond? Raymond O'Brien? What are you doin' here?" All of a sudden it seemed to me like half the town was wanderin' around on my mountain that night, and I could not wrap my head around exactly what was goin' on. Was there no end to this confusion?

"It's me, Billy May, and Darryl Lane and Eugene Cooper, too, so put your gun down, little lady. We're on your side." Raymond stopped when he got up to that bloody scene on my front porch. He whistled a low sound. "Although by the look of things, you didn't need no help. Damn, woman."

Behind him, Darryl and Eugene stepped forward for a better look, Darryl rubbin' the back of his neck, lookin' worried. Darryl always was a worrier. "Is it true, Billy May?" he asked me. "Them rumors about what they done to you?" He looked up at me, and his face was all screwed up with askin' the question. His hand kept on rubbin' at them muscles in the back of his neck, and I remember thinkin' he was goin' to rub the skin plumb off if he didn't ease up.

I looked at him straight. I was too tired to get into that question, and too out of sorts to come up with words. I didn't have no idea why Darryl was even there, on my mountain in the dark with a snowstorm comin', but there he was. Thirty years after I had last seen Darryl, I reckoned he had come to help me, and that touched me. I nodded at him. "It's true," I said, and I left it at that. There wasn't no need to say more.

Darryl's eyes flickered toward the busted up door. "Is it also true what they done to that girl?" He motioned towards the cabin, the rifle still in his hand. I nodded at him again, my eyes steady on him until he looked down first. We had come a long way from racin' across playgrounds and ringin' church bells.

"Well," he said after a minute, lookin' down at the bloody scene on the porch again. "I reckon they deserved what they just got."

Beside him, Eugene pushed his hat back on his head and nodded his agreement.

"Justice, Billy May," he said to me. "This here ain't nothin' but justice." He spat on the ground near Jimmy's remains. "And it's about damn time."

"Don't give her all the credit," yelled Sue Ann from her seat at the table inside the cabin, startlin' everyone in the yard. None of the men had even known she was in there. "Jimmy was mine. I killed him, and I enjoyed ever' minute of it."

While Darryl and Eugene looked at each other, their eyebrows raised up high, Corinne started to laugh, not the kind you laugh when you're amused by somethin', but the kind you laugh when you've been just about shocked out of your sensibilities. There was a cry buried down in that laugh.

John Paul tightened his arm around her shoulders and then peered up at me, a questionin' look on his face. *What the hell has happened here? What the hell is goin' on?* His face was askin' me them questions, but he didn't say a word. Them men had at one time been his friends, and I felt a little bit sorry for him, havin' to see all that, and havin' to learn what they'd turned into. That could not be an easy thing for a good man to know. I couldn't explain it all to him, so I just held up my hands and shrugged. While we stood there over that mess, the first snowflakes drifted their way down, landin' in puddles of blood that was still steamin' in the cold night air. I was not sorry about them men, and, Lord help me, that is the truth.

Down the mountain, in the quiet little valley below, Mr. Smith remained on the couch in the Johnson's living room where John Paul had ordered him to stay several hours before. John Paul had refused to let him come along, had insisted he stay and rest, and had even ordered him to call Dr. Hayden. Mr. Smith had refused to call the doctor, though, insisting he would be fine as soon as he rested.

Waiting in the darkness, Mr. Smith lapsed in and out of consciousness. He had to get up, had to get to Billy May, needed to save the girl. Agitated, he thrashed his head from side to side, moaning in his confused state as the pain ravaged his chest.

Then suddenly Marla was there, sitting beside him and shimmering in the darkness, telling him it was all okay; Billy May was safe, and so was the girl. She held his hand—oh, how he had missed the feel of her soft hand in his, the fingers so long and fine!—and smoothed his wrinkled brow, her touch a cool and refreshing breeze.

"You did good, Gerry," she said. "You saved 'em all." She smiled at him, that sweet smile he had loved so much, her freckled nose wrinkling the way he adored, her cowlick curling up over her right ear as it always had. She leaned forward and kissed him lightly on the mouth, teasing him, and it was the sweetest kiss he'd ever had. She stood then, and tugged at his hand so that he stood with her. Holding her hand, he followed her into the soft light, his heart no longer hurting, but bursting with happiness.

Chapter Forty-Three
The aftermath

The light from the oil lamp created dancin' shadows on Corinne's face as I took a seat across from her and pushed a cup of coffee over the rough wooden table. "Better drink up," I said, keepin' my voice quiet. "This night ain't over yet."

Corinne sat back and sighed, reachin' gratefully for the cup. Corinne had always been a girly thing, and that night she was far out of her natural element. I wondered what was goin' through her mind. Over on the bed, Sue Ann moved in her sleep, groanin' softly, while next to her, up against the wall, Jessie slept soundly in spite of the events of the night.

I had given them both the lettuce tea, and it was workin' its magic on them, allowin' them some rest. I rose to bend over Sue Ann and check the poultice I had applied to the wound in her shoulder. The bullet had gone clean through, missin' her vitals, but it was still bleedin', and Sue Ann's face was hot to the touch. She was a tough one, Sue Ann was, livin' through not only the recent injuries, but all of them old ones we had seen.

"When do you reckon they'll get back?" asked Corinne, while I placed a cold, wet cloth on Sue Ann's forehead.

I looked over at the splintered door. The men had patched it back up into place for a temporary fix, but I would have to rebuild it later. Yet and still, at least we wasn't completely open to the night. There wasn't no hint of mornin' showin' yet through the cracks, but occasional snowflakes continued to blow in, meltin' on the floor where Old Mongrel licked 'em up. I shrugged. "I don't know. Maybe another hour? It's hard to say. They don't know their way down, and in the dark, with the snow still comin', it'll take 'em longer than it should." I settled again at the table across from Corinne. "Do you think he'll come? Dr. Hayden?"

She puckered up her lips, exhalin' a long, tired breath. "I know John Paul will do his best. He ain't above usin' guilt, if that's what it takes."

I stood up again and paced around the cabin, goin' from the broken door to the wood stove, cravin' a cigarette but not wantin' to leave Jessie. "It's all right, Billy May. Go smoke, why don't you? I'll keep an eye on Jessie and Sue Ann." Corinne held the coffee mug in both hands, warmin' her hands up with its heat. The door was in place, but the cold wind still managed to sneak its way through the busted up planks. In spite of the fire in the stove, the cold was takin' over the cabin; I could see Corinne's breath when she spoke to me.

I shook my head. "No, I cain't leave right now. I don't know that I want to go out there, anyway, but I know I don't feel right smokin' inside in front of Jessie. It's a terrible habit. It ain't ladylike at all, is it?"

Corinne smiled at me. "Billy May, when was you ever ladylike?"

I shrugged again, then looked over at Corinne. "I ain't been out there since they left. What's it like?"

Corinne blew on her cup, sippin' at the coffee. "They cleaned it up pretty good," she said. "Whatever stains was left will be covered with snow now. Where did they take 'em, do you know?"

I ran a hand through my hair, unable to relax. When the shootin' had stopped and the world settled down, I had found myself surrounded by all them people from my childhood. It was a strange, strange feelin', let me tell you. I hadn't seen most of that crowd for thirty years, and I wondered how on God's green earth they had all managed to be up on my mountain that night.

Osda adenedi, my momma said in my head. The good spirits, and I knew it was true. I had so many people lookin' out for me that night, not just the ones in this world, but the ones in the next one, too. I had not known that, not until then. I had not known that there was people lookin' out for me.

The men stepped up quick-like, takin' control of the situation, and I let 'em. In ordinary times I would have fought against it, but these was not ordinary times, and to tell the truth I was relieved to have the help. First, Raymond pulled them dead bodies around the side of the cabin, out of Jessie's sight. Then John Paul, Eugene, and Darryl pieced together the door the best they could in a hurry and reattached it to its frame, blockin' at least some of the wind and snow from the cabin and the injured ones inside.

Corinne and me tended to Sue Ann and Jessie, and I set my herbs on to boil, gettin' my poultices ready for Sue Ann and her injuries, both new and old. Aside from the broken door, the cabin looked the same as always, blanketed with a cleansin' layer of snow. Except for all them people millin' about up on my mountain, you wouldn't never know nothin' had happened.

I settled Sue Ann in the bed next to Jessie and wrapped up her shoulder with a hot slippery-elm poultice. "Sue Ann," I said to her, "you're goin' to need more care than I can give you." Sue Ann didn't argue with me; she recognized she needed more than I could do for her.

"Dr. Hayden," she had said. "Can you get me to him? He's a good doctor. He don't get involved, but that might be a good thing in this situation."

"You cain't make it down the mountain," I told her. "We're goin' to have to try to get him to come up here."

Sue Ann frowned, sweat beaded on her brow. "I don't know if he'll do that. Like I said, he don't like to get involved, and climbin' up a mountain in the middle of the night is pretty involved."

Corinne come over to Sue Ann then, gently touchin' all them bruises evident on Sue Ann's chest and face. "Does Dr. Hayden know about these?" she asked.

Sue Ann looked down at them marks coverin' her upper body, some fresh, some already healin'. She nodded. "He knows. He cain't help but know. There's too many for me to hide, and I get tired of tryin'. Besides, he looks at them, looks at *me* like I'm from another planet. But he don't say nothin'.'"

"Well, then," Corinne decided. "He owes this to you. We'll send John Paul to fetch him. We'll tell him he owes you, for all the times he didn't do nothin', and we'll pray that that works. We need to get him to take a look at Jessie while he's here, too, Billy May. Are you okay with that, honey?" Corinne reached over Sue Ann and patted Jessie's shoulder.

Jessie nodded, her green eyes big in the glow of the firelight. "But is he goin' to hurt me?" she asked.

I leaned over the bed and took her chin in my hand. "Honey, he ain't goin' to hurt you, and I'll be right here with you. Anytime you want him to stop, we'll make sure he stops. But he needs to check on you to make sure you're healin' okay. All right?"

Jessie nodded again, givin' in, trustin' that I would keep my word. That couldn't have been easy for that little girl, and it touched my heart. I was sure she wasn't used to folks keepin' their word.

While we put the cabin back to order, Sue Ann and Jessie propped themselves up in bed, sippin' their tea. I fixed some coffee for the rest of us, but the men told me they didn't have time. They was still makin' plans. They had gathered on the porch, talkin' low among themselves. I didn't know what they was sayin', and I didn't ask. I reckoned they'd tell me when they was ready, and they did. A minute later Raymond stepped through the doorway and approached me, puttin' his hand on my arm.

"Billy May, we're goin' to get rid of the men," he said, his voice too low for Jessie to hear. "And then we're all goin' to pretend nothin' ever happened. Them boys deserved what happened to 'em, and then some. They'll be rottin' in hell for what they done to you, and to her," he nodded towards Jessie, who was sittin' up next to Sue Ann, readin' quiet-like from her book.

"What are you goin' to do with 'em?" I whispered, and I was worried. I had killed a man that night. I didn't know what might happen to me if I got caught, but I was more worried about what might happen to Jessie. Where would she go if I was taken away? She didn't have nobody.

Raymond looked down at me, and his face was serious. "Shaft number twenty-seven," he said to me, watchin' for my reaction. He knew that mine had killed my daddy, and Corinne's, too.

There was a part of me that didn't want them ugly men nowhere near my daddy's final place. I didn't know exactly what I thought of heaven and hell back then, but I knew there was spirits, both in this world and in the next. My daddy's sprit was down in that shaft; I knew it because he'd been talkin' to me my whole life. But as I thought more on it, I realized that was exactly the place them men needed to go. It seemed to me them men had been workin' with the devil, and I didn't see no reason he'd take to punishin' 'em since they was doin' his work for him. My daddy, though, he was big and he was strong.

Lord, I'd have hated to be them men facin' my daddy's spirit down in that shaft.

The more I thought about it, the more I figured he'd just been down there waitin' on 'em all them years, so he could finish up his business before movin' on. *Here they come, Daddy*, I told him in my head. *Get ready for 'em.*

Then I heard him answerin' me. *Ta me reidh, mo chailín beag*, he said. *I'm ready, my little girl.*

And I will tell you the truth, though it don't cast me in a very charitable light: Even in the middle of all that was happenin' that night, the thought of my daddy gettin' ahold of them men was near about enough to put a smile on my face. It was a bad way to think, there ain't no doubt about that, but I reckoned after all I'd been through over all them years, I deserved that smile, and I knew my daddy would agree. I hugged him in my mind, and he hugged me back in his strong arms. Yes, he did.

"That's as close to hell as we can get 'em," Raymond said then, and I surely agreed with that; that mine was an evil place. "Seems like a good spot, and won't nobody ever find 'em there. Our story is that they just took off and left their families behind, little Jessie, and Sue Ann and her boy. No one knows where they went. Prob'ly whorin' around somewhere, knowin' them two. You understand?"

I couldn't do nothin' but nod; I was overcome with so many feelin's in that moment. Not even thinkin', just reactin', I grabbed Raymond's neck in a hug, standin' on my toes to be able to reach him. He was different; he was bigger and taller and stronger than the boy I had known, but he was still Raymond. "I thank you," I said. "I don't know why you're doin' all this, but I thank you."

Raymond tightened his arms right around me and picked me plumb off my feet. "Damn it, Billy May," he said, squeezin' me. "We'd have helped you before, too, but you was too quick to leave. You never give us a chance. Hell, we didn't even know what had happened; one day you just wasn't there no more." He set me back on my feet. "It's good to have you back." He gave me one more squeeze and let me go. I hid my face away from him; I do not like to cry in front of people. He turned around and joined back up with the men on the porch. They had work to do.

Sittin' at the table with Corinne I told her what the men had decided to do with the bodies. She didn't say nothin' at first, just grunted that she'd heard me. After a minute she leaned forward, reachin' out to touch my cheek. "Billy May," she said, "please look at me."

I was dizzy at that touch; her voice was echoin' in my head. *Do you feel it, Billy May?* "Corinne," I said, suddenly afraid of her. I drew away, jumpin' to my feet, nearly upsettin' my chair when I did. "Don't."

She shook her head, pullin' back her hand. "No, Billy May. I'm not. I'm sorry; I won't touch you." She smiled a sad little smile. "I won't touch you," she said again, and I sat back down in my chair, rubbin' my hands on my dungarees; they was sweatin'.

"I got enough guilt without wreckin' your life again," she said. "I just need to let you know, sorry don't even begin to cover it. Now let me finish," she said, wavin' away my protest. I didn't want to open all that up again, but Corinne was bound and determined to have her say. She always was a stubborn one. "Let me finish," she repeated. "This has been weighin' on me a long time, and I'm goin' to say what I need

214

to say and then I'll shut up about it" She set down her mug and looked at me. "I need for you to know it was real," she said. "It *is* real."

I looked down at my hands, rubbed at the calluses there, glanced at the bed to check on Jessie and Sue Ann and seen Jessie restin' peacefully, Sue Ann fitfully.

Corinne started talkin' again. "What I said to you that day, it was real. I ain't never been ashamed of that. What I *am* ashamed of is everythin' that happened next. I would have never...I just didn't know...."

"Corinne," I interrupted her again. "Let it go. It was a long time ago. Neither one of us could have known what they'd do."

Corinne took a deep breath and wiped at her eyes. "But Billy May, it was my lie. I started it all, and it was my lie that caused all this." She held her hand out, indicatin' the cabin. "I threw you to the wolves. I was a coward. All I could think when Willy was there screamin' at me was that I couldn't never face my family. I couldn't never let them know. They'd have been so upset; they'd have disowned me, every last one of 'em. But you," she breathed out hard, "you didn't have a family. So I said it was you.

"I didn't stop to think about how much it would hurt you or about what might happen. I had no idea they'd do what they did. I swear I didn't." Corinne stopped, and I could see her throat workin' when she swallowed. I sat there quiet, not movin', my hands balled up tight in my lap. I didn't know what she wanted me to say.

Corinne took a breath and kept on goin'. "I should have spoke up then, afterwards. I should have come to you. Lord, how I've regretted that I didn't. But I was so afraid."

I shook my head, leanin' forward towards Corinne. "Corinne, it wouldn't have done no good for you to speak up. How could that have helped? What difference would it have made?"

"It would have let you know I loved you, Billy May. It would have let you know you wasn't alone. But I was too afraid of what everyone would think." Corinne rested her head in her hands. "In a little town like Cedar Hollow, it don't matter who you really are, you have to be who they expect you to be; that's the only way they'll ever *let* you be." She sighed, and it was a lonely sound. "My whole life, I've been livin' by somebody else's idea of who I'm supposed to be. It takes a whole lot of courage for a person to live by her own ideas, and Billy May, I ain't never been the courageous one."

She lifted her head up and put her hands back around her coffee cup, turnin' it around in slow circles on the wooden table. "All these years," she said, lookin' down into her coffee, "so many times, I've wanted to come up here, to be with you. But I was too afraid, not just of what you would do, but of what everyone else in town would do, too."

She paused and looked up to see me. "Today, though," Corinne swallowed again. "Today I finally found some courage. And now I'm prepared to do whatever you want me to do." She leaned forward and looked into my eyes, her own blue eyes blazin' at me. "Do you understand what I'm tellin' you, Billy May? It's up to you where we go from here. It's all up to you. I will do anythin' you want."

I felt in my shirt pocket for a cigarette, pullin' one out, in desperate need of a smoke. My hands was shakin' so I couldn't get that cigarette up to my lips. I set it back down on the table. I rubbed my palms along the thighs of my dungarees, rockin' slightly in the wooden chair. I was beside myself with not knowin' what to say to her. I ran my hand through my hair, picked up the cigarette again, and stood up. Gettin' a box of matches from a shelf on the stove, I lit up. I didn't like to smoke in the cabin; it was such a small place it filled up quick with stale smoke, gettin' into everythin'. But I needed somethin' to occupy me, somethin' that would distract me away from Corinne sittin' there in my cabin, sayin' those things to me.

I paced to the window, opened the shutter, and looked out into the night. The pain I felt was nigh unbearable; I will admit that. I couldn't say nothin' to Corinne, couldn't speak through that pain, couldn't breathe with it sittin' on my chest the way it was. Why was she sayin' those things to me?

"They oughtta be here before too long," I said when I

could, and my voice was thick. "It must be gettin' on toward...."

"Billy May!" Corinne interrupted me, her voice an angry whisper. "Don't you dare go hidin' from what I just said to you."

I spun around to look at her, and I was angry, angrier than I had ever been at her. "Well, what do you want me to say, Corinne? Do you really think I'm goin' to ask you to do somethin' that hurts everybody else? Ain't there been enough hurt? I ain't goin' to do that, Corinne; I ain't goin' to be responsible for somethin' like that."

I scrubbed my hand through my hair and took a drag on the cigarette, exhalin' hard, pacin' again. "There is some things in this life I just ain't never goin' to have," I told her. "I have had thirty years to get used to that idea; it ain't goin' to change."

She didn't say nothin', just sat there watchin' me. I threw the remains of my cigarette into the stove and paced angrily around the cabin, takin' it all in as I did. Thirty years I had been there, on that mountain. Life had been hard and it had been lonely. In the beginnin' it had been all I could do to force myself to get up and live, one minute at a time. I had grieved hard for everythin' I'd lost, Momma and Daddy, my town, my friends, and yes, my innocence, too. I had been robbed of a normal way of life.

But while I was pacin' that cabin, I seen that my life had also been good durin' them years, and to tell the truth a part of me was surprised to see it. I had had Polly, and Old Mongrel. I had had the mountain and my wildlife. I had had a peaceful existence, livin' as myself without worryin' about what other people thought of me.

I was able to be myself in a way that I couldn't as a girl. Life had not turned out the way I had thought it would; little girls grew up, married, and kept house, and as a child I had always accepted as a matter of course that that's what I would do, too. Even when I knew that didn't feel right to me, I had still accepted that it was what I would do; it was what girls did.

No, life hadn't turned out as I had thought it would, but

maybe that was for the best. Maybe, I thought, lookin' out the window again, maybe in some ways I had been happier those last thirty years than I would have been if life had turned out the way I had expected it to. Maybe the life I ended up with had been more true to who I was.

And there was Jessie. My eyes rested on the girl, the dog finally givin' up on the snowflakes and curled up below her feet. I stood for a minute and drank in the sight of her, the anger drainin' from my body. It had all led to this; how could I regret it?

I turned back to Corinne, and my voice was softer now because I had found some peace. "You know it cain't happen, Corinne. It just ain't meant to be."

Corinne still didn't say nothin', just watched me like she'd been doin', and her face was sad, but it was also acceptin'. She wanted to reach out for me, I could tell, but she wouldn't. She understood how unfair that would be to me.

I sat again, straddlin' the chair across from her, and rubbed at my eyes. I was tired. I rested my elbows on the back of the chair and lowered my head to my arms. "When you get right down to it," I said after a minute, raisin' my head, "at the end of everythin', all any of us really want is to be remembered by somebody."

I stopped, not knowin' how to explain what I meant. "It's a terrible thing, to think everybody you loved has forgot about you. You remembered me; I know it now. And them others, too," I motioned to the door. "I have been touched tonight, and I am blessed for it." I smiled at Corinne, and it was a real smile.

Corinne smiled back, with a little shake of her head. She was tired, too, plumb exhausted, I could tell. I glanced over at Jessie, then back at Corinne. I reached out and took Corinne's cold hands in my own, and she held fast to me.

"There is some things I ain't never goin' to have, Corinne," I told her again. I nodded towards Jessie. "But I also got some things I never thought I would, and I reckon it all balances out in the end."

I raised Corinne's hands up to my cheek and pressed

them there, closin' my eyes for a minute. Then I lowered her hands back down to the table. "Go home, Corinne. That's where you belong."

There was a quiet knock at the door, followed by John Paul's voice and the sound of boots against the porch floor, stompin' off the snow. I let go of Corinne's hands and she wiped her eyes, and they was so blue, sparklin' with tears in the light from the lamp. I stood up and went to open the door for John Paul and Dr. Hayden.

I do not remember a time when I did not love Corinne.

Chapter Forty-Four
Two months later
Cedar Hollow, West Virginia, 1975

The bell above the front door of Mr. Smith's General Store jingled, and Jessie Russell and J.J. Williamson raced to offer assistance. From behind the counter, Sue Ann smiled, watching them both with pride. Although her arm was still in a sling, it was healing nicely, and at her appointment that morning Dr. Hayden had told her that within another week or so it would be as good as new. "Then will you come back to work?" he had asked, and Sue Ann had shaken her head no.

"I believe I need a change," she had answered. "I appreciate what you done for me, but I need a fresh start." Dr. Hayden had nodded, sad to lose Sue Ann's assistance, and sadder still that he hadn't done more for her when she had needed it. Sad, too, he admitted only in his most secret heart, because he had begun to develop quite a fondness for Sue Ann Leary Temple Williamson. Now that he thought of it, though, it might work to his advantage that she was no longer his employee. He smiled at the thought.

From Dr. Hayden's office, Sue Ann had gone straight to the general store, where she had been helping Billy May get moved in and set up for business. She still couldn't get over Billy May moving back to town, but Billy May had been adamant. She didn't want Jessie isolated on the mountain. "The mountain was what I needed," she had explained to Sue Ann, "but it ain't what's good for Jessie. She needs a normal life, with school, and friends, and a community where she feels like she belongs. It's time for me to move on."

Billy May had rented her mountain to a wealthy family from New York who wanted their own oasis from the city for those times they could escape. Sue Ann could only imagine how hard that must have been for her, but Billy May never let on. She didn't know what Billy May made from the rent, but she imagined it was a good sum. Billy May financed Mr. Smith's General Store with the profits, and she and Jessie moved into the upstairs apartment.

Watching the children assist June O'Brien with her last minute Christmas shopping, Sue Ann felt happy for the first time in many years. She still had difficulty sleeping at night, expecting Jimmy to come crashing into the bedroom at any moment to yank her up by her hair or drag her off the bed for another beating. Slowly, though, with the passage of time, she was learning to relax and let her guard down, and J.J. was positively thriving, both from the calm that had descended over the household and from his blossoming friendship with Jessie. Just last night he had stayed late at the store, up in the apartment with Jessie while she worked with him on his reading. Already, Sue Ann could see an improvement.

With the help of friends, Sue Ann and J.J. set out to transform their little home, erasing all the bad memories and replacing them with new ones. They had painted inside and out, repairing screens and doors, papering the kitchen and sanding and staining the floors with a warm oak finish. With Corinne's help, Sue Ann had sewn new curtains and bed sheets, and the Cedar Hollow Baptist Church Quilting Bee had donated two beautiful quilts, always ready with a helping hand to assist single mothers, particularly those who had been abandoned by their no-good husbands. To Sue Ann's amazement, the house was beginning to look, and feel, warm and cheerful, almost as if Jimmy had never been there.

As Raymond had predicted, no one in the little town had been too surprised to hear that Roy and Jimmy had taken off. After all, everyone knew they were trouble makers. Some folks had been surprised they'd stuck around as long as they had. The town had pulled together to help the poor children the men had abandoned, offering support in the best way they knew how. Never before in her life had Sue Ann been the recipient of so many casseroles.

Sue Ann turned at the sound of a footstep on the stairs and saw Billy May galloping her way down from the upstairs apartment, Old Mongrel following slowly at her heels. Sue Ann regarded her new friend with amusement. Billy May still sported the dungarees and flannel shirts she had worn forever, and she still, more often than not, had a home-rolled cigarette in her hand. Even as a girl, Sue Ann remembered, Billy May had always preferred pants to dresses. Her hair was still cropped short, her face devoid of makeup. But nonetheless, something about Billy May sparkled. Sue Ann smiled.

Just yesterday, Billy May had handed Sue Ann a lifeline. Running her hand through her hair and looking nervous, Billy May had confessed to Sue Ann that she needed help running the store. "I can do the organizin' and the stockin', but I never was good at math. I need help with the orderin' and the financials. I know you've worked for Dr. Hayden for a long time, but if you have time for extra work, I surely would appreciate your help."

Sue Ann had laughed aloud. "Billy May Platte, you are the answer to my prayers," she said. "I'll quit Dr. Hayden's when I go for my appointment tomorrow. I appreciate him comin' and lookin' after me that night, but I am needin' somethin' different. This is the perfect solution, and you know J.J. loves helpin' you out."

Billy May had cocked an eyebrow at Sue Ann. "You been wantin' to quit Dr. Hayden's? Does this mean y'all are about to start datin'? Because you know he's sweet on you."

Sue Ann blushed. "Billy May! What on earth are you talkin' about? The last thing I need right now—the very last thing—is a man. I think me an' J.J. will just take a little time to be together without anyone else comin' around tryin' to control things."

Billy May smiled. "Y'all do that," she said. "But when y'all get tired of that, I imagine Dr. Hayden will be waitin'." Sue Ann had slapped Billy May on the hip with the apron she had been holding, telling her to shush. "Don't wish a man on me, Billy May. I'm needin' some time to myself." But she had blushed in spite of herself.

223

Now Billy May quietly joined her behind the counter and the women surreptitiously watched the children, who were at that very moment persuading June O'Brien to purchase Old Spice cologne for her husband, Raymond. Studying Jessie, Billy May reflected on the past weeks. The physical wounds had healed, but Billy May knew the emotional ones were another matter entirely. In spite of that, she was pleased to see that on this day, at this time, Jessie sounded like any young girl surrounded by friends. They would deal with the rest as it came.

"He'll smell so nice, Mrs. O'Brien," she was saying. "And the green bottle is so pretty!" At this last, J.J. rolled his eyes, prompting Jessie to elbow him in the ribs. "Don't you roll your eyes at me, J.J. Williamson!" Jessie frowned at him. "I am tryin' to *sell*!"

Across town, Officer Wimbley rolled his patrol car to a stop outside Peggy's Diner. It was early for supper, but as always, the town was so deathly quiet he decided to pass the time in the diner, where he might at least catch the latest gossip. Why, just a couple of weeks ago he had learned that the old grocer, Smith his name was, had passed away. From what he'd heard, Billy May Platte had come back to town and bought the store. She'd turned back up with a daughter, which had surprised the living daylights out of Officer Wimbley, since he had had her pegged as a homo. But who could tell these days? Men with long hair, women with hairy legs...the world was going to hell in a hand basket, that was for sure, with no one seeming to know who was a man and who was a woman, not even the people themselves.

Officer Wimbley gingerly stepped over a patch of ice and pulled open the door to the diner, entering into the warm, fragrant room with a sigh of relief. He settled his considerable bulk onto a barstool at the counter and looked around the room. A couple of grizzled old men, retired miners, judging by the cough, sat at the opposite end of the bar, smoking and drinking coffee as they discussed the fishing over on Rugged Creek. They nodded towards Officer Wimbley before resuming their discussion.

Sam Peeler, the barber from across the street, waited patiently at the counter for his cheeseburger-to-go. "How do," he said by way of greeting, and Officer Wimbley responded with a hearty, "Good, good. Gotta get over to see you, later." He made a mental note to stop in before his shift was over. He was due for a cut.

Over in the back corner, Eugene Cooper and Darryl Lane played a game of pool with some other men, fresh from afternoon shift change at the mine. The men waved a hand in greeting. On the opposite side, Dr. Hayden sat alone, reading the paper and picking at a piece of apple pie, a glass of sweet tea neglected in front of him, the melted ice overflowing onto the table. He didn't look up at the jingle of the bell, apparently lost in thought.

Farther up, towards the front of the diner, the mechanic's wife (Johnson, he remembered) sat with an elderly woman, probably her mother, engrossed in an animated conversation. Officer Wimbley sighed. Nothing ever changed in this little town. Catching Peggy's attention, he ordered a piece of key lime pie.

From the second booth back, Corinne looked up briefly as Officer Wimbley entered, then continued her conversation with her mother. She was in the process of planning a big Christmas dinner and wondered which turkey dressing would be better: cranberry or cornbread?

Mrs. Lorraine Pruitt, visiting with her daughter for the holidays, observed her only surviving child with wonder. Corinne's cheeks were pink and there was a sparkle in her eyes that Mrs. Pruitt hadn't seen since...well, since that ugly business so many years ago. She knew Billy May was back in town, but she hadn't yet stopped by to see her. She also knew that Billy May had taken in Roy Campbell's girl when he and Jimmy Williamson had skipped town, but this news didn't surprise her. Billy May had always had a generous heart.

She was anxious to see Billy May, but had promised Corinne she would wait until Corinne's Christmas dinner. Sue Ann Williamson and her boy, Billy May and Jessie, Raymond and June O'Brien and their youngest daughter Bella, Eugene Cooper and Darryl Lane and their wives and passel of little ones, all were planning to attend. Corinne had even invited Dr. Hayden, who, to everyone's surprise, had shyly agreed to come. Mrs. Pruitt wasn't sure what had brought about this change in Corinne, although she had a good idea. She wasn't, after all, as naïve as they had all believed. Regardless of the reason, she was happy to see it. It brought her old heart a sense of peace, seeing Corinne so happy. She smiled to herself and settled back in the booth to listen to Corinne as she debated the pros and cons of pumpkin pie versus sweet potato.

Chapter Forty-Five
Jessie
Huntington, West Virginia, 2010

Jessica Russell McIntosh, Jessie to her friends, growled in frustration and tossed her cell phone onto the passenger seat of the rented SUV. Ever since she had headed south on interstate 64 out of Huntington Tri-State Airport, cell phone reception had been spotty. For the last ten miles, surrounded by the rock walls of the carved up mountains, it had been all but nonexistent. Jessie was desperate to reach the hospice. After a delayed flight out of Los Angeles, a hold up in baggage claim, a mix-up with the rental car, and now this, she had quickly gone from desperate to frantic.

Her last communication with Corinne Johnson had been early this morning, when Mrs. Johnson reported with a catch in her voice that Billy May was hanging on by a thread. *Damn* it, she thought for the thousandth time. If only Billy May had told Jessie—had told *anyone*—she was sick, Jessie would have come home immediately, would have cared for Billy May, and would have had time to say *good-bye*, for God's sake. But Billy May, being Billy May, hadn't said a freaking word, not even to her friends, not until the night three days ago when she had been unable to breathe and had finally called Corinne for help. Damn it all to hell.

Jessie pushed harder on the gas, straining the engine up the steep grade. She had last been home five months ago, for Christmas, and she had noticed at the time that Billy May seemed weaker, but she was, after all, nearly eighty years old. Aside from the weakness and an occasional cough, she had seemed the same as always. Same jeans, same flannel shirts, same spiky hair, though white now instead of black, and same dark eyes, sparkling with humor. And, of course, the same cigarette habit, which Jessie had nagged her about for years now. And look where *that* got her, Jessie thought petulantly.

They had had Christmas dinner at the Johnsons', as had been their tradition for decades. John Paul Johnson, Jr., now known simply as John, had flown in with Jessie from L.A., where they had just completed work on a movie touting some big name stars, John as director, and Jessie as producer. Neither was married, John Jr. because it wasn't legal for him to marry his partner, and Jessie because after struggling through nearly a decade of marriage, her husband had finally decided that he did want children, after all. Since she was unable to provide them, he had decided to look elsewhere. *Cest la vie*, she thought now, swerving impatiently around a slower car. As it had turned out, Jessie had been strangely relieved to see him go.

Jessie had enjoyed Christmas in Cedar Hollow, taking comfort from the traditions started so many years ago. The Johnsons had become like family over the years, and she always enjoyed seeing them on her frequent visits home. She had missed seeing the Johnson's older daughter, Chrissy, at Christmas, but these days Chrissy was obligated to stay in Atlanta for the holidays, where her own children and grandchildren now gathered to participate in their own traditions.

Her old friend J.J. Williamson, his sweet wife Bethany, and their twin teenaged boys had flown in from New York, barely making their flight on time when J.J.'s art gallery showing lasted longer than expected. J.J.'s mother, Sue Ann Leary Temple Williamson Hayden, and her husband Dr. Hayden, Graham to his friends, had completed the group Jessie always thought of as her extended family. The end chair had been left open out of respect for John Paul, as it had been ever since his passing eight years before.

Thinking back on that dinner now, Jessie realized that Billy May must have known about the cancer even then. She wanted to be angry—anger, after all, might override some of the suffocating sadness threatening to burst out of her

228

chest—but she couldn't. Billy May was Appalachian through and through, strong, stoic, and above all else, private. Of course she had told no one; it wasn't in her nature. Oh, Billy Momma, she thought, reverting back to the pet name she had had for Billy May. Please, please wait for me.

Jessie was forced to disengage the cruise control, suddenly hemmed in by news vans on all sides. She felt an unexpected flash of anger at the sight. Another mine explosion, this one outside of Charleston, had happened just three short weeks before. The Upper Big Branch mine had killed 29 people by the time all was said and done, and doubtless left hundreds of others devastated.

That was the thing outsiders didn't know, she thought bitterly. The devastation didn't end at the close of the news hour, nor did it end at the close of the funerals. It went on for generations, affecting everything and everyone from that point on. The President of the United States had ordered an investigation, but what was to investigate? The mines had always taken the lives of West Virginia's men and women, and they would continue to do so.

Jessie honked angrily at the vans hemming her in. Come and get your story, she thought. Raise your ratings and sell your papers, and then leave us the hell alone. Jessie herself had produced a movie about a mine explosion set in the 1930s, loosely based on what she knew of Billy May's history, but that had been a labor of love. Jessie had wanted, more than anything, to make the loss real to the rest of the country, to show people, no holds barred, what West Virginians suffered in the mines. The movie had been a huge commercial success and had solidified Jessie's place as a sought after Hollywood producer. Jessie had used the proceeds to begin a nonprofit organization aimed at helping families left behind by the men and women killed in the mines. The Platte Foundation, as it was called, was already assessing the latest mine explosion and readying funds for assistance.

These vultures, the ones surrounding her as she sped down the interstate, were here simply for a quick story, a way to fill a five minute timeslot on the evening news before moving on to weather, or traffic, or whichever one of the Hollywood jet set was most recently spotted drunk and pantyless.

And what of West Virginia then? Well, West Virginians would do what they had always done; they would draw together and take care of their own. They would gather up the pieces and move forward the best they could, leaning on each other for support, understanding that it was only a matter of time until it happened again. What else could they do? After all the news reporters and rubber-neckers had moved on, appetites satiated, to the next big tragedy, West Virginia would once again be alone in her grief.

Sensing a gap in the caravan, Jessie stomped the accelerator and shot through the opening, reaching again for her cell phone, throwing it to the floor in frustration when the signal refused to cooperate.

This time I surface to feel a soft kiss on my cheek, and I smile without openin' my eyes. Corinne. I open my eyes, then, and sure enough there is Corinne, her cornflower blue eyes as pretty now as they was when I met her nigh seventy-five years ago. Now, them blue eyes is shinin', the skin around 'em crinklin' like crepe paper when Corinne smiles down at me.

"She's almost here, Billy May," she says. "Her plane landed about forty-five minutes ago. She called from the interstate, but then we lost signal. But she's almost here." Corinne pats my arm.

"Was she mad at me?" I ask, and my voice is raspy. "I was goin' to tell her, but the timin' never was right."

Corinne nods. "About as mad at you as the rest of us was. She's got a temper, that girl. But she knows you, Billy May. She was mad, but she wasn't surprised that you kept it to yourself." Corinne lowers herself creakily into the chair at my bedside. Corinne is old now, but she's still a girl to me. "She's terrified, Billy May. She don't want to lose you."

I press my lips together. I don't want to speak of these things. I don't want to think of Jessie bein' sad. "She's a good girl," I say. "She's strong; she'll be okay." And she was, too. Oh, the years hadn't always been easy—far from it. Jessie had her fair share of demons to battle. But we'd done okay, my girl and me. Yes, we had. I look over at Corinne. "You'll be all right, too," I say. "Y'all will have to be there for each other."

Corinne wipes at her eyes. "Damn it, Billy May, you wasn't supposed to catch me cryin'." She offers me a wobbly smile through her tears. "I know I'll be all right, but I'll miss havin' you to bicker with, you crotchety old mountain woman." I smile back at her and reach my hand out to hold onto hers. We sit that way for a while, just two old women bein' content in our silence.

I know that people think I hated to give up my mountain, and I suppose in some ways I did, but in the end it wasn't nothin'. I needed Polly and that mountain to heal me; that is the truth. But once Jessie came along, I didn't need that mountain no more; it wouldn't have been right for her.

I had been brought up to think life has a certain track; we have our childhood, we meet someone and get married, and then we have children and watch them grow up. Once they is grown, we dote on our grandchildren, and until we die, that is our life. Everyone I had ever known had that life, and they seemed to like it, but what do I really know about them and their secret thoughts?

Maybe they thought they was supposed to like it, and so they did. In all these years, I have figured out that life ain't a line. It's more just a bunch of stops and starts; sometimes it swings back on itself, sometimes it runs ahead forward, and sometimes it goes sideways. I reckon I've actually lived three lives: First, I was a child, and then I was learnin' to come back to myself, and then I was wholly myself, and that was the best part. Whatever the path is that most other people is meant to take, that path wouldn't have never worked for me. I know that now. But I also knew it might work for Jessie; she wasn't like me. I had had to give her that chance.

———————

At the *whoosh* of the opening door, Starlette looked up from the stack of charts she had been updating. Thank goodness, she thought. This has to be her. The woman was tall, much taller than Ms. Platte, and her hair was long, hanging past her waist in shining, chestnut colored waves. She was dressed in an emerald green blouse in some sort of shimmering material, silk, maybe, and a white pencil skirt, closely fitted to her slim hips. As she approached the desk at a run, Starlette noted that her eyes, almond shaped, were the same stormy green as the blouse. She was, in a word, beautiful, in spite of her obvious agitation and the fine lines radiating out around those phenomenal eyes. Starlette stepped out from behind the nurse's desk to greet her.

"Are you Ms. McIntosh?" she asked, but the woman was nodding even before she had completed the question. "She's waiting for you; her friend just left." Starlette pointed, "It's the room to the left of the desk. Go on in." Starlette stepped back out of the woman's way, misty-eyed and grateful that it wasn't too late. She didn't know the relationship between this woman and Ms. Platte, but whatever it was, it was obviously special, and she felt honored to witness it.

Jessie realized the pretty little nurse, with her kind face and smooth, brown skin, must have been waiting for her. She nearly ran over the woman in her haste to get to Billy May. Skidding to a stop, she took a deep breath and tried to compose herself before entering the darkened room. It wasn't too late. Billy Momma was still here. She stepped forward, letting her eyes adjust to the gloom.

Drapes were drawn across the windows, blocking the afternoon sun. The room was cool and quiet, unnaturally so, Jessie thought. The tiny woman in the bed hardly resembled the strong little mountain woman Jessie had considered her momma all these years. She was so frail, diminutive under the tucked in covers. Her cheekbones stood out starkly against her pale cheeks, the skin stretched tight. Her hair had thinned, and Jessie could see glimpses of scalp through the wisps. Then suddenly Billy May opened her eyes, as dark and glittering as they'd always been, and Jessie's breath caught in a sigh of relief. She rushed forward to kneel at Billy May's side, laying her head on the old woman's lap. "Billy Momma," she said. "Billy Momma."

———————

I open my eyes to see *adawehi,* an angel, standin' in the doorway, an angel whose green eyes is wide and afraid, and she has tears runnin' down her cheeks. "Jessie," I try to say, but the word cain't seem to work its way out of my throat. Then Jessie is at my side, and I am strokin' her hair the way I always did. "Billy Momma," she is sayin', over and over again, and my heart swells.

This is my life, has been my life, and nothin' else matters, nothin' else could possibly matter more than this. "Jessie," I finally manage, and Jessie raises her tear streaked face and looks into my eyes, stormy green meetin' black. "I love you, Jessie." My voice catches, rough in my throat. Even after all these years, I am not used to such words. I stroke the girl's hair. Funny how, even now, I still think of Jessie as a girl. "You gave me life, little girl. I love you."

Jessie sits up then, and places her hands softly on either side of my face, strokin' my cheeks gently and chokin' back a sob. I revel in her touch, crusty old mountain woman though I am. "No, Billy Momma, you gave me life," she says. "You saved me. I love you back, Billy Momma, more than life itself."

We rest then, Jessie on the bed beside me, holdin' me close as I float to the mountain top one last time.

Epilogue

The funeral of Billy May Platte was held on a spectacular spring afternoon at the Cedar Hollow Baptist Church in Cedar Hollow, West Virginia. Billy May hadn't been Baptist, strictly speaking, but for those who preferred any other denomination, Cedar Hollow remained limited, given that there was one church, and one church only. The old cemetery hadn't changed much over the years. The markers were still cared for, the grass still neatly clipped.

An American flag still snapped in the breeze over the area reserved for the mountain's sons, and now daughters, of war. More markers were there now, and more land had had to be bought to accommodate them, as young men and women returned home for their final rest, having sacrificed their lives on battlefields in Iraq and Afghanistan. The gods of war still demanded their sacrifices.

The wildflowers Billy May had so loved were brilliant in the warm afternoon sun, and Indian paintbrush flamed along the side of the mountain. The majestic oaks and elms surrounding the ancient little chapel had just unfurled their new green leaves to the fragrant mountain air. Billy May was laid to rest next to Pauline Henley Crutcher, just as she had wanted, across the way from the joint resting place of Sue Ann Leary Temple Williamson Hayden and Dr. Graham Hayden. J.J. Williamson had designed Billy May's marker according to Jessie's specifications, with first an engraving of a soaring seagull, and then the following:

Wilhelmina Platte
Billy May to her loving friends

Billy Momma to her loving daughter
February 6, 1931 – May 12, 2010
May you spread your wings and soar.

And finally, because Corinne Johnson had positively insisted, had absolutely refused to give in and had gotten downright aggressive in her insistance:

We remember you, Billy May.

The entire population of Cedar Hollow seemed to have turned out for the funeral, 212 by the last census, the growth most surely attributed to the extreme proliferation of the Pritchett family. It comforted Jessie to know that so many people had loved Billy May, sharing stories of Billy May as a young girl, of Billy May as a middle-aged woman, and finally, of Billy May as a septuagenarian, the eccentric character of the town.

Standing by the gravesite at the conclusion of the service, Jessie wiped discretely at her tears, and then suddenly John Johnson was at her side, elegant in a gray suit, his salt and pepper hair exquisitely cut. He draped an arm lightly around her shoulders, and she leaned against him, taking comfort in the embrace. She had often bemoaned his sexuality, teasing him that if only he weren't gay, she would have proposed years ago.

They worked well together, had ever since he had enticed her to California, straight out of Marshall University. He was already in the movie business by that time, having fallen into it almost by accident. As a delivery man, his muscular physique and leading man good looks had caught the attention of a casting director. He had started out with small parts and worked his way up to bigger parts, but his true passion had been in directing. His first gig had been a documentary chronicling the Civil War and the secession of West Virginia. That had been such a success he had moved onto bigger gigs until eventually his reputation was such that he was given the opportunity to direct a big screen movie. That was the beginning of what had turned out to be an immensely satisfying career.

With John's help in those early years, Jessie, too, had managed to get a foot in the door, first with commercials, and then with a brief, ultimately forgettable stint in a short running soap opera. Like John, however, she was most comfortable behind the scenes.

Over the years, John had invited her to work on several projects with him, and the teasing relationship that had taken root when she was but a traumatized girl sharing Christmas dinners with his family had grown into a deep and abiding friendship. Now, gratefully leaning against him, she sighed, "Steve is one lucky man."

John smiled. "I doubt he would agree with you at the moment. He seems to have gotten himself corralled by Raymond O'Brien. That man must positively bathe in Old Spice."

Jessie snorted, laughing through her tears. "I think I may have contributed to that obsession years ago," she said.

As she craned her neck to search for John's partner, she was interrupted by the sudden clanging of a bell. Startled, she looked towards the sound, shading her eyes against the afternoon sun, and then gasped in surprise. There, framed in the open window of the bell tower, was none other than John's mother, Corinne.

How on earth had she managed to climb all those steps? Before she could ask John what his mother could possibly be thinking, two elderly gentlemen joined her at the window. As the bell continued to chime, Corinne, Eugene Cooper, and Darryl Lane all raised a shaky fist towards the sky, as if in tribute to Billy May. Somewhere high above the deep sound of the bell, Jessie could hear the tinkling sound of Corinne's laughter.

"Your mother...." She said, turning her head towards John, leaving the question hanging.

"And yours, too," he replied, eyes twinkling down at her.

Jessie wiped her eyes, attempting a weak smile as she looked at him. "They were quite a pair, weren't they?"

"Oh, they certainly were. Much more than you know," John responded, struggling, but failing, to suppress an impish smile.

Intrigued by his tone, Jessie turned to face him full on in the shade of the elms. "What do you mean? John? What are you saying?"

John didn't answer, only smiled more broadly, his hair ruffling in the breeze.

Realization dawning, Jessie smacked him in the chest with both hands. "Shut *up*! You can't be serious."

"They really were quite a pair," he answered softly. "They loved each other, you know."

Jessie stared, stunned, mouth agape. "Since when?" she demanded, struggling to regain her composure. "This whole time?"

John shook his head quickly. "I think they had probably loved each other for years, maybe since they were children; who knows? But they didn't act on it until recently. After the children were raised and their duties were done. After my father died and they had waited a respectable amount of time."

"How do you know this?" asked Jessie, incredulous. "Did your mother tell you? Am I the only one who didn't know?" She ran a hand through her hair in an agitated gesture eerily reminiscent of Billy May.

John reached towards Jessie, pulling her close and massaging her shoulders tenderly. "Of course not," he soothed her. "No one knew but me, and no, she didn't tell me. But I knew. For heaven's sake, Jessie, who better than I to spot a clandestine love affair?" He smiled down at her, his expression ironic.

Jessie pulled away and turned, staring at him, unbelieving at first. Slowly, though, things started to make sense; missing pieces of the puzzle finally came together. Squinting, shading her eyes, she turned to look up at Corinne and the two men in the bell tower, steadily ringing the bell, framed against the clear blue sky.

Jessie had always worried about her Billy Momma, had not wanted her to be alone. But she hadn't been; she had been loved. *We remember you, Billy May.* The words echoed through Jessie's memory, calling forth a cold night and a hushed conversation. *When you get right down to it, at the end of everythin', all any of us really want is to be remembered by somebody. It's a terrible thing, to think everybody you loved has forgot about you.* Now Jessie understood.

All of a sudden, Jessie felt lighter than air, positively giddy with the knowledge. A laugh of pure delight bubbled up past the tears in her throat, joyfully escaping and meeting up with Corinne's tinkling laugh, spiraling high above the Appalachian Mountains. *We remember you, Billy May.*

Book Club Discussion Starters

1. "Seem like when you try to explain somethin' important to somebody else, somethin' you hold close to your heart, they don't always right away understand the importance, and that is a frustratin' thing." This was Billy May's reasoning when she chose not to answer the nurse's questions about her visitor. What does she mean by this? Does it diminish the importance if we have to explain our thoughts and feelings?

2. Billy May communicates often with her deceased loved ones through her thoughts. Are these communications real? Or is this simply a tool for Billy May to use to combat her loneliness?

3. Billy May describes her mother as an unhappy woman, and we know from Lorraine Pruitt that Suzanna wasn't given to displays of affection. What sort of mother do you think Suzanna was? Did she do an injustice to Billy May?

4. Lorraine Pruitt states that once you grow old, "...all the lies you'd told yourself to simply make it through the days were no longer content being silent." Is this true? If so, why might that be?

5. In Billy May's memory, her father takes on an almost larger-than-life persona, as Billy May's champion and hero. How might this be different if he had lived? Would he have saved Billy May?

6. Willy Pruitt was the ringleader of the attack on Billy May, yet his guilt drove him to suicide. Was the attack out of character for Willy? Was he simply a misunderstood, angry

young man?

7. John Paul is described several times as a good man, yet he was hesitant to believe his old friends could cause such harm. He's also described as a good husband, yet he's very out of touch with Corinne's needs. Is he truly a good man/husband?

8. Billy May once states that while she no longer feels sad for the woman she is, she continues to feel sad for the girl she was. What role does Jessie play in healing Billy May?

9. Billy May cannot remember a time when she did not love Corinne, although it was Corinne's betrayal that caused the attack on Billy May. How is it possible that Billy May continued to love Corinne? Should she have forgiven Corinne?

10. Once Jessie realizes the true nature of the relationship between Billy May and Corinne, she feels "giddy with the knowledge." Why might this be?

More Great Books by
Melinda Clayton

Return to Crutcher Mountain, Cedar Hollow Series, Book 2

Entangled Thorns, Cedar Hollow Series, Book 3

Shadow Days, Cedar Hollow Series, Book 4

Blessed Are the Wholly Broken

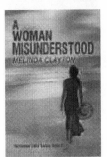

A Woman Misunderstood

Making Amends

Appalachian Justice is Clayton's debut novel in the Cedar Hollow Series, which also includes Return to Crutcher Mountain, Entangled Thorns, and Shadow Days. Clayton's other works include Blessed Are the Wholly Broken, A Woman Misunderstood, and Making Amends. In addition to writing, Dr. Clayton has an Ed.D. in Special Education Administration, is a licensed psychotherapist in the states of Florida and Colorado (on retired status), is a writing tutor for Pearson/Smarthinking, and teaches classes for Southern New Hampshire Unversity's MFA program.

Manufactured by Amazon.ca
Bolton, ON